DON'T BE CAREFUL

A Jamie Austen Thriller

TERRY TOLER

Don't Be Careful
Published by: BeHoldings, LLC

Copyright © 2022, **BeHoldings, LLC**
Terry Toler
All rights reserved.

Book Cover: BeHoldings Publishing
Contributing Editor: Donna Toler

For information email: terry@terrytoler.com.

Our books can be purchased in bulk for promotional, educational, and business use. Please contact your bookseller or the BeHoldings Publishing Sales department at: *sales@terrytoler.com*

For booking information email: booking@terrytoler.com.
First U.S. Edition: September 2022

Printed in the United States of America
ISBN 978-1-954710-15-3

OTHER BOOKS BY TERRY TOLER

Non-Fiction

How to Make More Than a Million Dollars
The Heart Attacked
Seven Years of Promise
Mission Possible
Marriage Made in Heaven
21 Days to Physical Healing
21 Days to Spiritual Fitness
21 Days to Divine Health
21 Days to a Great Marriage
21 Days to Financial Freedom
21 Days to Sharing Your Faith
21 Days to Mission Possible
7 Days to Emotional Freedom
Uncommon Finances
Uncommon Health
Uncommon Marriage
The Jesus Diet
Suddenly Free
Feeling Free

For more information on these books and other resources visit terrytoler.com.

Thank you for purchasing this novel from best-selling author Terry Toler. As an additional thank you, Terry wants to give you a free gift.

Sign up for:

Updates
New Releases
Announcements

At terrytoler.com

We'll send you a copy of *The Book Club*, a Cliff Hangers mystery, free of charge.

For Donna with love.

My editor, best friend, biggest fan, and loving wife.

These books would not exist if not for you.

1

Normally, the three men standing in front of me would be dead by now.

They didn't know that I'm Jamie Austen. The foremost female CIA killer in the world. Actually, the foremost female CIA killer *trainer* in the world as of three weeks ago.

Which was why I hadn't acted up to this point.

One of my trainee's, Kaley Presley, was standing next to me. To my right. I started out calling her Kale, like the vegetable. She didn't like it. So I quit doing it.

Kaley was nineteen and on a fast track to becoming the second most lethal female CIA killer in the world.

If she wasn't already.

Curly had been my mentor. I was now in his job at The Farm, where CIA recruits were trained. Sort of in his job. He trained the recruits with the most potential. Brad, my CIA handler, asked me to train Kaley. Supposedly the best of the best.

I was supposed to turn her into me in three weeks. How was that possible? It had taken me years to learn what I knew now.

I did the best I could. She was good, but I hadn't seen her in a real life or death situation. Until now.

Kaley and I went to dinner in Alexandria, Virginia. A pizza place in a reasonably safe neighborhood. If there were such a thing in the Washington, D.C. metro area. When we came out of the restaurant, we had to walk past several alleys to get to our car.

Three men stepped out of the shadows and blocked our way.

It would've been humorous except one of them pulled a gun. The one in the middle.

The moron demanded our money. He couldn't possibly know we were armed as well. Although our guns wouldn't be necessary. We had other lethal weapons at our disposal. Elbows. Knees. The heels of our feet. The palms of our hands.

I wasn't sure why these three men were still standing on their feet.

Kaley had already failed the first part of the test.

I would've taken the gun from him. Twisted it so it broke his trigger finger. I tried to include that move every time somebody was stupid enough to shove a gun in my face.

After that, I would've pushed his nose back into his brain with my elbow, while kicking the man to the left with a side kick to the stomach. Trusting Kaley took care of the guy on the right.

If she didn't, then in one motion, I would've taken the gun and pistol-whipped the last threat on the right side of his face. Then kicked him in the ribs when he fell to the ground. Called the police so the coroner could scrape their remains off the sidewalk.

At least, that's how I pictured it going down in my mind. These things were fluid. One had to improvise. Maybe the order was different. The blows were directed to another part of the body. If the need arose.

The end result would be the same.

I wasn't the least bit worried that the three wouldn't face that outcome.

Because they were imbeciles. Barely twenty years old. Wannabe tough guys. I'd faced down hardened terrorists. These boys weren't going to do anything to me.

Unless the gun went off accidentally. Which was always a worry.

The one with the gun held it loosely. He waved it around like he was some sort of bad guy in a movie. I could knock it out of his hand before he could blink twice. But then it could hit the ground and go off and hit one of us.

Besides, I was waiting for Kaley to act first. This was an opportunity for her to use the skills I taught her.

"Give me yous' money," the man said. "All your jewelry. Take off that wedding ring and give it to me, Blondie."

Did he just call me Blondie?

It almost caused me to laugh out loud. I was tall with blonde hair. I don't remember ever being called that name. It almost made me forget the absurdity of his demands.

Mentioning my wedding ring brought an image of Alex, my husband, to mind. This guy couldn't possibly know that I'd kill him before I'd give him my wedding and engagement rings.

If Alex had been there, the guy would've already been on the ground, writhing in pain.

Threatening to take my rings were fighting words. Although brandishing a gun was not a welcoming gesture either.

I was starting to get impatient. Not sure how much more guff I was willing to take off this guy.

What was Kaley waiting for?

Beating up the three was easy. Two were standing with their hands in their leather jackets. They looked cool. Like tough guys. But that's not a good strategy if you're about to get in a fight. I could hit each of them two or three times before they could get their hands out of their pockets.

They also might have guns. Probably did. Kaley should disable them before the other two had time to draw theirs. Three guns pointed at us might be problematic. It certainly tilted the odds more in their favor.

Was Kaley waiting for me? Out of respect for her elder and mentor. Did she think I had seniority?

Was she frozen in fear?

I wouldn't have thought that. I'd put her through the ringer over the last three weeks. I taught her advanced hand-to-hand combat. Krav Maga. Fighting with knives. Even swords. We'd practiced every type of gunplay.

We spent several hours on how to take a gun from someone. It wasn't that hard.

When Brad first asked me to train Kaley, I was skeptical. My CIA handler told me she had the potential to be as good as I am.

Kaley was better than I had expected. She made tremendous strides in a short time. She did remind me of a younger me. Without the blonde hair. Hers was red. We were about the same height.

And now she was in a real life or death situation. Except for the danger, this was a good thing. It'd test her skills. I couldn't have scripted it any better.

I tried my best to simulate these situations for her. The training at The Farm was dangerous. But an injury would only happen by accident. I never let it cross the line. We used real bullets in our training but with every possible precaution in place.

The guy standing in front of us brandishing a weapon wouldn't use such precautions. While the chances of us dying were actually quite slim, it was a possibility.

Kaley should've already taken care of the situation.

The longer we waited, a gun could go off by mistake. Her foot could slip on the gravel and the disabling blow she aimed at her target could come too late.

Disarming a gunman required precision. I'd made her practice it dozens of times until she got it right. Curly made me practice it until my whole body ached and I could barely climb into bed or get up the next morning. I was with him for six months. Not three weeks.

How could I teach her what Curly taught me in that short period of time? Kaley had already had the six months training at The Farm. But not with someone like Curly.

She suddenly shifted her weight to her back right foot.

I grimaced inside.

She had changed her angle of attack. I knew why she was doing it and wanted to correct her on the spot. She intended to disarm the gun, so it'd be pointing away from me. But it wasn't the path of least resistance.

She obviously hadn't learned a thing I taught her.

The better strategy was to turn to the right.

I wanted her to step forward, not back. Raise her hands in surrender. Close the gap. Turn her body to the left. Facing me. Use her right hand to grab the gun. Point the gun down. Twist the gun, breaking the man's finger. Maybe his wrist. Maintain the grip on the gun, kick the guy on the right in the groin. Turn and face the middle man. Reestablish her balance and kick him in the stomach or knee.

I'd take care of the third assailant. The one on the left. He wouldn't even know what hit him.

But Kaley was being careful.

The very thing I told her not to do.

The first thing I said to her when we started the training was, "Here's the most important rule. Don't be careful. Careful will get you killed."

A Curlyism. He drilled it into me. It became a creed for us to live by.

Anyone could learn the moves. Things were different when guns were blazing. Careful caused you to take precautions. To hesitate. What we did had risks. Ironically enough, careful compounded the risks, not made them go away. The ability to throw caution to the wind in the heat of the battle and trust your instincts was the difference between a good operative and the best. Sometimes the difference between living and dying.

Few of us had it.

Kaley turned to the right, so she had her back to me. Grabbed the gun with her left hand so it'd be facing away from me. She twisted it upward and away from her body instead of down. That was fine. I heard the sound of breaking bones. Finger and wrist. A violent and painful move.

She already knew that move when she came to me and executed it well.

The low life cried out in pain. Kaley twisted further and yanked downward, dislocating his shoulder. It'd take a surgeon several hours to fix it. If he could. The man fell to his knees. His arm dangling to his side.

5

But now the angle was wrong to take out the assailant to the right. He pulled his hands out of his pockets.

As I suspected. He had a gun.

Kaley let out a muted scream.

2

The man raised his weapon to fire.

Kaley reacted like a cat. She ducked as the bullet flew over her head. In a fluid motion, she swept the man's feet out from under him. She'd want to grab the gun away from him but still had the other man's gun in her hand. So she had to improvise.

Hopefully, she didn't try to wrestle the gun away from him. She didn't.

Instead, Kaley kicked him in the head, knocking him unconscious. The gun fell to the side. With the adrenaline flowing, she turned and kicked the middle gunman with the bum shoulder in the groin. For good measure. He'd be walking funny for months.

My guy was already on the ground. Knocked cold. His hands were still in his pockets. I dispatched of him as soon as Kaley turned sideways.

She was jumping up and down. Excited. Like a boxer. With her hands in front of her. She taunted them. Daring one of them to make a move. I remembered that feeling. It never went away. Even after all these years.

In a gunfight, adrenaline surged. It pulsed through your veins like someone turned on a fire hydrant inside of you. It'd take several hours for it to go away.

My threat wasn't serious enough to cause my heart to accelerate at all. Although the gun shot caused me some slight angst.

I took out my phone and called Brad. Not 911. The cops would take us down to the station. Interrogate us. We'd have to lie about who we were.

Too many complications.

Brad told us to leave the scene. Make sure we weren't seen on any security cameras.

He'd make a call to 911 as soon as we were safely away. From an anonymous number, so the call couldn't be traced. An ambulance would come. We didn't want the three boys to die on the street, so I checked to make sure their air passages were open and they could breathe.

I was satisfied they'd live. Mine probably wouldn't remember what happened.

We got in the car, and I drove away. Neither of us said anything.

I was fuming inside.

It took all my self-control to keep from going off on Kaley. I had many choice words flying around in my head. Mostly things Curly said to me when I screwed up. Less the four-letter words Curly was famous for.

Kaley was lucky. I wasn't as mean as Curly, but I intended to tear into her.

First things first. *Calm down.* We usually didn't debrief on a mission until the adrenaline was gone. Too easy to get into our own physical confrontation or say something we regretted in the heat of the moment.

I stopped at a convenience store and got a caffeinated soda and energy drink for Kaley. A concoction Curly taught us. It helped with the adrenaline. A bit counterintuitive. Loading your body with caffeine actually calmed the raging hormones on the inside.

Kaley was clearly still on edge.

"How did I do?" she asked, after we were on the road again. Almost smugly. Like she was proud of herself.

I hesitated. I really didn't want to have this conversation so soon after the confrontation. It'd be better to discuss it in the classroom when cooler heads would prevail.

I couldn't help myself.

"You did everything wrong," I blurted before I could stop myself.

Her eyes widened and I could see her go through a progression of emotions. First disbelief. Then confusion. Then anger. Her forehead burrowed and her jaw clenched as she settled on being mad at me as the prevailing emotion.

"What are you talking about?" she said. "I took out those two guys the way you taught me."

I shook my head.

My tone matched her anger. "What's the first rule I taught you?"

Her eyes were distant as she clearly tried to remember.

I raised the tension in the car even further. "The first day I met you! What did I tell you? The most important rule. I told you not to forget it. And you did."

"Don't be careful," she said, with a little bit of the bravado taken out of her sails.

"That's right. You were being careful back there. It could've gotten us both killed."

"How was I being careful? I evaluated the situation and came up with a course of action. The results speak for themselves. We're alive aren't we?"

"You turned your body to the right. Not to the left. With your back to me."

"That was so the gun wouldn't be pointed at you. I was protecting you, Jamie."

"You were being careful."

"How is that being careful? That's being smart."

"That's being stupid."

"I can't believe you're angry with me for saving you from taking a bullet. I put my body between you and the gun. Thank you very much. That's what you should be saying. Not railing on me."

"You put both of us in greater danger by doing so."

Kaley let out a sigh of disgust. "I didn't see you doing anything about the threat."

"I was waiting to see if you were ready to deal with it. I guess I was wrong."

"You're jealous. There's a new kid in town who's better than you. And you can't handle it."

"Don't flatter yourself. You'll never be as good as me. I've forgotten more than you'll ever know. If we let you in the field, you won't live long enough to amount to anything."

I immediately regretted the harshness.

Her sassiness was a good thing. I'd been careful not to work that out of her. She needed it in our profession. Confidence was good. Overconfidence was bad, cockiness could get you killed. So could insecurity. I didn't want Kaley doubting her abilities. I wanted to fire her up inside, so she'd be resolved to get it right the next time.

Curly was relentless in the pursuit of perfection. I'd been bitter at him at times. Once I got in the field, I appreciated it.

Kaley was good. I didn't doubt that. But she wasn't ready for prime time.

Might not ever be.

I'd lost my confidence in her. Don't be careful was the most important rule as a CIA operative.

She didn't get it. It's an intangible that can't be explained.

She didn't have it. Probably never would.

I'd let Brad know tomorrow.

I was wasting my time with her.

3

Alex and I were called to headquarters to meet with Brad, our CIA handler. He needed to coordinate mission details for Alex and his team. Surprisingly, he wanted me there as well. I thought we would be talking about Kaley. Instead, he had a file for both of us which meant I was going on a mission as well.

I couldn't imagine what mission it might be.

After I won gold at the Olympics, my face was seen around the world by billions of people. When Brad extended an offer to start up AJAX again, the CIA only wanted Alex. Not me. I was damaged goods as far as working undercover was concerned.

I didn't think so and had vehemently protested.

My protestations fell on deaf ears. Inside the CIA, anonymity was of the highest priority for obvious reasons. Operatives had to be clandestine to be effective. While I understood the reasons for the precautions, I felt them unnecessary.

So far, I hadn't been recognized once in the states. The only time I was recognized on foreign soil was at a restaurant in Italy. Someone from Israel came up to me all excited, but I insisted I wasn't the person who won the gold medal at the Olympics in Bavaria. I only looked like her. That seemed to satisfy the lady although she walked away with a confused look on her face. Or maybe a disappointed one.

I was a hero in Israel. Or at least the woman who won the first gold medal in Israeli women's Olympic history was the hero. But no one knew where that woman was. Her location was an international mystery. She'd disappeared off the face of the earth. No television appearances. No sightings at all.

Saul Geller, the Director of Mossad who organized and ran the mission to the Olympics, tried his best to contain the fallout. All kinds of conspiracy theories had erupted. The woman had been kidnapped by Islamic forces. She'd died in a plane crash flying home. The closest one to the truth was that she was a spy and was in hiding.

It's possible some of the intelligence agencies in the world had figured it out and knew I was the woman. MI 6 certainly knew. As did Mossad and the CIA. Which was why CIA Director Ryan Coldclaw nixed the idea of me coming back on board in an official capacity.

Ryan's mother was acting director when I started and she loved me before she passed away. I helped Ryan get his start with the CIA. Went to bat for him with Curly and Alex when they wanted to cut him loose.

I'd been proven right. Ryan wouldn't be in his position if not for me. He knew that and would do almost anything in the world for me. I expected him to take my side on the issue.

He didn't.

Too great a risk.

Maybe later. Eventually, the dust would settle, and I could go back to normal. At least that was everyone's hope.

I wondered if that was happening already. Since Brad had a file in his hand for me.

"Who wants to go first?" Brad asked, waving the two files in the air.

"Ladies first," Alex said.

"Why should I go first just because I'm a woman?" I retorted. Not allowing a smile on my face even though I was kidding.

Alex looked at Brad, who looked at me, then shrugged his shoulders.

"Okay then," Alex said. "Age before beauty."

"You think you're better looking than me now?"

I was purposefully ratcheting up the tension in the room with the playful banter.

"Look at this face," Alex quipped, putting his hand to his chin, and turning it from side to side for us to look at.

"Oh please."

"I'm using a new skin cream. It takes away all the lines."

It was well known that, between the two of us, Alex was the vainest. He spent more time getting ready in the morning. Even though my hair was longer, he primped his more. He'd also been working out like a fiend. He was in the best shape of his life, and I was enjoying his six-pack abs. Although, I had to limit my number of compliments, or his head would swell up bigger than the room.

I came back from the Olympics in world class shape as well. Three weeks with Kaley had gotten me back into mission shape. The soreness in my muscles aside, I'd never felt better.

"I think Alex should go first," I said. "He's right. Ladies first."

He twisted his lips to the side in a snarly gesture.

"What's the cream called?" Brad asked. "I could use some."

I rolled my eyes. Alex saw me.

"And there it is, folks," he said slowly and with added emphasis. "The daily eye roll. I wondered when I'd get it." He looked at his watch. "What took you so long?"

"It's not daily," I said.

"Yes it is. Brad, every day I say or do something that causes Jamie to roll her eyes at me."

"I didn't roll my eyes at you yesterday."

"That's because we didn't see each other. You were still at The Farm with Kaley." His voice had a whiny tone to it.

"Actually, now that I think about it, I did roll my eyes at you yesterday," I said. "I thought of something you did before I left home to go to The Farm. I rolled my eyes for effect."

"I'm glad I wasn't there to see it."

13

"Anyway, you go first, Alex," I said, barely able to contain a grin. "Either way you win. Age before beauty or ladies first."

"Hey!"

"You're the one talking about skin cream."

"I can't help it if I'm aging better than you."

I rolled my eyes again.

"A double eye roll! One of these days your eyes are going to get stuck in that position. Then what are you going to do?"

"Eyes can't get stuck. That's only if you're crossing them."

"The two of you sound like an old married couple," Brad said. "It's sickening. That's why I'm divorced. You guys should consider it."

I shook my head. "Not happening. The only way Alex is getting out of this marriage is in a coffin."

"Ditto."

"You guys need professional help."

"Nah. We're just in love," Alex said, reaching out his hand and taking mine. I pulled it away playfully.

"She can't resist me."

"It's the skin cream I can't resist."

I pushed him on the shoulder playfully.

"Can we get down to business?" Brad said roughly. "Alex, you'll go first."

He handed Alex a file. Alex didn't even open it. Probably because he was the one who came to Brad with the mission specifics and already knew the details.

"We're headed out tomorrow," Alex said. "On the AJAX plane."

"Who's we?" I asked.

Alex and I hadn't had a chance to talk about it. I'd been at The Farm. Now that I was done with Kaley, he was leaving on a mission. Which stunk since we hadn't been together much since the Olympics.

That's how our life used to be when we both worked for the CIA. We mostly passed each other coming and going. I'd go on a mission while he was at home. When I got back, he was already gone. Vice versa. It seemed like that pattern was starting up again and we'd only been back with the CIA for three weeks.

"A-Rad, Bond, and Colonel are going with me," Alex said.

"That's a lot of firepower," I said.

I assumed they were going after Pok if Alex felt the need to bring the A team. I wanted to ask where he was going, but we never asked each other about the specifics of our missions. Protocol was "need to know" basis. Even for spouses.

Brad must've not cared because he said, "How sure are you that Pok is in Vietnam?"

"A hundred percent," Alex said.

"It didn't take long for you to find him," Brad said.

"I would've found him sooner, but he had me in South Korea on a wild goose chase."

Not literally. Alex meant on the internet. He didn't actually go to South Korea. Alex and Pok were two of the foremost computer hackers in the world. Alex insisted that he was the best. From my observations, I'd say that was accurate. And not just because Alex was my husband.

Pok was slightly behind Alex in skill. Evident by Alex finding Pok when he didn't want to be found. The North Korean should've been more careful. Alex intended to kill him this time. I hoped he succeeded. Pok had been a thorn in our sides for a long time.

What Alex said next floored me.

"I even know where the three billion is," he said. "It's actually closer to five now. I can take it anytime I want."

I sat forward in my chair.

"That's our money," I said. "Pok stole it from us. Why don't you take it back now?"

"I will. But I don't want to alert him that I'm on to him. If I take the money, he'll leave Vietnam and I'll have to track him again. I want to kill him first and then get our money back."

"That makes sense."

"Are we good with that?" Alex asked, looking at Brad. "I mean that's our money."

"I don't care as long as you don't run into any problems with the IRS."

All of our other assets had been stolen by the former CIA Director Fuller who was now rotting away in jail. We recovered some of them. Our yacht. Our two planes. All the paintings I had acquired on behalf of AJAX.

Pok stole the money when Fuller came after us and Brad brought Alex back to the CIA to track Pok down. The lowlife hacker was wreaking havoc on the worldwide financial markets and the CIA had an interest in bringing him down.

For Alex, it was personal.

"Do you have everything you need from me?" Brad asked.

"We're using the same credentials we had before. Back when we were going to South Korea. We never used them. If that's okay."

Brad nodded.

Alex took a piece of paper out of his pocket and handed it to Brad, who unfolded it and looked it over.

"What's this?" he asked.

"That's our new tail number for the flight transponder. I have to assume that Pok is tracking our plane. So I hacked into the FAA site and changed the tail number so Pok won't know we left the United States. He'll think our plane is still on the ground. I'm giving you the number so you can track our movements. Or in case we get into trouble."

"I'd appreciate it if you wouldn't admit to a federal crime in my office," Brad said, with a barely noticeable grin. He was only half kidding. "I'd rather not know when you hack into an American government organization."

"So you don't want to know that I read all your emails and text messages?"

Alex was grinning from ear to ear so Brad would know he was kidding. Although Brad and I both knew Alex could do it if he wanted to.

"If you do, you have way too much time on your hands. Those are boring."

"I found a few things I can use against you. If the need arises."

Brad laughed, but didn't comment.

"As soon as we're wheels up, we're going dark," Alex said. "I won't have any communication with anyone until Pok is dead. Not even you Brad. I have to assume Pok is watching my every move. I'm not going to give him the chance to get away again. I should've killed him when I had the chance."

We had several chances to kill Pok.

I regretted that we hadn't taken them.

Hopefully this time, Alex would get rid of the threat once and for all.

4

"What do you have for me?" I asked Brad. "I thought I wasn't working for the CIA anymore. Other than training Kaley. Which I'm finished with by the way."

The words were dripping with sarcasm. I wasn't happy about not being part of the CIA and Brad knew it.

I could still do missions. But I was on my own. Since I'd been training Kaley, I hadn't had a chance to plan one.

"I want you to go to Alaska," Brad said, startling me.

Alex let out a guffaw.

I was tempted to roll my eyes at him but resisted. I didn't want it to lose its effect.

"Watch out for Grizzly bears," Alex said.

I ignored him.

"The CIA can't operate on U.S. soil," I said. "The last time I checked, we still owned Alaska."

"This isn't a CIA mission. I'm putting it on your radar. I know you've been itching to get back at it."

"What's the mission?"

"Twelve girls have gone missing in Denali National Park."

"Where's Denali National Park?" Alex asked.

"Mount Mckinley," Brad said. "It was renamed several years ago."

That seemed to satisfy Alex. Or at least he didn't ask another question.

"I've heard about the missing girls," I said. "Authorities think it might be a serial killer on the loose."

Brad shook his head.

"It's a sex trafficking ring. They take the girls from Alaska to Russia. As you know, it's only fifty-five miles to Russia across the Bering Sea at the closest point. There's a huge demand for American women in Russia right now. I guess the men are getting tired of the teenage middle eastern girls being trafficked. Apparently, the oligarchs will pay top dollar for an American beauty."

"Tell me about it," Alex said. "I'm paying top dollar for one myself."

That comment deserved an eye roll, but I wasn't sure if it was meant as a compliment or as a snide remark, so I let it pass. My mind had already shifted to full operational mode. It felt good to have an actual mission with a target. Rescuing girls was my passion. This was right in my wheelhouse, and I was excited about it.

"So that means I'll have to go into Russia to find them," I said.

That made the mission extremely dangerous. Which was probably why the CIA hadn't acted. Since I wasn't leading the sex trafficking division, the results had dropped off significantly. He didn't have any effective women operatives to go into Russia to rescue the girls.

I could see why Brad wanted to pawn it off on me. I also wondered if he was grooming Kaley for that position. A twinge of jealousy rose up inside of me, but I tamped it down.

"That's right," Brad said.

The best of both worlds for Brad. He'd get the job done, but have plausible deniability if things went south.

"Do you know for a fact that the girls are still alive?" Alex asked.

"They will be," I said. "Those women are like currency. They wouldn't go to all the trouble of kidnapping them and then kill them. Not when they can make a lot of money by selling their bodies to the highest bidders over and over again."

I grimaced.

An old feeling returned that hadn't been there for a while. That disgusting nausea that came over me when I thought of what traffickers did to women. The only way I kept my sanity for the last few months when I couldn't run missions was not to think about it.

Once I was in mission mode, I no longer held back the emotions. The rage was what drove me to success. I'd do whatever it took to get those girls back.

"I agree with Jamie," Brad said. "The girls are alive. We have satellite images of where they're being held."

Brad handed me the file in his hand.

"I'll go there and get them out," I said with confidence that had suddenly returned. I was afraid of losing it if I was on the sidelines for too long. "What's the plan?"

"You do it however you want," Brad said. "You have full mission control. I'd rather you go to Alaska first though and find out who is behind the operations in America. Dispose of them. Then go to Russia."

"I'll do it."

I was ready to walk out the door and get on a plane at that moment.

"I want you to take Kaley with you," Brad said.

"Nope. No way," I said, shaking my head violently from side to side. "She's not ready."

"Your job was to get her ready," Brad said. "You've had three weeks. I thought the training was going well. There's only so much you can teach her at The Farm. Nothing like a real life mission to get her feet wet."

"I don't think she'll ever be ready for that kind of mission. She can handle undercover work. Hand offs. Meets. Flipping assets. She's got the skills to take care of herself if she runs into trouble. I don't recommend using her to rescue girls and run full blown missions. I don't think she has what it takes."

"That's disappointing to hear. Is this because of last night?"

"What happened last night?" Alex asked.

I told them both the whole story. Although Brad already knew most of the details.

"It's your mission," Brad said. I could hear the disappointment in his tone. "You always get to choose who you want with you. I'm not sending you into danger with someone you don't trust."

"Thank you."

We went through a number of mission details and then left.

As we were walking out of the building, Alex said, "Jamie, I think you may be overreacting."

"About what?"

"About Kaley."

I rolled my eyes at him.

5

Curly had warned me on more than one occasion not to get married.

"Have all the sex you want," he said, "but avoid marriage like you avoid getting shot in the head with a bullet."

His own failed marriages aside, which almost certainly provided the bitterness behind the words, his advice was backed by statistics. The divorce rate among spies was astronomical compared to the general population.

For obvious reasons. We were away from each other for long periods of time.

Our job title was Pathological Liar.

Meaning almost everything we did in the field was a ruse. Lying became so second nature to us, bringing that same mindset home was easy. Lie to your spouse, even when the truth served you better.

Alex and I vowed to never do that to each other, but that wasn't always possible. I liked to think of it as acting, not lying.

Curly's strongest admonition was, "Whatever you do, don't marry another CIA agent."

So much for that rule.

When he learned Alex and I were getting married, he said, "I give it six months. Maybe a year."

We somehow defied the odds and were still together. I'd even say that we had a good marriage. All things considered.

Curly even admitted it before he died.

"The two of you were meant for each other," he said. "You're the only two people on this earth who could stand being married to the other."

We weren't sure if he was complimenting us, but we took it as such.

Curly did warn us about something. The three of us were at The Farm one night, sitting in some chairs outside his residence. One of the few times I'd ever seen Curly relaxed. Alex and I had recently returned from our honeymoon.

"Watch out when one of you is getting ready to leave on a mission," he said, sternly. "It's a dangerous time for your marriage."

"Why Curly?" I asked. "What happens then?"

"One of two things," he said. "You'll either have a huge fight or make love like rabid dogs. Either way means your marriage is doomed for failure."

"I like the sound of the rabid dog thing," Alex said.

I probably gave Alex an eye roll that night. I don't remember. It may have been too dark for him to see it. We were sitting next to each other on a porch swing. Curly was in a rocker across from us. Staring off in the distance most of the time. A beverage of choice in his hand.

"Nope," Curly said. "That kind of sex is great if you're not married. It's bad if you're married and do it right before a mission."

"Why?" I asked.

"Emotions run high right before a mission. Leaving hurts. It's bad enough when you're not married. You're leaving your house. Your dog. The bed you sleep in. You're in strange places. Getting shot at. You never know if you're even coming home. It might be the last time you ever see your house. Or dog. Or wife."

It almost sounded like Curly was tearing up. We'd never seen him emotional before or this philosophical. It seemed like a shift was happening in our relationship.

Curly was going from a mentor to almost a father figure. Alex grew up without a father or mother. His parents were killed in a car accident when he was a teenager. My mom died of breast cancer when I was seventeen. I didn't know where my father was. I never met him other than to talk for twenty minutes or so one time.

My dad was a famous astronaut. He was chosen by NASA to go on a one-way mission to the ends of the universe in search of intelligent life. I'd never see nor hear from him again. I missed him desperately even though I didn't really know him.

Curly was filling a void. He wasn't loving and affectionate like a father might be. But he'd give his life for me. I would for him as well. I think he cared for me like a daughter.

He continued. "Leaving is harder when you're married," Curly said. "The pain of leaving is intensified."

"I can see that," I said.

I'd felt it, although I'd never taken the time to analyze the emotions. Even when Alex and I were engaged, I hated being apart. I didn't know what it was going to be like now that we were married.

"Don't ever leave mad," Curly said. He had stopped rocking and looked over at us.

"If we're leaving each other to go on a mission, why would we fight?" Alex asked.

"It's a coping mechanism," Curly said. "If you're mad at your husband or wife, it makes it easier to see them go."

"I would think it'd make it harder," I said.

"It does. As soon as you're out of their sight. Once you get on that plane and are in the air, you feel guilty. Regrets overwhelm you. You're miserable the whole time you're away from each other. You can't wait to get back to apologize."

"I can see where that's not a good thing," I said.

"It's worse than that. You're distracted in the field. Distractions get you killed. If you're the spouse left behind, you become bitter. Angry. Resentful."

"So the best thing to do is have sex like rabid dogs," Alex said. "Then you don't feel bad when you leave. You feel good."

Curly shook his head from side to side with emphasis.

"Nope. It's even worse than the first scenario."

"That doesn't make sense," Alex said. "How could great sex be worse?"

"When you leave, you're all in love. Feeling all mushy inside. That makes it harder. It's painful to leave someone you're that close to. You wonder if you're ever coming home to her. You miss her. You're lying in a fox hole with a bunch of sweaty men. The whole time, you're pining away for her like a silly schoolboy."

Alex reached over and took my hand and gave me an affectionate look. Then put his arm around me. I scooted closer. We were still in the honeymoon stage. Madly in love.

I was interested in what Curly had to say.

"That's when you make mistakes in the field," Curly said. "You start being careful. You quit taking risks. You have a wife at home waiting for you. Careful gets you killed in the real world."

"I can see that," Alex said.

"It'll mess with your emotions," Curly said. "Especially when you come back. You think things are going to be like they were the night you left. You'll be all hot for each other. You're not. She's a different person. So are you. She gets used to a daily routine that you aren't part of. You coming home disrupts her daily life. She's excited to see you at first, then you're just annoying to her. She can't wait for you to leave again."

"That's not going to happen to us," Alex said.

"She might even have a new boyfriend. Somebody to take your place. It's called transference."

"I didn't know you were a trained psychologist," Alex quipped.

I wondered if that had happened to Curly and that's why he was divorced.

"Like I said, don't get married," he said sharply.

"Too late," Alex said, squeezing my hand. "That won't happen to us."

The conversation had stayed in my head all these years. I remembered it like it was yesterday. Since that day, I'd tried to make sure Alex and I had a good send off. We didn't fight, but we also didn't rip each other's clothes off. I tried to make our last night normal.

I wanted to make sure he left satisfied and feeling loved, but not distracted by me. Like Curly said. Distractions can get you killed.

Alex must've remembered the conversation as well. We never fought before a mission.

I'd almost messed that up this time. When Alex said that I was over-reacting about Kaley, I'd snapped at him.

"You weren't there," I said. "I know what I saw. Kaley was being careful. She doesn't have what it takes to be in the field in my opinion."

"The girl is only twenty years old," Alex argued. "She disarmed two gunmen with her bare hands. Sounds like she's ready to me."

"She's nineteen," I said, correcting him.

"That makes it even more impressive."

"One of the men got a shot off. We could've been killed."

"But you weren't."

"But we could've been."

"But you weren't."

"Stop saying that! If she can't handle two punks in Washington, D.C., how's she going to handle trained Russians with machine guns."

"Take her with you and find out."

"I'm not taking her with me. The decision's been made. I'm going alone."

"I think it's a mistake."

"Don't tell me how to do my job! It's none of your business. I don't tell you how to run your missions."

Alex put his hands up in surrender and didn't mention it again.

6

I immediately regretted the harsh tone with Alex.

Especially when it created a coolness between us. The entire evening we'd been cordial but distant. I didn't want us to leave that way. Curly was right. It could affect both our missions.

We were in our bedroom, packing. It wouldn't take long. We both traveled light. Alex didn't need much since he was going on our plane. It already had toiletries, clothes, weapons, and ammunition.

What I needed in the way of mission supplies would be waiting for me at a CIA safehouse in Fairbanks, Alaska. I was traveling commercial first class, but whatever I took from home had to fit in one backpack. We never checked our bags.

"Don't forget your skin cream," I said, trying to lighten the mood.

"It's already packed," he said, in a friendly enough tone. Kind enough to let me know he was mostly over our tiff.

That gave me the opening I was waiting for. "I'm sorry I snapped at you earlier," I said.

"You were right. It's none of my business. I shouldn't tell you how to run your missions."

"Thank you for that. But I do value your opinion. Why do you think I'm overreacting?"

"Oh no. I'm not going there."

"Why not? I'm asking your opinion."

"I don't want you to get mad at me."

"I won't. I promise. I'll listen to what you have to say and then tell you why you're wrong."

I was grinning so he'd know I was kidding.

He tried an eye roll.

"You really don't know how to roll your eyes, do you?" I said.

"Yeah I do. See."

He turned his head in a jerking motion up and to the side.

I laughed. "That's not an eye roll. That's a head roll. Your eyes never moved."

I thought about teaching him how to do it but decided I'd rather not. That was one area where I had the upper hand and I intended to maintain it.

My backpack was full, so I zipped it up and went to stand next to him while he finished neatly folding his clothes and organizing them in his suitcase. My clothes were thrown into my backpack.

We'd argued about that before. "Mine would get wrinkled," he said.

I didn't care. I could always iron them. Not that I would in this situation. I was going deep into the woods of Denali National Park. I didn't think anyone would notice a few wrinkles on my shirt.

"Alex, tell me why you think I'm overreacting, or I *will* be mad. I really want to know."

He stopped what he was doing and looked deep into my eyes. Probably trying to decide if it was safe to do so.

"All right. I agree that being careful will get you killed. I also agree that Kaley's best move was to turn to the left and not to the right."

"I'm glad we agree. Then why am I overreacting?"

"Because Kaley wasn't killed. Neither were you. The bad guys were on the ground within seconds. Everything turned out alright in the end."

"We were lucky the bullet missed us."

"No you weren't. You said Kaley ducked to avoid it. That's skill. Not luck."

"The thug shot wildly. She was lucky he didn't know what he was doing."

"Exactly. She handled the situation and came out unscathed. Considering all the factors."

"Whoever is on the other side of the gun may not miss the next time."

"You'll never know unless you give her a next time."

I could feel the frustration rising. I would get angry if I let it continue to gain momentum. So, I tamped it down.

Alex didn't get it. Just because we weren't killed, didn't mean we couldn't have been. Kaley put both of us at risk. I wasn't sure what point he was making.

I took in a deep breath to make sure my tone was measured. My words were going to be sarcastic. "So are you saying that I should take Kaley with me until we both get killed? It's a little late then, don't you think?"

Alex stopped what he was doing and took my hand and sat me down next to him on the edge of the bed.

"The intangible that you and I have is not what you think it is," Alex said.

"What do I think it is?"

"You think it's our skill that keeps us from dying."

"That's what it is. You and I have that intangible. We can go into the worst situations and come out still standing. That's the 'it' factor. Kaley doesn't have that."

"Forget Kaley for a minute. Let's talk about us. There have been a dozen times when I thought I was going to die."

"Me too. Probably more than that."

"But you didn't die."

"I know. That's the intangible."

"It is, but it isn't."

"You're not making sense."

"When you were on that plane, flying over Cuba, about to parachute into the eye of a hurricane, you almost died, right?"

"Almost. I came within five feet of not making it to the shore. I probably would've died in the swells."

"A gust of wind could've pushed you back into the water."

"Right. Then I would've died. What's your point?"

"You could've jumped out of the airplane five seconds later and you wouldn't have made it to the shore. You would have landed in the waves and been killed."

"I know that, Alex. I'm still not following you."

"You think the reason you're still alive is because of your skill."

"It is. That and the intangible. I was able to take a hopeless situation and survive it."

"With a little luck."

"Curly said to make your own luck."

"My football coach said that luck was when skill met opportunity."

"Exactly."

"Don't think so highly of yourself."

Now I was starting to get mad. He squeezed my hand. I pulled it away. Maybe I shouldn't have brought it up. We couldn't have this conversation without fighting.

"Hear me out," Alex said in a soft tone. He clearly was trying to keep things from escalating into a fight. "You're the most skilled operative in the world."

"I thought I was second," I said, jokingly. Feeling the tension subside somewhat. "You always said you were the best."

"We're talking hypothetical here."

"Continue."

"You parachuted out of a plane into the eye of a hurricane. But by the time you were to the shore, you were in the hurricane. Any normal person would've died."

"I know. I have skills. I still don't understand. Please help me." I was beyond frustrated.

"Skill played a part in you surviving the jump. But when you were still in the plane, you can't tell me you knew if you waited five more seconds to jump, that you'd die."

"Of course not."

"That's my point. It's not all about us. The intangible is that we always survive. That's what makes you and me different. That's the intangible. No matter what we're facing, we somehow survive it."

"I think I'm beginning to understand."

"Remember when I crossed the North Korean border and walked right up to Pok's cyberlab and turned myself in."

"That was stupid."

"Yes, it was and I survived it. Remember when you were in Hong Kong and the sniper missed hitting you by a few inches?"

"I still get chills thinking about it."

"That had nothing to do with you. If the sniper's aim was better, you'd be dead."

"He's dead now."

"My point exactly. For whatever reason, we always win in the end. Or at least we have so far."

"And you're saying Kaley has the intangible because she survived the attack last night. The bullet didn't hit her."

"I don't know if she has it or not. She's only nineteen. That was her first opportunity to prove herself. You think she failed. I think she succeeded. She used her skill to dodge the bullet. But luck was on her side as well."

"She wouldn't have been in that situation had she not made a mistake in judgment."

"You and I have made more mistakes on missions than any humans alive. You and I both should've been killed a dozen times."

"At least."

"But we weren't. Kaley should've turned to the left, but she turned to the right. So what? She got the job done. And she did it skillfully. With precision beyond her years. Thanks to your incredible training."

"I see what you mean."

"That's why I think you should take her with you."

I wrapped my arm around his neck and kissed him. Gently.

"When did you get so smart?" I said.

"Since I started using that skin cream."

"You've never been more attractive to me than you are right now."

"That's because of the skin cream as well. I need to stock up on that stuff."

"No. It's because of what you were saying. You're brilliant. It makes me want to rip your clothes off."

"What's stopping you?"

Nothing stopped me. Even though Curly said not to, we were like a couple of rabid dogs on the bed that night.

7

Waking up a trained CIA spy was something you had to do with great care.

As operatives, we were trained to always sleep with a gun on the nightstand next to us. More than one operative had been killed in a hotel room bed in the middle of the night. Some operatives slept in the closet for that reason. Or the bathtub. That gave them the element of surprise.

I never did that. I valued a good night's sleep.

Curly taught me how to wake up, secure my weapon, aim, assess the threat, then fire. All in less than four and a half seconds. Which was the amount of time Curly felt I needed to kill the threat before he killed me. I got it down to under three seconds. Which meant somebody I knew, including Alex, had better not get cute and try to startle me out of a deep sleep as a joke.

That was a good way to get killed.

Kaley was asleep in her hotel room. I'd dropped Alex off in the wee hours of the morning at the hangar where our AJAX plane was housed. Before the sun was up.

"Don't be careful in Russia, Jamie," he said after we kissed goodbye.

"I won't," I said. "Don't miss me."

"That'll be hard to do after last night."

The previous night had been intense and passionate.

"There's more of that waiting for you when you get home," I said, sending him off with another big kiss.

My heart ached as I watched him walk toward the plane. I sat there for a minute or so even after he disappeared from my sight.

I missed him already.

It was getting harder to be away from him. It'd been awhile since we'd gone on separate missions.

For whatever reason, I had a weird feeling about his mission. I didn't voice it to him, even though it had been nagging at me since the night before. We never spoke of those types of things. I didn't want to put it in his head. It might distract him. Cause him to lose a split-second edge.

Enough to cause a disaster. A self-fulfilling prophecy.

It was probably nothing anyway. Every once in a while, Alex and I both got an ominous feeling about things. A sixth sense. Like we knew something bad was going to happen. It did about half the time.

Which meant half the time the feeling was wrong, and the worry was for nothing. The other half, the disaster did happen, but we lived through it. So I tried to shake it off and not worry about it.

It couldn't linger in my mind. Otherwise, it might affect my mission. So I did what I was trained to do best. Compartmentalize my emotions. Lock them in a vault. Nothing I could do about it. Alex was going on the mission no matter what. Whatever happened, happened. I knew he'd do everything within his power to come back to me safely.

I'd do the same. If I worried about him, I'd be the one not coming home.

I didn't stay to watch his plane take off. Instead, I left and tried to get him out of my mind. My mission was dangerous enough without having to worry about him.

Thirty minutes later, I stood outside the door of Kaley's hotel room. I could open the key card door since I had a card, but thought better of it. She didn't know she was coming with me to Alaska. As far as she knew, I was done with her. I had disparaged her to Brad. Told him that she wasn't ready for the field.

That was how I felt. I still hadn't changed my opinion. But Alex had been insistent. His arguments were sound and he talked me into taking her.

I hoped I didn't regret it.

Since Kaley had no ideaI was coming, I didn't want to burst into her hotel room and wake her up from a deep sleep with a flurry of activity. Like Curly did to me on several occasions at The Farm to see how I would react in that situation.

I could imagine myself sprinting across the hotel room, throwing off her covers, and depositing her on the floor. Then jumping on top of her and pummeling her with rabbit punches. To show her she wasn't ready for the field. Berate her for not having her gun on the nightstand. For not being prepared to deal with a threat.

If this was real-life you'd be dead! A good training technique.

Did she remember what I taught her? To always sleep with her gun next to her. No matter what. Even in a Virginia hotel room where there were no threats. To develop the habit. Alex and I could be on vacation, and we still followed protocol. One hundred out of a hundred times.

But what if Kaley was prepared? What if she had paid attention and her gun was on the nightstand. She'd practiced securing her weapon and had gotten it down to under six seconds. Not bad for a rookie.

It's hard to simulate a deep sleep though. You can't really practice it at The Farm. Not with a live gun. So she practiced the moves while she was awake.

I hadn't been so lucky. One of the things I hated most about Curly's training was when he woke me from a deep sleep. Curly didn't care that my gun might be loaded. He was confident he could get to me before I could secure it.

I wasn't sure how Kaley might respond in a real-life situation. More than likely it'd take her ten seconds or so to react.

Maybe less if she was prepared.

The procedures were standard.

Gun on the nightstand. She was right handed, so I told her to sleep on the right side of the bed. Try not to toss and turn. Sleep facing the right. The barrel of the revolver was to be facing away from her. So with one motion, she could reach, secure the gun, aim, then determine the nature of the threat before she fired. You didn't want to kill the maid.

If it was a threat then take it out.

More than likely, I could get in her hotel room and secure her weapon before she could reach it. Part of me wanted to try. But what if I couldn't and she was better in real life than she was in practice? What if she didn't recognize there was no threat in the dark? What if she fired by accident?

Not a good way to start a mission.

So I knocked on her door.

If she remembered her training, she'd secure her weapon, stand to the side of the door, and ask who it was. Not open the door or look through the keyhole. A good way to die. All a threat had to do was wait to hear a noise inside, then fire a bullet through the keyhole, and splatter an operative's brain matter all over the hotel room.

Opening the door was equally stupid. The threat had an easier target. Aim and fire. Dead.

I knocked a second time. Not loud. I didn't want to wake the guests on the same floor.

I heard footsteps coming from the inside. Like she was tiptoeing. Like I had taught her to do.

Kaley didn't look through the keyhole. I could tell. Looking cast a barely perceptible shadow from my vantage point.

So far so good. I was impressed.

I heard a groggy voice. "Who is it?"

I tried to think of a funny comeback. The Big Bad Wolf. Housekeeping. Your worst nightmare. Something stupid like that. I resisted the urge to try and be funny.

"It's Jamie."

The door cracked open.

I pushed it all the way open. Roughly. Then bolted through it and into the room, leaving Kaley standing at the entrance. She had her gun in her hand. Dressed in shorts and a tee-shirt. As I trained her. Always sleep with clothes on in case you have to make a quick getaway.

"What are you doing here?" she asked, after closing the door behind me.

"Get dressed," I said, turning the lights on ignoring her question. I wanted to reestablish the trainer/trainee relationship immediately.

"Why?"

"You're coming with me."

"Where are we going?"

"Need to know basis."

8

"Pack your bags. Brush your teeth. Get a move on it," I said to Kaley.

"I don't understand. Brad said you didn't want anything to do with me."

The words had a bitter undertone to them.

"I don't. But I'm going to give you a chance to redeem yourself. See if you can prove me wrong."

She perked up.

"I want that chance. I won't let you down a second time."

"Then get moving before I change my mind."

She gathered her things, changed clothes, and was ready within two minutes.

Neither of us said anything the entire way to the airport. Kaley was probably afraid to ask questions for fear of making me angry again.

I wasn't even thinking about her. My mind was occupied. Between trying to get rid of my worry about Alex and his mission and formulating a plan for my own. Now that Kaley was with me, I had more options.

When I looked over at her, she was looking straight ahead. I could sense the coolness between us. Brad said she'd been extremely disappointed when he spoke with her the night before. She was practically in tears. I almost felt a twinge of guilt when he told me.

I genuinely liked Kaley. To her credit, she had been a model trainee. Enthusiastic and obedient. She sopped up my instructions like a sponge.

She knew my reputation and was respectful. Too much so. I tried to get her to question me some, so she'd better understand why we did what we did. I didn't want a mind-numbed robot in the field. I wanted someone who could think for herself.

Eventually, I was able to pull it out of her. Except for the problem outside the pizza joint, I thought she had tremendous potential.

"Leave your weapons in the car," I said, once we pulled into long-term parking. "Guns. Knives. Leave anything that you won't be able to take through security."

If we had CIA credentials, we could carry our weapons on the plane. Technically, the CIA had nothing to do with this mission. We were traveling under fake passports, provided by Brad, but he'd keep no record of assisting us.

Everything was outside normal channels. Kaley was still a recruit, and I was an independent freelancer.

"Where are we going?" she finally asked.

No reason not to tell her. I'd already made the point that I was still the boss. I couldn't help but tease her, though.

"We're going to an island," I said. "Where we can lay on the beach and sip rum runners." I said it in as sarcastic a tone as I could muster.

"Seriously. What are we doing here?"

"Do you want to go on a mission or don't you? Let me know now. If you don't, I'll get you a cab and you can go back to your hotel room and go to sleep."

"Yeah. I mean, no. Of course I want to go. But I don't understand. Brad said you cut me loose. You said I wasn't good enough. Never would be."

"I changed my mind. Don't make me regret it."

That seemed to satisfy her. She clammed up. Probably thought she was on thin ice with me. That I would cut her loose if she said the wrong thing. That wasn't true. She was going on the mission no matter what.

We put our weapons in the trunk along with anything in her backpack I thought she didn't need. Brad would have weapons for us once we arrived in Fairbanks, Alaska. I'd called him the night before and told him I was taking Kaley with me.

Brad was glad to hear the news. He had a lot invested in Kaley. Expectations were high. But my words held a lot of weight. It would've taken Kaley a long time to dig herself out of the hole and prove herself.

I told him to let me tell her.

I had a new resolve.

Kaley was going to be good enough. My life depended on it.

Our mission was to rescue the twelve girls. That was priority number one. My second priority was to get Kaley ready. If humanly possible. I'd consider it a failure if I couldn't bring the best out of her.

I wondered if Curly ever had any of those same doubts about me. If he did, he never gave up on me. Even when I screwed up.

Now I'd take it as a personal affront if I couldn't help Kaley reach her potential. Like somehow, I was the one who failed. Not her. Alex reinforced that in me the night before. His football coach always said that if they lost a game, it was the coach's fault. Not the players. Not the assistant coaches. Not the refs. The buck stopped with him.

If the players weren't good enough, it's because the coach didn't recruit well enough. If the assistant coaches weren't good enough, then the coach didn't hire the right people. If the players were good enough but didn't play up to their potential, then the practices weren't hard enough leading up to the game.

If they won, the players got the credit. If they lost, the coach took the blame.

That's how I looked at it.

Kaley was going to succeed.

Losing wasn't an option.

Of course, where we were going, failure meant death. Or the rest of our lives in a Russian prison. Brad wasn't going to come after us if we ran into trouble. There wasn't a cavalry that'd be called in. The President wasn't going to initiate any prisoner swaps. Not right away.

The only thing I could count on was that Alex would search high and low until he found me. Probably dying in the process. A Russian prison was our worst nightmare. The only thing worse would be an

Iranian prison. We all knew ending up in a Russian prison meant years of torture.

Nothing anyone could do to get us out. Even if they wanted to. Attacking a prison with hundreds of armed Russian soldiers wasn't an option. Escape wasn't either. Death was the only way out of the misery.

So I needed Kaley to come through. Or we'd both be in trouble.

I might regret taking her with me. She might regret it even more.

I went to the ticket counter and purchased her a first-class ticket. I thought about making her sit in coach but decided against it. I needed her morale up. I spent three weeks at The Farm breaking her down. Destroying her confidence.

Now I had to build her back up.

We were on a mission together. I was the leader, but she was a valuable part of the team. I'd still joke around with her, but my bossy attitude would be gone.

Once we were on the plane, my tone changed. I began treating her like I treated A-Rad or Bond. We were a team. The sooner I made her feel a part of it, the better she'd be.

She definitely noticed but didn't say anything.

Once we were in the air, I took out the CIA file and handed it to her.

"What's this?" she asked.

"This is our mission."

She opened the file and began to rifle through it. Inside were pictures of the twelve kidnapped girls along with details of their backgrounds.

"Memorize that file," I said. "Study every face."

I'd already memorized them. Their faces were etched in my mind. For motivation. Not that I needed it, but I liked knowing everything about them.

It created the rage I needed to go scorched earth on the human excrement who were holding them. Depraved men who didn't deserve to take another breath on this earth.

The girls were from various backgrounds. Most were visiting the area. Jogging or hiking in the Denali National Park. They'd come there for an adventure. Alone. To become one with nature.

Most were nineteen to twenty-five. College students or young professionals taking a vacation to Alaska.

"These girls were kidnapped off the trails," I said. "We're going to find the guys who kidnapped them."

"There are hundreds of miles of trails. How are we going to do that?"

I pulled the map of the park out of the file.

"Most of the girls went missing about the same distance away from the visitor's center. I think that's where the bad guys staked them out. We'll go there first and see what we see."

"Then what?"

"We're going to bait them out."

"What's the bait?"

"Not what, who. You."

"What do you mean? How am I the bait?"

"Every day, you're going to go to the Visitor Center, make yourself seen and heard, then you're going to head off on a trail. Alone."

"By myself?"

"Yep. Hopefully, they'll make their move and try to kidnap you."

Kaley's eyes brightened. I could hear the excitement in her voice.

"Then I take them out," she said excitedly.

I shook my head.

"Nope. You play along. I want them to take you to Russia. That's where the girls are being held."

"You want me to voluntarily go with them?"

"Yes. Resist slightly. You have to make them think you're untrained. A normal young woman, hiking the trails. Don't let them know you have skills."

"How do I resist the urge to break their necks?"

I liked what I was hearing.

"Being a good spy is acting," I said. "Playing a role. You have to make them think you're vulnerable. That they can control you. But you are always in control. You can break their necks anytime you want. But they can't know that."

"What weapons will I have on me?"

"None."

"Can I have a gun?"

"No."

"Why not? It says here that you can carry a firearm in the park."

"I don't want you to carry a gun. You'll be tempted to use it."

"So I allow them to kidnap me, but I have no weapons?"

"You always have a weapon."

"Oh right. My hands, feet, elbows, knees. Everything is a weapon." She said it sarcastically. Mimicking my voice.

"Not just that. Anything at any time can be a weapon. A rock. A branch lying on the ground. A strong twig is as good as a knife if stuck in the side of someone's neck. Remember, the bad guys will have guns. Take theirs if you need one."

"But you said I'm not allowed to resist."

"That's right. Don't resist unless you have no other choice."

"These girls are being trafficked. Am I supposed to let them have sex with me?"

"No. The rules of engagement within the CIA are clear. Women are not permitted to subject themselves to prostitution. Men operatives aren't allowed to have sex with prostitutes. Even if it gets us in the inner circle. Those are some lines we won't cross."

"Even if it blows my cover?"

"Even if. If at any time, you feel like your life is in danger or you are in immediate risk of bodily harm, including rape, then you act. Not before."

"Where are you going to be?"

"I'll meet you in Russia."

"You're not going to be there if I need you?"

I heard the first hint of fear in her voice.

"No. You're on your own. Let them take you all the way to Russia. I want to see how they get the girls across the Bering Sea. Keep your eyes and ears open. You'll be the best person to gain intel. I want to know how many men are involved in these operations. Remember their faces. Height. Weight. Build. Take a look at their IDs if you get the chance."

"I can do that."

"Kill them if you have to. But preferably, I want them to take you all the way to the prison in Russia where they're holding the other girls. Once you're with them, then formulate a plan to get them out. I'll help you from the outside once you get free."

"I can do that."

"I'm counting on you."

"You can."

"Don't forget rule number one."

"I won't. Don't be careful."

9

Denali National Park

Kaley didn't understand the "don't be careful" nonsense. Was she supposed to be careless? The CIA trainer before Jamie constantly criticized her for being too reckless. Taking too many chances.

While she'd learned a lot from Jamie, that's one thing that didn't make sense and she disagreed with. An operative needed to be smart. Cagey. Skilled. Not a no-holds-barred shoot from the seat of your pants loose cannon. That seemed like a sure way to die.

It certainly didn't make sense now.

Kaley was hiking on a trail about six miles from the visitor's center. Deep in the woods of the Denali National Park. With only one weapon. A knife. The only reason she had it on her was because she hid it from Jamie. It seemed irrational to wander off into the middle of nowhere unarmed.

She felt like a worm wiggling on a fishhook.

Kaley was the bait.

What a stupid idea.

That's not how she'd do it if she were in charge. Rescuing the girls was a righteous mission. Kaley was on board with that. Even willing to risk her life for the cause.

But they knew where the girls were in Russia. Why not go there and get them out? The path of least resistance. Save the girls. That was the ultimate mission.

Kaley understood the desire to take down the organization inside the United States. But why not turn the tables on the two men? Hunt them down. Interrogate them until they spilled everything they knew about their organization.

A gun could be persuasive when put on the side of someone's head. That seemed like a much better plan. But this was Jamie's mission. She was in charge. Kaley had to do what she said. Brad had made that crystal clear.

That didn't mean she had to like it. Especially since she was the one hiking alone on the trails. Taking all the risks. Why was she the one put in harm's way? Why not Jamie? It seemed like Jamie only brought Kaley along so that she didn't have to put herself at risk. It didn't seem fair.

Was the great American hero losing her nerve?

Kaley tried to put these bitter thoughts out of her mind and focus on the task at hand but they kept surfacing. Like Old Faithful that had to erupt from the pressure every few minutes. Apparently, Jamie's approval was the gateway into her career with the CIA. That also seemed unfair. Why was one person given that much control over her life?

Jamie was supposedly the best CIA operative ever. Kaley intended to take that moniker away from her. In the meantime, she had to pay her dues. Prove herself. This mission was her first opportunity to do so. If Jamie was the gatekeeper, then Kaley had to figure out how to get past her.

By succeeding on this mission. Whether she liked it or not.

Focus.

Two men were nearby. She could feel it.

Jamie had spotted one of the men at the Visitor's Center earlier that morning. She motioned for Kaley to go into the lady's restroom.

"He's the man wearing the red Wisconsin Badgers shirt," Jamie said. "The one with the binoculars around his neck."

"I saw him. He looks like a tourist."

"That's what he wants you to think."

"How do you know it's one of them?"

"Bad guys have a look. He's nervous. Fidgeting. He keeps touching his hip. Where his gun would normally be. He picks up a brochure, pretends to look at it, then puts it back. He doesn't keep any of them and doesn't actually read what's in it."

"I didn't notice."

"You'll learn to notice these things. Mostly, it's the eyes. You can always tell a bad guy by the eyes. Pure evil. That's one thing they can't hide."

"I never saw his eyes. He kept looking away."

"That's what I'm talking about. You're a pretty girl. Guys will notice you. He tried not to make eye contact with you."

"He was standing close to me."

"He's checking you out. He also has a partner. I saw him out by the car. Smoking a cigarette."

"How do you know they're together?"

"That's my job. The vehicle is not a rental car. It has a local license plate. I memorized the number. I'll have Brad look it up."

"Why would the guy be wearing touristy clothes if he lives in Alaska?"

"Exactly. Now you're catching on."

"What do you want me to do?"

"I want you to go back out there. Go to the information desk and ask for a map. Talk louder than normal so the man can hear you. Work into the conversation that you're alone."

Kaley felt her heartbeat tick up a notch. For the first time, it felt like she was on a real mission. She did as Jamie suggested and got a map along with a few admonitions from the park ranger.

"Be careful out there," he had said.

Jamie says I'm not supposed to be careful.

Kaley forced back a grin.

"Are you camping overnight?" the ranger asked.

Wisconsin guy moved closer. So he could overhear the conversation. Now that Jamie had identified the man for her, Kaley could clearly see what she meant. She was kicking herself for not spotting him first.

"Wearing the red shirt was stupid," Jamie had said. "It makes you stand out. He should be wearing camouflage clothing."

The man was so close, Kaley could've reached out and touched him. She answered the ranger's questions, not bothering to raise her voice since the man was nearby. "Yes. I'm going to spend several days in the backcountry."

"Are you here alone?"

"Yes. My friend was supposed to come. We're in college. You know. On summer break. One last vacay before we get back to the grindstone. She had a death in the family. I decided to come by myself. For the adventure. Yes. I'm going to be camping under the stars for several nights."

Almost immediately, Kaley realized her mistake. She was talking too much. Trying too hard. Like the guy in the Wisconsin shirt. He was trying too hard not to be noticed. She was trying too hard to get his attention.

And she didn't have any camping gear on her. No tent or supplies. Hopefully, the bad guy wouldn't notice.

"Make sure you have plenty of food and water in case you get lost," the ranger said. "You always have the mountain as your focal point. If you do get lost, try to find a clearing where you can see the mountain."

"I'll be fine. I have a map and a compass. I won't get lost."

"Do you have bear repellant?"

"Yes."

She lied. Then realized a second mistake. She should've said no. The bad guy didn't need to think she had something on her that could be used as a weapon.

"Do you have a whistle?"

"No."

"Do you have a weapon?"

"No."

I have a .44 magnum.

She left it in the trunk of the car in Washington, D.C. She wished she had it now. That gun would blow the man's head off. The one standing so close she could hear him breathing. He was looking at some post-cards.

Having clearly targeted her.

So far, so good.

This was fun. Jamie was right. It was like acting. Kaley was playing the role of dumb college student perfectly.

The ranger continued with his fatherly instructions. He was clearly concerned about her. That helped the persona. The bad guy had to be chomping at the bit. Feeling like he'd found his next victim. A beautiful but naïve young woman. The Russians would pay top dollar for some-one like her.

"Don't drink the water from the streams," the ranger said. "At night, keep your food a hundred feet away from your tent. Have something to keep you warm. The nights are cold even in the summer. We get snow twelve months out of the year. None is in the forecast, but you never know."

Blah. Blah. Blah.

Kaley wasn't even listening. She was thinking about the mission. How she'd play the part when Wisconsin man made his move on the trail.

The ranger looked her up and down. He seemed skeptical. Like he could tell she wasn't ready to go out in the deep woods by herself.

Hopefully, Wisconsin man would be thinking the same thing.

Kaley found it hard not to look at the bad guy. To keep her normal tone and appearance.

She accidentally looked his way. He quickly turned his head to the side away from her. He was tall and skinny. Not Russian. Defi-nitely American. Dusty blonde hair short on the sides with longer bangs brushed off to the side. A smoker. Kaley could tell by the smell and lines on his face.

He didn't seem like much of a threat. Not what she had imagined. The guy was a weasel. Kaley could twist him into a pretzel and not break a sweat. It'd take all her self-control to let this man touch her without breaking his arm.

It did give her some confidence.

Jamie was right. This was dangerous, but Kaley could handle every threat if the need arose. She could disarm weasel guy before he knew what was happening. If he restrained her, she knew how to get out of handcuffs and zip ties.

The men wouldn't kill her. They were kidnapping her to take her back to Russia. Kaley was worth more to them alive than dead.

Once she was in Russia, that's when things would get dicey. Even then, Kaley had the advantage. While outnumbered, she had surprise on her side. They didn't know about her skills. If they locked her in a jail cell, she knew how to pick any lock. She could also fake a sickness and lure a guard into the cell where she could disarm him. Once she had a weapon, she could fight her way out.

The better tactic was to sneak out without them knowing. Get the other girls and find a way of escape. She was confident she could do so.

Jamie thinks I'm not ready. I'll show her.

Kaley was getting ahead of herself. The men hadn't even tried to kidnap her. She wasn't sure they were even going to.

"Which trail has the fewest people on it," Kaley asked the ranger. He pointed out two options.

"Excellent. I go to a college with sixty thousand people. I'm ready to get alone with nature."

"You be careful out there," the ranger said again. "Be sure to write your name and information and put it in the box outside. Write down the number for an emergency contact in case you get in trouble. Write where you're headed."

I'm trying to get into trouble.

"I will."

Kaley couldn't help but grin. She was headed to Russia. After her Oscar winning performance in the Visitor Center, she was certain the men would follow her.

They had.

She could feel it.

Her heart began to beat faster.

It wouldn't be long until they made their move.

10

Kaley veered off the main trail. To make herself seem even more vulnerable to the men. The trail wasn't busy, but she didn't want to run into any other hikers.

This was her opportunity to use her training. If she was the bait, she had to make sure they took it. She made herself appear as vulnerable as possible.

Where was Jamie? Was she following close behind?

Kaley didn't want Jamie to rescue her. That'd only reinforce Jamie's point. That she wasn't ready for the field.

Was this a test?

Was that why Jamie insisted Kaley go out alone?

Everything was eerily silent around her. She could almost hear a pin drop. She could hear her heartbeat pounding in her ears.

Kaley had wanted to wear radio communication in her ear or a tracking device. Jamie was against it.

"You can't have anything on you that would tip them off that you are undercover. That'll get you killed immediately."

"I'll get rid of the device somehow."

"Can't take that chance. If they search you and find it, they'll shoot first, and ask questions later. You've seen their faces. They won't let you live."

"I'll take them out like I took out the guys at the pizza place."

That thought brought up a source of contention in Kaley.

Why was Jamie so upset about what happened that night? Kaley thought she did good. She disarmed the men, put them in the hospital, and protected Jamie at the same time. The one man got off a shot, but Kaley had anticipated it and ducked. Then made him pay for missing her.

What was the big deal? Her first trainer would've thought she did the right thing. Not Jamie. She was so upset she told Brad that Kaley would never make it as a field operative.

Of all the nerve.

She was crushed when Brad told her. She'd been so angry at Jamie, they would've had a confrontation had Jamie been around.

This was her life. Didn't Jamie know that?

Kaley had nothing else. She grew up without a father. Her mother was a drunk. She was the one who took care of her. The roles were reversed. The child took care of the parent. Thankfully, she didn't have any brothers or sisters she had to stay around for. Once she was old enough, she got out of there.

The CIA program was her lifeline out of a miserable life. And she was good at it. For whatever reason, Jamie Austen didn't like her. She intended to prove her wrong.

Starting now.

Kaley slowed her pace. If the men were following it'd give them time to catch up to her. Jamie had taught her how to spot a tail, but in no uncertain terms warned her not to use the techniques today. The men could have no idea that she had any skills whatsoever.

She resisted the urge to look back. She kept her focus on the makeshift trail in front of her. Almost to the point that she wasn't able to enjoy the view around her. The first part of the trail had been steep. It opened up into a rock outcropping overlooking a large tundra field. Kaley could see wildlife at a distance.

Moose and elk grazed on the other side of the field.

"Stay over there," Kaley said.

Interestingly enough, Kaley was more afraid of the wildlife than the men with guns. She wasn't trained to fight a bear. She did buy a can of repellant, but it only worked if the bear was within a few feet of her.

Kaley heard a noise behind her.

The sound of twigs breaking.

Showtime.

She steadied her pulse the way Jamie taught her. She'd dreamed of this moment. Her first encounter with a bad guy. The three scumbags at the pizza joint aside, this felt like a real-life mission. The stuff from which movies and legends were made.

Jamie Austen had such a reputation. The baddest female operative in the world. The most deadly female assassin on the planet. Kaley intended to take that moniker from her. In time.

Admittedly, she was impressed with Jamie while they were at The Farm. Jamie taught Kaley a lot. Taken her skills to a new level. But Kaley was the one in harm's way on this mission. She had yet to see any of Jamie's skills in the field.

To this point, Jamie was making Kaley do all the heavy lifting.

Maybe her mentor had lost a step. Jamie might not be as confident in her abilities as she once was. That might be why Jamie was a trainer now and not in the field. She wasn't as good as she once was.

Stand aside for the new kid in town.

Kaley definitely felt a presence behind her.

She heard a noise that sent chills down her spine.

Not what she expected to hear.

She turned and faced her worst fear.

Not the man in the Visitor's Center.

A Grizzly bear.

Staring right at her.

11

Washington, D.C.
Oval Office

Brad had been to the White House many times, but it still hadn't lost its mystique.

It wasn't the room itself. The Oval Office was relatively small considering it's the office of the leader of the free world.

The furnishings, if in any other office in America, were average at best. The history behind the various artifacts on display was what made them priceless and gave Brad a feeling of awe when he walked into the room.

The President's desk sat in front of three windows and four massive gold curtains. The most interesting piece in the room from Brad's perspective. He wanted to walk over and sit in the President's chair and pretend. If only for a moment.

He resisted the urge to do so.

Brad knew the history. The Resolute Desk, as it was known, was given to President Rutherford B. Hayes in 1880 by Queen Victoria of England. Made from the timbers of the British frigate Resolute, hence the name. The desk was a thank you to America for sending seamen to the arctic to free the Resolute when it became stuck in the ice.

First lady Jaqueline Kennedy had the desk restored and placed in the Oval Office. The desk was removed after her husband's assassination and traveled as part of an exhibit for years before being returned to the White House. Current President, Don Kemp, had the desk brought out of storage.

A bit of irony.

John F. Kennedy sat behind that desk contemplating what to do during the Russian Missile Crisis and the Bay of Pigs. America and President Don Kemp faced a similar crisis now.

The purpose of today's meeting.

Brad looked around the rest of the Oval Office. Taking it all in. Still unable to wrap his mind around the fact that he was in that room. Participating in such a high-level meeting. One in which the fate of the world potentially rested.

He sat on one of the two sofas that faced each other. Not knowing if he should sit there or in two sets of four wingback chairs positioned at both ends of the sofas separated by thin tables. Normally, the President sat in one of those chairs which was why Brad chose that strategic position.

He fidgeted. The sofas were surprisingly uncomfortable. He attributed it more to nerves.

He needed a distraction.

The Oval Office grandfather clock stood next to the northeast door of the room. Brad wanted to stand and walk over and look at it but also resisted the urge. The President and his boss, CIA Director, Ryan Coldclaw, could walk through the closed doors next to the clock at any moment. The ones that led to the President's private office. Ryan was briefing the president on the latest intelligence information Brad had gathered which would no doubt set the entire west wing on fire once it got out.

Brad tried to imagine what it was like for President Kennedy when he faced a similar crisis to help him regain his focus. Facing the same enemy. Russia. Who decades before attempted to move nuclear weapons into Cuba.

Kennedy ordered American warships into the Caribbean Sea to

block them. A stand-off occurred. The Russians eventually backed down and retreated.

What would President Kemp do?

Probably order a similar show of force. That's what Brad would recommend if he were asked his opinion. He might be. Depending on the direction of the meeting.

A portrait of President Reagan hung over the fireplace. Brad tried to imagine the meetings that took place when Reagan and his advisors tried to navigate through the Cold War. Reagan took a hard line with Russia as well. The most prudent tactic in Brad's opinion. The only thing the Soviet Union responded to was strength. Any weakness was exploited.

Why did America keep dealing with the same threat?

Because, in this instance, Kemp's predecessor was weak. Drew lines in the sand but didn't respond when Russia crossed them. To be fair, there was no permanent solution to the Russian problem. Not when both countries possessed nuclear weapons.

Brad strained his neck to do a full circle survey of the room. He closed his eyes momentarily and pictured what it was like for Roosevelt, Truman, Kennedy, Nixon, Reagan, Bush and others. He imagined the advisors of the presidents giving their opinions.

It sent a bolt of anxiety pulsing through him when he realized he was one of those advisors in this current crisis.

He'd always been nervous when he met with the President. Thinking about the current situation made him even more so. He changed positions on the sofa several times. Crossed his legs. Then uncrossed them only to cross them again seconds later. He began to wring his hands. Then wiped his sweaty palms on his pants. He straightened his suit and tie. Several times. Brushed his hair to the side and patted it down on the sides and back.

Reminded himself to breathe.

This was his job. What he was good at. Gathering information and analyzing it. He was prepared for such a time as this. He had to keep reminding himself. If he couldn't take the heat, then he should get out of the Oval Office as fast as possible and never look back. He signed up for a job with the CIA working in terrorism. Winning the war against the bad guys was his life's calling. He had to trust his instincts and abilities which were good.

As he moved up the career ladder, his decisions seemed to have more and more weight attached to them. The world was always on the precipice of war. It'd been centuries since the world didn't have a conflict going on in some part of the world.

The U.S. hadn't declared a formal war with Russia, but had imposed severe financial sanctions on the current regime. Those sanctions were as close to a war as you could get without firing a shot. They had decimated Russia's economy. Backed them into a corner.

The Russian President was like a fox in a tree with dogs surrounding it.

What else could the fox do but fight his way out?

That's what Russia was doing now. Desperate people took desperate actions.

What was their next move? Brad tried to organize his thoughts. How should America respond? He'd almost certainly be asked.

What about a preemptive strike? That was not his first inclination. Diplomacy first was the best policy.

Maybe the room would bring out the best in all of them. Give them the wisdom they needed.

How many times had the fate of the world rested on the decisions made in the Oval Office? Would that be the case in this instance as well? Would the president make a decision based on Brad's advice?

What if his advice was wrong?

He felt a wave of anxiety come over him a second time. The thought sent shivers down his spine. It felt like a weight was suddenly on his shoulders. Like an elephant was sitting on his chest, as he was having trouble breathing.

Why was he there? Was he really qualified?

He'd been lucky. His main job to that point had been managing Jamie Austen and Alex Halee. He'd overseen them since the beginning of their careers. While he had other operatives under his purview, the pair were his most notable. For many reasons. Mostly because of their successes for which he got a lot of credit within the Agency.

Most of which he didn't necessarily deserve. He pretty much sent them on a mission and they did whatever they wanted to do, ignoring his advice. Most of the time, things turned out for the best.

The only blip in the radar was when corrupt CIA Director Fuller took charge of the Agency. He promoted Brad from field analyst to assistant to the director, mostly to keep an eye on him. Then went after Alex and Jamie, who still somehow managed to end up on their feet. With some help from Brad.

It had been a fortuitous promotion. Fuller was in jail now and the new CIA director, Ryan Coldclaw, kept Brad in the position. He'd become Ryan's right-hand man. Together, they were transforming the Agency. Rather, reestablishing the things in the past that worked.

One of the first things they did was bring back Alex. Reinstated AJAX and allowed Brad to work with Jamie as a freelancer. She might eventually come back into the fold, but he'd discourage it. Jamie was better when she was on her own. Unshackled from the bureaucracy.

Brad hoped Kaley could be an adequate replacement and fill the void inside the Agency. While she might not ever be as good as Jamie, he'd take seventy percent.

It felt good to be working with Jamie and Alex again.

Alex initially found the threat with the Russians. He was the foremost computer hacker in the world. He'd only been back with the CIA for three weeks when he discovered secret communications within Russian war channels.

The Russians were moving ballistic missiles into the Kamkutz Peninsula. Only a few hundred miles from Alaska. The satellite images confirmed the intelligence. That's why Ryan brought it to the President with such urgency. That's why something had to be done. Soon.

The door opened, interrupting his thoughts. His heart skipped a beat when Ryan entered the room, then the President followed. The atmosphere in the room ticked up a notch.

Brad stood to his feet. President Kemp waved his hand dismissively.

"Keep your seat, Brad," he said. "You don't have to stand when I enter the room."

"Good morning, Mr. President," Brad said. "The Director would fire me on the spot if I didn't stand."

"Well, you can sit down now," he said with an engaging smile.

President Kemp was a good-looking charismatic type. He'd won the presidency with the largest number of popular votes in history and the largest margin of victory since Reagan. Not a small feat considering how polarized the country was.

He ran on a pledge to be tougher on Russia. The sanctions were one of his first acts. They'd been swift and ruthless. The Russian economy had been brought to its knees.

The Russians were obviously escalating the situation by moving the missiles into position where they could strike the west coast cities. They could strike them from their previous facilities, but Russia was bringing them to the peninsula for effect. To show how serious they were. A bit of bravado and showmanship.

Only God knew if they intended to follow through on the threat and fire them. If they did, hopefully aimed to land in the middle of the ocean. A shot across the bow so to speak.

Could they even take that risk?

The President's pledge to be tough on Russia would be tested now. Brad had to be sure the President didn't overreact. He was known as a bit of a hot head. Impulsive.

President Kemp walked behind his desk, took a look at his messages, then came back around and sat in one of the wingback chairs next to the sofas. Ryan sat on the couch across from Brad.

The President and Ryan both sat on the edge of their seats, so Brad assumed the same pose.

"Ryan has briefed me on the situation," the President said. "He wasn't shy on the details. What do you think we should do Brad?"

He couldn't stop his heart from racing.

12

Brad took a deep breath and reminded himself to talk fast.

President Kemp was a high strung, type A personality. No nonsense. Didn't like it when people wasted his time. He had an uncanny ability to assimilate facts quickly and draw conclusions.

Brad, on the other hand, was a deep thinker. Contemplative. An analyst. He made decisions slowly and carefully. After he had all the facts. It might take him six months to buy a blender.

He wasn't even sure he had all the facts now. He probably didn't.

They certainly didn't have six months to act though. The president would expect Brad to have an opinion for him now.

Rather than answer the question directly, he thought he'd give background information to support his position.

"We intercepted messages that Russia was moving ballistic missiles into the Kamkutz Peninsula," Brad said, starting with what he knew the president already knew.

Brad anticipated the interruption and paused.

"Are we certain there are no nuclear weapons in the mix?" the President asked.

"Yes. To the extent you can be certain about weapons in a foreign country."

"Pop-off intends to use them as leverage," the President said. "To get us to remove the sanctions."

He'd already figured out the obvious.

The Russian President's name was Yasha Popov, but Pop-off had become the disparaging nickname given to him because of his constant blustering and bloviating.

Popov leveled a new threat at the United States almost daily. He was becoming like Iran and North Korea who continually spewed out venomous threats at the United States and Israel. The only difference was that those two countries had no way of backing them up.

Something that wasn't the case with Russia. They had as many nukes as the United States.

"He's within days of having the missiles in place," Ryan said.

"Would he launch them?" the President asked.

Ryan looked at Brad for his opinion.

"I wouldn't put it past him," Brad said. "What does he have to lose? The sanctions are crippling his economy. If they continue, he could be thrown out of power. The Russian people are hurting and losing confidence in his leadership."

"We'd respond," the President said. "He must know that."

"Proportionately," Ryan answered. "That's what he's counting on."

"I hate that word," the President said. "If I go to war, I like to use overwhelming strength so that the enemy learns a lesson."

Brad's biggest fear. An overreaction could cause a nuclear war.

"Even then, an attack would hurt us more than it'd hurt him," Brad answered.

"What would the damage be to the U.S.?" the President asked.

Ryan answered. "He'd hit the west coast cities. I suspect that his initial attack would be restrained. He would want to walk a fine line. Enough to hurt us, but not enough to provoke us into a full scale war the Russians couldn't win."

"No one would win," Brad added. He didn't want to use the word nuclear even though it had to be in the back of everyone's minds.

Ryan nodded. "Popov would hit the closest cities. In California, Oregon, and Washington. He might not target the big ones to limit the casualties."

"None of those states voted for me anyway," the President quipped.

Brad and Ryan both chuckled nervously.

Fortunately, the conversation wasn't being recorded. At least as far as Brad knew. Some presidents in the past had secret video cameras inside the Oval Office. That practice had been discontinued for obvious reasons. Things were sometimes said that the involved parties wouldn't want in the hands of their political enemies.

"Be that as it may," Ryan said, "Popov would sacrifice a couple of his cities for ours. He will calculate that Americans don't have the political will for such a fight. Even if the damage was minimal, it'd be all over the news. Your poll numbers would plummet."

"I'm not worried about that. I don't run for reelection for three and a half years. That's an eternity in political years. I want to make sure Popov knows I mean business."

"There's always a preemptive strike," Ryan said. "You could take the missiles out before they're in place."

"Or you could make a phone call to the Russian president," Brad said. "Threaten him. Let him know we know what he's up to."

Ryan gave Brad an annoying look. Like he wasn't pleased with that idea.

Brad was certainly aware there were people in high levels of government who profited from war. Ryan wasn't one of them, but leaned to the hawkish side of the issue. The President, on the other hand, was elected in large part because of the big money donors in the defense industry.

They were counting on him getting the U.S into some kind of extended conflict. Not nuclear. That'd put everyone out of business. But a tussle with ballistic and cruise missiles was perfect for them. At 1.5 million dollars a pop, missiles were a huge profit center.

"What about sending in a Seals team and destroying the missiles?" the President asked. He clearly preferred action over words.

"Too dangerous," Ryan said. "They'd see them coming from miles away. It's on the peninsula. There's no good way to get to it. You'd be better off destroying the missiles from a distance. With a cruise missile."

"I'll meet with my generals. We'll develop a plan. At the very least, we can move a warship into the area. Two can play the intimidation game. If the Russians persist, I'll blow the peninsula into oblivion."

"Jamie Austen is there," Brad blurted out.

"What's she doing in Russia?" the President asked.

"She's on a mission to rescue those twelve girls who were kidnapped in Alaska. They were taken to Russia."

"I thought she wasn't with the CIA anymore."

"She's not," Ryan answered. "This is her own mission. And a high value CIA recruit is with her. Brad's right. We can't bomb the areas with them there."

"Where she's going is in the same area where they are setting up the missiles," Brad explained. "About thirty miles away at an abandoned Russian prison. You can't blow up the area without risking killing Jamie, Kaley, and the twelve Americans being held prisoner."

The president rubbed his forehead. "Then get her out of there," he said.

"With all due respect," Brad said, "I don't think Jamie would leave. Not without the girls."

"She'd disobey a direct order from the President of the United States?"

"Like I said, she doesn't really work for the CIA anymore," Brad said. "Even when she did, Jamie has a mind of her own."

No one said anything for a few seconds. The silence was awkward, so Brad continued.

"I have a bigger worry," Brad said, taking advantage of the lull.

"What's that?" the President asked.

"Jamie might see all the activity in the area and wonder what's going on. I can't guarantee that she won't act on her own."

"That'd be a suicide mission," Ryan said.

"Would she listen if you called and warned her?" the President asked.

"No," Ryan and Brad answered simultaneously.

Jamie was going to do what she was going to do. That's how she was wired. Hopefully, she went into Russia and got the girls out as quickly as possible without noticing any of the Russian troop movements.

Hopefully, before either side started firing missiles.

13

Denali National Park

The two men were following me, not Kaley.

So much for best laid plans. I was certain they'd follow the younger girl. I'd sent her off on one of the trails from the Visitor Center and expected the men to be right behind her. I intended to follow behind at a distance in case Kaley ran into trouble she couldn't handle.

We had set the plan in motion. Kaley headed up the trail. The two bad guys met at their car and discussed it. Instead of following her, Wisconsin red shirt man came back inside and started scoping me out. I had to improvise quickly.

Such was the life of a spy. Constantly thinking on your feet. Pivoting on a dime.

I had to immediately transition into the vulnerable female, so they'd at least follow me. If they didn't, we were back to square one. No way we could come back to the Visitor Center and hang out again. They'd get suspicious.

This was our chance.

I had a license plate number and snuck a couple of pictures of the men when they weren't looking. We could pursue that thread, but who knew where that might lead. The plates could be stolen. The men might not be in any of our databases. Finding them in the woods of Alaska would be like finding a specific salmon in a stream.

This was our best chance to get to Russia. If they kidnapped me, then the plan was still operational. If they didn't, then I had to figure out a way to take them down and question them. Force them into telling me how they transported the girls to Russia.

No way was I letting the two scumbags out of my sight.

Kaley was on her own. Unfortunately, I had no way to contact her and let her know about the change of plans. She'd eventually figure it out. Somewhere out on the trail a few hours from now.

At least she was out of harm's way. I was back to going it alone. Which was fine by me. One less distraction. That's probably how I should've proceeded anyway. Always follow my first instinct. I should know that by now.

I hung around the Visitor Center for a few minutes, then set out on my own trail. The men followed right away. Staying a distance behind, thinking I wouldn't notice them.

Almost comical, the way they handled the surveillance. These men were amateurs. Even then, I had to remember they had successfully kidnapped twelve young girls without getting caught.

Curly said to never underestimate your enemy, no matter how inept they appeared on the surface. A stray bullet can kill you as easily as one aimed from a deadly sniper.

There'd be no need for guns. Mine was in the backpack. As was my laptop. Nothing in there would tell them I was CIA. I'd make it easy on them.

At least that's what they'd think.

I'd be unlucky number thirteen eventually. The odds were pretty high they wouldn't make it out of this alive. Once we landed in Russia, I intended to kill both of them. Otherwise, they'd come back to America and prey on other unsuspecting women.

This was their last rodeo so to speak. I intended on making it eventful for them.

The trail turned steep. We went up a rocky crag. I hadn't thought that through. It'd be easier for them to snatch me on flat ground.

My mind was going in all kinds of directions. Why did they follow me and not Kaley?

Was it because I was older? Did they think I'd be less trouble? Less able to defend myself?

That stoked my anger which was already at a boiling point the moment I saw their disgusting faces.

You're not that old, Jamie.

I still look good for my age.

I was in the best shape of my life. If those men knew how many men I'd killed over the years, they'd be running for their lives. Men with a lot more skill than these buffoons. Terrorists. Oligarchs. Sheikhs. Men with machine guns. Suicide bombers. Acid throwers.

A twinge of insecurity did flash into my psyche. I was getting older. Every time I looked in the mirror, I saw a few new lines forming.

I let out a hoot of disbelief. It's one thing for me to see the aging process happening before my eyes. Another to be reminded of it by a couple of lowlife scum with the morals of a meat cleaver.

A new resolve formed. As if I needed added motivation. I'd show them how old I was.

Now I was glad they were following me and not Kaley. It almost made me want to abandon the plan, run at them with my gun drawn, beat the tar out of them on the spot, and leave them on the side of the trail for the bears to eat. Go to Russia on my own.

But that wasn't a good plan. I had no mode of transportation. No way to cross the Bering Sea. They were my ride.

So, I brought my anger under control and focused. I'd get my satisfaction in seeing their faces right before I put bullets between their eyes.

My mind turned to Kaley. Would she be disappointed or relieved? That'd say a lot about how ready she was for this mission. Could she handle the twists and turns? What would she do when she realized the men hadn't followed her?

This would've been a good opportunity to test her skills. Curly threw me into the fire right away. It helped me grow up fast. Kaley needed such a test. That's why I sent her out as the bait. Trying to do the same thing Curly did to me. See what Kaley was made of.

For whatever reason, I didn't have the affection for Kaley that Curly had for me. I didn't think it was jealousy. I'd rather be my age with my skills and experience than to go back to that point in my career again.

I had no desire to be young again.

No. I think it was because Kaley didn't know what she didn't know. That she felt invincible. I had felt that way at first as well. Now I knew better. My blood would spill as easily as anyone else's.

Invincible?

Far from it.

Kaley had never experienced seeing her life flash before her eyes. Most people wilted under the pressure.

Her test would come at another time.

I looked back. The clowns had stopped at the last turn. Unable to keep up with my pace even though I had slowed it.

These yahoos were ridiculous. Even Kaley could've handled them. I could take them with one of my hands tied behind my back. Probably with both of them shackled.

I came to a complete stop and waited for them to start walking again. A nervousness came over me. What if they decided I wasn't worth the trouble and turned back? Maybe I should walk back toward them.

That's what I did.

My heart began to beat faster. It had hardly been stressed at all even though the trail was steep. But it got that way, when things heated up in a mission. I wasn't concerned about confronting the men. This was the easy part if there were such a thing.

Russia was a different story. I knew how dangerous it'd be once I was there. I could probably get myself in and out without much trouble. But how did I get the twelve girls out? Not only did I have to get them out of the prison where they were being held, but also to a safe rendezvous point where we could get back to Alaska.

My plan was to ride over with these lowlifes. Kill them. Hide their boat and use it to bring the girls back to Alaska. Hopefully able to avoid sonar and Russian patrols.

I wasn't comfortable with the plan yet. Not completely sure it would work. Of course, that plan had included Kaley. Now I'd have to rescue the girls and get them out by myself.

A thought suddenly rushed into my head. *Surely Kaley wouldn't be foolish enough to try and get into Russia.*

I felt myself shake my head no.

She'd have no way of doing so. She didn't have a ride. I'd taken it from her.

So what would she do?

Go on her hike. When the men didn't attack her, she'd come back to the Visitor Center. She'd wait for me at the car. I wouldn't return. It'd get dark. She wouldn't know what to do, so she'd call Brad.

Brad would figure I decided to go it alone and order her back home.

Satisfied that's the scenario that would play out, I decided to put Kaley out of my mind. Focus on the mission.

I startled the men when I came upon them.

14

I'd gotten a good look at them at the Visitor Center, but now I was within a couple of feet of them. They were in their late forties. One was already slightly balding. Both had slight pooches hanging over their bellies. They were each dressed in touristy clothes. Wore shorts with tee shirts. Wisconsin man's bright red Badgers tee shirt was hard to miss.

The slight bulges of their guns were clearly evident in the small of their backs. The worst place to carry a gun if they wanted to react quickly. Mine was in my backpack. An even worse place. But I'd put it there on purpose. I didn't want to scare them off.

They jumped when I walked right up to them. Then tried to act casual. I forced back a mocking smile.

I had a map in my hand. "I'm kind of lost," I said. "Can you two kind gentlemen help me?"

A damsel in distress act seemed like the best course of action. I accentuated it with a heavy southern belle drawl.

One looked at the other. I saw Wisconsin man nod. He must be the leader.

The signal was some kind of confirmation to activate the plan. That made me feel better. Things would go smoother if I didn't have to force them to take me to Russia.

The guy in the Wisconsin shirt came and stood next to me. I held my map out so we could both see it.

His breath smelled of onions and stale cigarettes.

"I think we're right here," I said shyly. "But I'm not sure. I think the Visitor Center is that way." I pointed down the trail.

"No, little lady. We're right here." He pointed to a spot on the map.

He was lying. Trying to confuse me.

I played along. "Oh dear. I *am* lost. It might not be such a good idea to be out here by myself. All alone in the middle of nowhere."

I saw two silly smirks. Like they couldn't believe how easy this was going to be.

I let out a huge sigh.

"How do I get back to the Visitor Center?" I asked.

Wisconsin man ignored the question. "What's a pretty little thing like you doing out here all by yourself? Don't you have a husband or a boyfriend?"

"Heavens, no," I said in as sickening an accent as I could muster. "Well. Here's the thing." I waved my hand in a feminine gesture.

"I don't have a boyfriend. I mean. I did. We broke up. We planned to go to Alaska together on a vacation. Stay in a nice hotel. But he left me for another woman. Can you believe that? I thought I'd show him by coming by myself."

"I can't believe that," Wisconsin man said, lustfully. "If you were my girlfriend, I wouldn't leave you for nobody else."

"Thank you. That's sweet."

I batted my eyelashes. I was making my own stomach crawl. The act was sickening. Against everything I tried to portray in normal life. Tough. Hard nosed. Every man's equal.

But I kept it up. No turning back now.

"Actually. It's kind of stupid," I said. "No one even knows I'm out here. This wasn't such a good idea. If I get lost, it'll be weeks before anyone will come looking for me. The ranger told me to fill out one of those cards, but I forgot."

It took all of my self-control to keep from grinning. They were fighting back the smirks as well.

Wisconsin Badger shirt guy looked over at his friend. I saw a wink and another nod.

Time to act. Fine by me. I was getting impatient as well.

"What's your name?" he asked.

"Jennifer Lee."

Curly always said to keep your cover name as close as possible to your real name. It'd make it easier to remember.

"I'm from Alabama. Roll Tide." I emphasized all four syllables of Alabama.

Alex would not be happy. He was the starting quarterback for the Stanford Cardinals. They lost the national championship game to Alabama. On a last second touchdown. I don't know why I said Alabama. It came out of my mouth like a burp. Before I could stop myself.

I probably said it because it'd be easy to remember as well.

I hadn't really thought through my cover. I'd been focused on making sure Kaley knew hers. She was Kathy Sanders from New Jersey. Nineteen. Attended Rutgers. Was in Alaska on vacation. She was supposed to come with a friend, but she canceled at the last minute.

I was making up my cover on the fly. Southern belle from Alabama. Distraught over a cheating boyfriend.

Surely I could've come up with something better.

It was working perfectly though. Wisconsin man took my arm. Aggressively.

I pulled away slightly and frowned.

"What are you doing?" I asked, letting fear wash over my face. Curly had taught me how to do that on demand.

"We'll show you back to the Visitor Center," he said.

"I can find my way back. Just point me in the right direction."

He gripped my arm harder. "We insist," he said roughly, no longer keeping up the pretense.

"You're hurting me," I said, trying to squirm away.

I tried to resist the appropriate amount. Even a frightened girl would put up a little bit of a fight.

"Shut up! You're coming with us."

"No I'm not. I hope I didn't give you the wrong idea. I'm not interested in you. I just want directions."

"Like I said, we'll show you the way."

He started walking me back down the trail. I tried to resist. I was being pulled along. I looked back.

He turned off the trail and began heading south.

"I thought you said the Visitor Center is that way," I said.

"We know a shortcut."

A couple suddenly appeared ahead of us.

The last complication I wanted.

Dang it.

The men tensed. So did I.

A gun was suddenly in my back. Things had escalated.

I might have to act. Innocents were now in the equation.

What would the men do?

"Don't say anything or you're dead," Wisconsin guy said to me.

I let out a little shriek for effect.

"I mean it. I'll kill you and the two of them."

The young couple walked toward us. The girl in front of the guy. Wearing heavy backpacks.

The gun in my back was problematic. It'd be easier if the man was a couple of paces behind me. If I had to take the gun from him, and make sure he didn't get a shot off.

The angle was the tricky part. I had to twirl with such speed that I could change the trajectory of the gun so it would fire away from the couple. And from me. Make sure my hand wasn't on the barrel so it didn't get burned.

The best thing to do was play it cool. Obey the man so he didn't have to act.

But the couple saw my face. And the two men. It didn't look right. I saw the girl frown. Almost stop walking.

Did the men see it?

These were witnesses. The men might kill them for that very reason.

The couple would remember a blonde who went missing. The bad guys couldn't possibly know that no one would ever report me missing.

I looked away so the couple couldn't see my face clearly. Also, not to give the bad guy a reason to fire his gun into my lower back. I could see them cutting their losses and killing all three of us.

Wisconsin guy grabbed my waist and pulled me closer. Like I was his girlfriend. The couple was upon us. I tried to avoid eye contact as they passed by us on the trail. They couldn't see the gun from their vantage point.

"How you doing?" Wisconsin guy said.

I smiled slightly at them.

When they were past us, Wisconsin man turned me so I was facing them. So they wouldn't see the gun.

When the couple was out of sight, I breathed a sigh of relief on the inside. The two scumbags let out noticeable audible sighs as well.

"Go get the car, Willy," Wisconsin guy said. "I'll meet you at the usual place."

A picture of Willy Wonka came to my mind. The second man sort of reminded me of the character in the movie.

It was also telling. Or it would be if I were an actual kidnap victim. They weren't trying to hide their names or identities. Meaning I was never going to see the Visitor Center again.

In my case, they were taking me to Russia. Never to be seen again. What did it matter if I knew their real names?

I'd sold them on my vulnerability. They obviously thought I was helpless since they were willing to leave me alone with Wisconsin guy.

Willy took off down the trail. In the same direction as the couple.

"Don't hurt me," I pleaded.

"You do what I say, and we'll let you live."

He grabbed my backpack. I instinctively flinched. It had the gun in it but nothing else that would give away my identity or skills. I'd say the gun was for protection from bears.

He jerked it roughly off my back. Then knelt down to go through it. Took his eyes off me. His gun dangled in his hand. What a fool. I could've killed him on the spot. The urge was strong, but I had to stick with the plan.

It was working. I'd be in Russia by nightfall.

15

The bear stopped on the trail and stared at Kaley. Then started lumbering slowly toward her.

She tried to remember everything she read in the brochure the ranger gave her at the Visitor Center.

If you encounter a bear. . .

Number one. Don't run.

Kaley sized up the massive grizzly. Not running didn't seem like good advice. Surely she could outrun him. She had agility on her side. He knew the terrain. She could climb a tree. In the back of her mind, she thought she read that a bear could climb a tree as well. He could probably push the tree over with his tremendous strength.

Was it a male? Why did she call it a he?

She couldn't tell from that angle. She only assumed it was. What did it matter? Did she care if she was killed by a male or female bear? The dumbest thoughts popped into her head at the most inopportune times.

It did matter. A female might be defending her cubs. In her experience, women could be the most vicious creatures on earth. Especially when defending their children or their man. Kaley looked around and didn't see any little ones. For whatever reason, that brought a wave of relief over her. Even though the bear was still walking toward her.

A male would be preferred, she decided. Most of her training had been geared towards killing men. She also had experience fighting off men in bars. Some with grabby hands. Although they didn't have the massive claws she saw on this monstrosity, who took each step like he had four pick axes attached to his legs.

Men didn't have those teeth either. Even from a distance, they were terrifying. She'd rather be facing down a terrorist with a handgun. Any day of the week.

Where were the two kidnappers? She'd momentarily forgotten why she was there to begin with.

Focus.

She needed to keep her mind on the immediate threat. And fast. If she was going to get out of this alive.

I can outrun him.

Her.

Either way.

Kaley was fast. She ran track in high school. Sprints. Hundred meters and two twenty. The shorter races were more her strong suit.

What about the bear? It didn't seem like he could get his big fat body started that quickly. She could get away from him before he got moving. For whatever reason, she couldn't make her legs move. They were frozen to the ground.

There had to be a reason why the instructions were so adamant in the brochure. *Don't run. Whatever you do. Don't do that.*

Then she remembered why you weren't supposed to run. Bears liked to chase prey. Running encouraged an attack. It exuded fear. Something Kaley was certainly feeling at that moment in bushels.

The bear was probably better running a long distance than sprinting. Which might be why running wasn't a good idea. He could wear her down. Pursue her as far as she wanted to run and eventually catch up when she ran out of adrenaline, which was now pulsing through her body like someone had released a pressure cooker valve inside of her.

What was the next instruction?

Number two. Make noise. Make yourself look bigger.

No.

Jamie's voice was suddenly in her head.

Arm yourself. Kill the threat before he kills you.

I don't have a weapon, Kaley retorted.

You're always armed. You always have a weapon.

She had dreamed about her first kill. With no idea it might be an eight hundred pound bear.

How could she kill him? Nothing came to mind.

She did have the knife. And the bear repellant. Attached to her belt. Careful not to make any sudden movements, she took them out of the belt and slowly positioned the bear spray in her left hand and the knife in her right.

The bear was still a distance away. Not in a hurry to kill her. Maybe he wasn't that hungry. Her stomach growled as if on cue. She'd been hiking for awhile and had forgotten to eat one of the power bars in her backpack that she had intended to snack on a couple miles back on the trail.

Maybe she could throw one of those toward the bear and distract him.

He'd swallow the bar whole. Then she'd be mad. He might kill her but he wasn't taking her food.

Kaley used the opportunity to survey her surroundings. The trail had leveled off. She'd come up a fairly steep ridge and was now walking parallel to the mountain. Behind her and ahead was another steep area that began a climb to the top of the ridge. Another reason not to run. The bear could probably ascend the mountain much faster than she could.

No sign of the two kidnappers. Kaley thought they were the ones following her. She suddenly felt a wave of disappointment. The bear was putting a significant kink in her plans. The Grizzly probably scared off the men.

The Grizzly was uncomfortably close now. Still thirty paces away, but Kaley imagined he could close the gap quickly if he wanted.

Make noise. Lots of it.

Kaley lifted both hands in the air and began waving them back and forth shouting at the top of her lungs. She tried to make herself look bigger. More intimidating. But didn't think it was working. Her hundred and forty pound five foot ten frame probably didn't look fearsome to the monstrosity which continued toward her.

The bear yawned. Was he bored? Or was it a laugh? Was he amused by her?

Kaley began to jump up and down. Wave her hands. Shouting even louder. Showed the bear the knife and bear repellant.

"You don't want to mess with me, big guy. I've been trained to kill a man a hundred different ways with my bare hands."

She'd heard Jamie say that. She couldn't wait to use it in real life. It sounded hollow now.

"I'm your worst nightmare," she said. Something she'd heard in a movie.

"Go ahead. Make my day." Another movie quote.

That made her laugh out loud.

What she wouldn't give for Clint Eastwood's Smith & Wesson Model 29 .44 magnum. The most powerful handgun in the world at the time. She'd settle for her own .44 magnum in the trunk of the car at Washington Dulles airport. Or the CIA issued Sig. That was in the car at the Visitor Center.

Jamie had a gun. She had insisted Kaley not carry one because she'd be tempted to use it. She also didn't want Kaley to scare off the two kidnappers. If they saw her with a weapon, they might decide to move on to an easier target.

Kaley pretended the knife was a gun and pointed it at the bear.

"Bang. You're dead."

Mocking the bear probably wasn't a good idea. Even if he didn't know what she was saying. The words did empower her. She felt a jolt of confidence run through her.

The bear stopped and observed. Moved his head from side to side and let out a menacing growl that sent shivers down her spine. The confidence dissipated as fast as it had come upon her.

Kaley started yelling even louder. Whatever she was doing had at least made him stop in his tracks. She wished she'd taken the rangers advice and bought a whistle.

Where was Jamie? Kaley figured Jamie would follow her. To check up on her and make sure she did everything correctly.

Jamie could kill the bear with her gun.

Kaley started to call out to her. Just in case she was nearby and hadn't seen the predicament Kaley was in. Then realized that'd make her look weak in Jamie's eyes. Like she was being careful.

If Jamie was nearby, she'd already heard the yelling.

What was she waiting on?

The reality hit her. No one was coming. Jamie would've already helped her. She was out in the wilderness of Alaska. Alone. Without a real weapon. Facing down a Grizzly bear.

Don't be careful, she heard Jamie whisper in her ear.

"Are you happy now, Jamie?" she said bitterly.

It seemed like she was being anything but careful.

Making noise worked for nearly two minutes. Or at least it seemed like the standoff lasted that long. A truce ensued. Kaley stared him down. He matched her glare.

Then she remembered.

Number three. Don't make eye contact.

That was against everything she'd been taught. Jamie told her to look her enemy in the eye. Watch his reactions. Look for tells. Meaning the eyes gave away intentions. You could see anger. Hate. Fear. When someone was about to draw or fire a weapon, they shifted their eyes. Back and forth.

Don't look a Grizzly in the eye, the brochure said. That's like a challenge to the bear. Like you are egging him into a fight.

She didn't want that. What was the proper demeanor in this situation? Should she act aloof? Disinterested? Should she look away? Pretending like she was out on a stroll?

Did a bear sense fear? Weakness? Did he even care? He was probably at the top of the food chain in the Alaskan wilderness. He didn't have to be afraid of anyone or anything but a hunter with a gun.

Which she didn't have.

He probably could sense her fear. Jamie said that was the worst possible thing a CIA operative could do when faced with a threat. Act afraid.

Kaley was breathing heavily. Her heart raced. Jamie taught her how to slow her heart rate. At the moment, she couldn't remember any of the instructions. Too many were running through her head at one time.

She started to turn and walk away. Maybe the bear wouldn't follow. Then she remembered the next instruction.

Number four. Don't turn your back to the bear.

Okay. I won't.

That stopped her in her tracks. Didn't make sense anyway. She wanted to keep her eyes on the threat.

The bullet that kills you is the one you don't see coming, Jamie had said. *Keep a watchful eye out at all times for any conceivable threat.*

It wasn't hard to see the threat in this instance. No chance that she wouldn't see the bear coming. The one that was going to kill her.

"You are not going to kill me!" Kaley said roughly. "Do you hear me? I'm talking to you. Don't come any closer to me. I have a knife."

She shook it at him.

The bear shook his head from side to side. Almost like he wasn't impressed.

"You think I won't do it, mister? Try me."

Again, she didn't think daring him to attack her was a good idea.

The bear started toward her again. A little faster this time. She practically screamed at him. Waved her hands more wildly. It didn't phase him. He kept moving forward. Stealthily. Like he wanted to prolong her agony.

Number five. Back away slowly.

She was already doing that. Instinctively. As soon as he started moving forward, she began inching her way backward. Trying to keep the same distance between them.

He was getting too close. Moving toward her with more of a purpose. Like he'd made a decision to attack.

She let out a shriek. He hadn't charged but had definitely decided she was worth the effort and not much of a threat to him.

Number six. Fight back.

That seemed like a last resort.

She had no choice.

A confrontation was inevitable.

Was this how she was going to die?

Never think that, Jamie said. *Always assume you're going to somehow survive.*

Jamie was all in her head.

Remember your training.

Act. Don't react.

Kill him before he kills you.

Don't be careful.

"Shut up, Jamie," Kaley said aloud. "Does it look like I'm being careful to you?"

Kaley switched the knife to her left hand and picked up a stone and threw it at the bear. Striking him in the nose. She let out a cheer when the rock hit its target.

The bear swiped his massive paw across his face. That appeared to annoy him more than anything else. At least he stopped walking toward her. She picked up a bigger rock and threw it. Sailing it over his head. The adrenaline must really be flowing. Kaley was normally fairly accurate in her throwing skills.

She was proficient in knife and ax throwing. A debate raged in her head.

Should she throw the knife at him or hold on to it in case she needed it for close-range fighting?

She didn't like her chances in a hand-to-hand combat situation.

She threw another rock to gauge the distance. Throwing the knife seemed like the best option. The bear was a big target. Would it phase him? The odds were good that she could hit the bear between the eyes with the knife.

Would that work? It'd have to penetrate the bear's skull. Ben seemed thick headed. She decided to hang on to the knife.

Ben was the name she'd given him seconds before. Gentle Ben. She'd seen reruns of a television show by that name. When she was a kid.

Wishful thinking. This bear didn't seem the least bit gentle.

He suddenly reared onto his hind legs. He looked like he was twenty feet tall even though that was impossible. Ben wasn't more than ten yards from her.

The story of David and Goliath popped into her mind. Something she remembered from Bible school as a kid. She felt like David. All he had was a stone to kill the giant. She had already tried that. A stone wouldn't phase the monster she was facing.

The knife might.

This was her opportunity. She could aim the knife at his underbelly. Without hesitation Kaley reared back and let it fly. Aiming slightly lower, figuring adrenaline might cause her to throw it high.

The bear let out a horrendous sound when the knife connected. Ben immediately dropped to his four feet.

Then charged.

16

The bear bounded toward her. His eyes filled with purpose.

She wasn't supposed to look him in his eyes, but she saw the rage. If she lived through it, she'd never forget the look on that bear's face. Determination. His mouth was open.

Kaley let out a scream that echoed through the mountains. Every ounce of her being was telling her to run away, but she held her ground.

I hope this bear repellant works.

Her hands shook. She fumbled with the release cap. This could be a scene out of a horror movie.

Kaley looked down and away from the bear momentarily. Things were happening in slow motion now. She threaded her finger into the release cap and flicked it off with force. Switching hands. Gripping the can of spray in her right hand.

The bear was so close she could feel the earth shaking from his powerful steps. Could hear his intense breathing.

For whatever reason, she remembered the instructions on the can. Spray the ground in front of the bear. If she sprayed the repellant in the air, the wind might blow it away or back into her face.

Her hand was no longer shaking. Kaley pushed the nozzle and immediately smelled the liquid as it came out. The bear was within five feet or so. He stopped in his tracks. His massive paws slid in the gravel on the trail helping him to stop on a dime. Maybe he was more agile than she first assumed.

Kaley could reach out and touch the bear. He was that close. Ben let out what could only be described as a sneeze. Then swiped at her. She stepped back, then forward and sprayed the bear in the eyes.

He let out a cry of pain. Or some kind of horrendous sound.

Kaley turned and began sprinting away. Totally ignoring instruction number one.

Instead listening to Jamie, who was shouting instructions at her faster than she could process them.

Run. Don't look back. Keep your eyes focused on getting away. Don't stop until you are safe.

The trail became a fork. Two trails. One went up the mountain. The other down toward a canyon. Where there was a stream. More bears might be drinking and feeding at the stream, so Kaley went up.

Always try to get the high ground when possible, Jamie had said.

Jamie was practically shouting in her ears. Almost like she was right there with her.

Kaley's legs were burning now at the sudden exertion. Her breathing was labored from the altitude. But she willed herself up the mountain. Afraid to look back. If the bear was following, she wasn't sure what she would do.

She slowed slightly to keep from slipping and twisting her ankle on the rocks. She came to a flat spot and decided to look back.

The bear had followed. She let out a muted scream.

It wasn't chasing at full speed but was clearly stalking her.

Jamie continued shouting at her. *Think through your options. When plan A doesn't work, go to plan B.* Kaley remembered the conversation like it was happening now.

"What if I don't have a plan B?" Kaley had asked Jamie.

"Then you die."

The point of the instructions was to always have a plan B.

You are never out of options until you're dead. Those words from Jamie reverberated in her head.

It made sense to her. She had options. Run further up the mountain. She still had the bear repellant.

Kaley began spraying the ground on the trail as she retreated upward. When the can was empty, she kept it in her hand rather than throw it away. It might be useful as a weapon.

Spraying the ground bought her some time. The bear turned around several times like he was going to leave. But he always turned back toward her. Relentless. She was nearing the top of the ridge. On the other side, she'd be running downhill. Did that give her an advantage? She wasn't sure.

The bear kept coming. Slower than before. The repellant caused him to hesitate.

Kaley was suddenly out of good options. Over the ridge was rocky. A fall would kill her. She couldn't beat the bear to the top at this rate. He was certainly a better climber than she was.

To her left was a fissure in the rock. Kaley looked over the edge of what was a cliff with a huge drop off. Her head spun as she looked down at the creek below. It had to be several hundred feet down.

Could she jump to the other side? The distance between the two rock outcroppings was about fifteen to eighteen feet. In high school, Kaley tried the long jump. Because of her ability to sprint. She'd gotten close to nineteen feet as a senior.

Could she make it? This was life and death. Not track practice where she was goofing around.

The bear was running now. Charging up the mountain toward her.

"I can't jump. It's too far."

Don't be careful, she heard Jamie say.

The impetus she needed. Kaley got a running start and leapt over the opening. Flailing her arms to give herself added momentum.

She landed on the other side and rolled.

It knocked the wind out of her. She scratched her arm. Cried out when her knee hit against a rock. She struggled to regain her breath.

When she came to a stop, she took a second before moving to assess the injuries. Satisfied she wasn't badly hurt, she scrambled to her feet. The bear was on the other side of the crevasse looking at her in puzzlement. Not sure what to do.

Kaley let out a whoop and a holler. Began mocking him. Trash talking.

"Take that, Ben. That's why I'm human and you're not. My brain is bigger than yours. You can't get me now."

She'd never felt this much energy inside of her before.

She paced around in a circle. The adrenaline pumped through her like she'd had several B-12 shots.

It felt exhilarating.

She understood what Jamie meant.

Don't be careful.

She hadn't been. She'd been brave. She threw caution to the wind. Jumped without even really thinking about it.

If she had been careful, she'd still be on the other side of the crevasse. Fighting for her life. A battle she'd certainly lose.

She couldn't wait to tell Jamie.

Then realized her problem. How am I going to get back to the Visitor Center without running into that bear again?

17

Brad had to deliver horrific news to his boss, Director Ryan Coldclaw.

And he was dreading it. Partly because of the nature of the intelligence information but also because he didn't have many answers to the barrage of questions he knew was coming.

He picked up the file he'd been working on for hours and flipped through it one last time. Satisfied, he left his office and walked down the long hallway to the director's office. More slowly than usual. Each step felt like a funeral march. Or a notifying next of kin kind of trek.

Telling Ryan would be hard. Breaking the news to Jamie would be excruciating.

A burning question raged in his mind. Hopefully, the director would make the decision and take it off his plate. When should they tell Jamie? She was in the throes of a mission. Probably in Russia at that very moment.

If they told her, she might drop everything and come back. The mission to rescue the girls would be on hold. Worse, she might continue on and be so distracted she got herself and/or Kaley killed.

On the other hand, if they didn't tell her, she'd be furious. Say she had a right to know her husband was probably dead. Brad didn't have a good argument against keeping that information from her for the sake of the mission.

But if they did tell Jamie, what could she do about it? Nothing. It might even endanger her life. Best not to tell her until she got back. Hopefully, Ryan would agree.

Brad opened the door to Ryan's office, took in a deep breath to calm his nerves, and walked into the main lobby. The director's administrative assistant was on the phone but acknowledged him with a smile and a slight wave. He dutifully stood inside the door until she was done.

When she hung up the phone, she greeted him warmly. After the pleasantries, Brad said, "I need to speak to the director."

"He's not to be disturbed."

"Oh well."

She nodded and picked up the phone. "Brad is here to see you. It's urgent."

He hadn't actually said it was urgent, but she could obviously tell from his tone and body language. He could feel all the blood drain from his face. If his shoulders and head drooped any further, they'd be dragging the floor. Or at least it felt that way.

He didn't remember ever feeling this much despair. Alex and Jamie were like family to him. He wouldn't be where he was without them. He felt the same way when Curly died. That was a loss.

But this was a catastrophe.

Curly was older. They were all surprised he lived as long as he did, considering his lifestyle. Alex was young and in the prime of his life.

"Give Director Coldclaw another minute," she said after she hung up the phone.

Brad slumped down in one of the chairs.

Pull yourself together. You are a professional.

If it was a minute, it passed by in a blur. Before he could think about it, he was standing and walking toward the open door to Ryan's office. His heart racing like a thoroughbred let out of the starting gate of a horse race.

The director closed the door behind him. The sound of the door shutting jolted him out of his funk. He needed to be composed. Choose his words properly. Keep his voice from cracking. Tears formed in his eyes. The CIA dealt with life and death situations all the time. This part of the job came with the territory.

Ryan would demand answers.

"Is this a behind-the-desk kind of meeting or should we sit in the comfortable chairs?" Ryan asked, somewhat soberly. Obviously picking up on Brad's demeanor.

"The information is. . . not going to be very comforting," Brad said. His voice cracked even though he had consciously told himself not to let it.

"The comfortable chairs it is."

Interestingly enough, the chairs and sofa in Ryan's office were more comfortable than those in the Oval Office. Mostly because they were designed for long meetings. Such was the nature of the intelligence service. Strategy sessions within the CIA could last for hours as information was analyzed ad nauseum.

In the White House, the President's time was planned out to the minute. Seldom did anyone other than his closest staff get more than a few minutes with him in the Oval Office. If an extended meeting was necessary, it was held in the conference room. The war room if necessary.

Maybe that's why the chairs and sofa were uncomfortable. No one wanted anyone in the Oval Office to get too comfortable. To stay longer than necessary.

This information might lead to another meeting with the President. He'd almost certainly want to know. More than likely Ryan would deliver the news by phone and Brad would not be required to make another trip to the White House. He wanted to get back to his office and get to work. To find more answers.

Figure out how to explain why they lost an operative under his watch. One of the two most valuable assets in the entire CIA by everyone's estimation. Made worse by the fact that Alex had only been back with them for three weeks.

Who would Brad send to kill Pok now?

Another question that would demand his full attention. Alex was probably the only person alive who could pull it off. Other than Jamie. But how could they risk sending her there? What kind of frame of mind would she be in?

He couldn't risk possibly losing both of them.

"What's going on?" Ryan asked.

"Alex Halee's plane is missing."

18

Alex's plane wasn't exactly missing.

Brad knew where it was. It had crashed in the Indian Ocean. It hadn't been recovered, meaning, technically, it was missing.

Brad had paused to let the words sink in after he told Ryan.

A few seconds passed before Ryan responded in a monotone voice. Showing no emotion at all.

"Presumed?" Ryan asked.

"Presumed to have crashed into the Indian Ocean," he said as clarification.

Ryan let out a notable heavy breath. Like someone had punched him in the gut. Brad knew how he felt. His stomach was tied up in knots.

Emotion for both of them was coming.

"Was this his AJAX plane?" Ryan asked.

"Yes. Although, the Malaysian authorities think it's a private cargo plane."

"Alex's handiwork, I assume."

"Correct. He changed the transponder number. He was on his way to Vietnam to kill or capture Pok. A Top Secret mission. It was in your morning briefing report."

"I remember."

"The plane took off from D.C. three days ago," Brad explained. "The same day Jamie went to Alaska. It stopped in Helsinki for fuel and supplies. Stayed there overnight. It left Helsinki and flew a direct route to the middle east, stopping in Istanbul. I'm not sure why. Probably as a decoy. In case Pok was tracking him."

"Alex was always one to cover all his bases."

Brad nodded.

"The plane took off from Istanbul this morning. It flew directly south to avoid Iran, Afghanistan, and Iraqi airspace."

"Of course."

"It flew over the Arabian Sea headed for Vietnam. It was tracked over India by local radar. Traveled over the Bay of Bengal. This is where things get sketchy."

Brad let out his own deep sigh and changed positions on the sofa. Suddenly feeling like he was sitting on a bed of nails.

"Sketchy how?"

"The plane was observed on radar by Ho Chi Minh ACC. At that point, everything appeared to be normal. It was handed off to them by the Kuala Lumpur ACC. Thirty seconds later, it disappeared from both their radar screens."

"Disappeared?"

"Disappeared."

"As in, it fell out of the sky?"

"Correct."

"That's strange."

"I know."

That's why it had taken Brad so long to bring the information to the director. He wanted to have as many facts as possible. Unfortunately, the information was hard to piece together. The foreign countries were not necessarily forthcoming. Brad had to draw his own conclusions. Really, he was trying to find some explanation other than a plane crash.

"Planes don't just disappear," Ryan said.

"We don't know for sure what happened to the aircraft."

"Then why do you think it crashed in the ocean? Was there any communication from the plane? Did you talk to Alex? Did he call you when they ran into trouble?"

"No. I haven't heard from him since the day before he left."

"No distress call?"

"Nothing."

"Sounds like an Alex sleight-of-hand. What if he only wants you to think it crashed?"

"I don't think so. Not even Alex could pull off this big a ruse. Like you said, plane's don't just disappear."

"You're not making sense."

"I know."

"No sign of trouble at all?"

"None. It was traveling at cruise altitude and true airspeed when it disappeared."

"What was the weather like?"

"Good. No clouds. Visibility was good. No rain or lightning in the area."

"That's strange."

"It gets stranger."

"How so?"

"Secondary radar picked up the plane. Momentarily, then lost it again."

"Could it have been a mechanical malfunction in the transponder?"

"I don't think so."

"How do you know?"

"We were tracking it as well."

"Why didn't you say so?"

"I was getting to it. I was watching it the whole time. Not in real time. After the fact. From our satellite. Standard procedure when my assets are on a mission. I always track their movements. Just in case."

"Then you know what happened to the plane?" Ryan said roughly.

The director was growing impatient. Brad needed to get to the meat of the information.

"Alex's plane turned right and started heading directly south. Out of the blue. For no reason. Satellites followed it all the way. It continued several hundred miles west of the Malay Peninsula. Past the island of Penang."

"Military radar in the region must've tracked it."

"I suspect so. The Vietcong are reluctant to turn over any military radar information. As you can imagine."

"Of course, they are. Even after everything we do for them."

Ryan's words had a hint of bitterness behind them. "What about Australia? They're our friends. They must've seen something."

Brad nodded, then shifted again. He pretended to be looking at his notes. Even though he had nothing written on them about Australia. Rather than answer, he pulled a map out of his folder. Leaned forward on the couch and sat the map on the table between them. Looking at it upside down.

"This map tracks the flight. From the time it left the U.S. until it went missing. As you can see, it made a sudden veer to the right."

"Any idea why?"

"None whatsoever. There's no logical reason for such a maneuver."

"Any indication that it came under fire from hostiles?"

"I haven't found any evidence of that. As far as the countries in the region knew, this was a civilian plane. No threat at all."

"It was a threat to Pok."

"I considered that. Perhaps Alex was discovered by Pok. Even with all the precautions. I don't know what Pok could've done about it, though. He doesn't have any military capabilities. Vietnam doesn't even know he's there. As far as I can tell."

"What did Australia say about it?"

Brad answered. "The Aussies picked up a signal which might be Alex's flight. But they couldn't be sure. The plane was out of range."

"But you had eyes on it the whole time?"

"The satellite followed the plane for two hours."

"Two hours?"

Brad pointed to the map. "Yes. It flew at a steady pace. Slowly losing altitude, until it disappeared in the middle of the Indian Ocean."

"Crashed, you mean?"

"I'm afraid so."

"What do you think happened to the plane?"

"Had to be a catastrophic cabin failure. Sudden loss of oxygen. My guess is that everyone on board was incapacitated immediately. Otherwise, they would've tried to contact me or take some kind of action to prevent a crash in the ocean."

"What do you need from me?" Ryan asked.

"Authorization to send military planes into the air to look for wreckage."

"What assets do we have in the region?"

"The Nimitz and the U.S.S. Ronald Reagan are in the vicinity."

"How can we do so without making this look like an international incident? I don't want anyone to know it was a CIA plane."

"I would say we do it discreetly. We have the last known location of the plane. Our birds can fly over the area under the guise of a training mission."

"Let's do it. I'll notify the President. He'll authorize it."

"Thank you."

"How many souls were on board?"

"Four. Alex. Colonel. A-Rad and Bond."

Ryan let out a groan. "That's the whole crew."

"I know."

"That's four of our best men wiped out at once."

"I know."

"That's a huge loss."

"I know."

"Is that all you have to say for yourself? I know?"

"I'm at a loss for words as well. It's incomprehensible."

"Does Jamie know?"

"Not yet, sir. I was hoping you'd give me some direction on that front. She's still in Alaska. Probably in Russia by now."

"Things are heating up there. More missiles are headed to the area."

"I know."

Ryan gave Brad a slight glare. Brad hated to say "I know" for the umpteenth time but didn't know what else to say.

"I don't think I could get in touch with Jamie even if I wanted to," Brad said. "Her plan was to infiltrate the sex trafficking ring by letting herself or Kaley be captured."

"That doesn't sound like a good plan."

"That's Jamie's idea. You know how she is. 'Don't be careful' and all that."

Ryan was trained in the field by Jamie and Alex. The pair convinced Curly to let Ryan work with him in Costa Rica. That's where Curly died. Ryan was there at the time. The three, Jamie, Alex, and Curly had left their indelible mark on Ryan.

He was holding up well considering this news would be as devastating to him personally as it was to Brad.

Ryan would certainly know about the "don't be careful" mantra. It had been drilled in him by Curly, then reinforced by Jamie and Alex. The whole CIA had embraced the motto. A saying probably first coined by Curly as far as Brad could tell.

"I guess you need to call her and tell her," Ryan said. "She has a right to know."

Brad shook his head.

"That's what I thought. But if I try to contact Jamie, I have to assume the bad guys have her phone. It might compromise her situation."

"Hmm. You're right. We can't take that risk."

"That's what I was thinking. We're better off waiting for her to contact us. I don't think her mission is going to take that long."

"You don't want her distracted."

"No, sir."

"I hate to leave Jamie out there twisting in the wind like that though. Maybe going into Russia wasn't such a good idea. Not with all the missile activity."

"She doesn't know anything about the missiles."

"Let's hope she doesn't see them. The whole area is crawling with Russian troops."

"Jamie can take care of herself."

Ryan nodded. "Still. I wish she wasn't alone over there."

"She has Kaley with her."

"Kaley's new. We don't know what we have in her yet."

"There's no way to send backup. Not with all the missile activity in the region. It's too dangerous."

"I just pray to God that we don't lose Jamie too."

"I know."

Brad didn't know what else to say.

19

Denali National Park

The sex trafficker was treating me like a Hebrew slave. Minus the whip. He was verbally mocking me and occasionally pushing me from behind for effect.

I wanted to knock his mouth to the back of his head.

Something I could easily do. My hands were still free, for obvious reasons. He couldn't exactly walk on a trail pointing a gun at a woman whose hands were bound. If we were to run into other hikers, he'd have a serious problem. So would I. I didn't want to put any innocents in harm's way.

To get his kicks, he had resorted to bullying. Acting like Mister Tough Guy. Except for the gun, it was all bravado. In a matter of seconds, I could have him on his knees bawling like a baby, begging me not to kill him.

When I didn't think it could get any more annoying, he resorted to blonde jokes.

"How do you keep a blonde in the shower all day?" he asked me.

I didn't answer.

"You give her a bottle of shampoo that says rinse, lather, and repeat."

He roared laughing. I kept walking. Ignoring him. Between Alex and Bond, I'd heard many blonde jokes over the years, including that one.

"I'd like to take a shower with you," he added, lustfully.

It took all of my self-control not to launch my own comeback and verbal assault. A dozen or more clever lines popped into my head.

Mostly, I wanted to tell him I was married. My husband was the first thing that popped into my mind in these situations. He was lucky Alex wasn't there or his face would already be rearranged.

Telling him I was married would be problematic. For whatever reason, sex traffickers didn't like to target married women. Their clients saw them as damaged goods. Also husbands went looking for their wives. Formed search parties. A missing married woman drew too much attention and jeopardized their operations.

Young single girls were the ideal profile to target.

For that reason, I wasn't wearing my wedding rings. I also didn't want to damage them in a confrontation. Although my diamonds could do severe damage to a man's orbital socket.

"What did the blonde say when she found out she was pregnant?" he said, as I groaned inside.

He paused, waiting for an answer that would never come. I rolled my eyes. Of course, he couldn't see it since my back was to him.

I knew the answer. I'd heard it before. *Are you sure it's mine?*

I wouldn't give him the satisfaction.

He delivered the punchline then pushed me from behind when I didn't say anything or laugh. I stumbled forward slightly. Never in danger of falling. I was in danger of blowing the whole mission and spinning around and elbowing him in the jaw. So he'd be eating all his meals out of a straw for the next six months.

Not that I intended to let him live that long.

I bit my lip and tightened my jaw and reminded myself to stay calm. Focus on the bigger picture.

"I wouldn't mind getting you pregnant," he added.

In your dreams.

I'd die first.

Which was true. Curly taught me how to withstand torture. Including sexual assault. I told him it wasn't necessary. I decided long ago that no man other than Alex would ever touch me. I'd never been with any-one other than my husband and never would. I'd kill anyone who tried to have sex with me. Even if it ruined the mission.

Even if I died in the process.

I was stubborn that way. I was perfectly fine going to heaven sooner if that was my fate.

The kidnapper poked me in the back with his gun.

That sent a dose of panic pulsing through my veins. The man wasn't being as careful with the gun as I'd like him to be. I'd much rather be facing down a gun than having one stuck in my back. Guns could go off accidentally. He could slip and fall. Pull the trigger by mistake.

I'd been perfectly compliant. He had no reason to be aggressive. I'd played the part of deer in the headlights perfectly. Dutifully resigned to my fate.

"Why are blondes so easy to get into bed?" he asked as the verbal barrage continued.

Shut up.

"Who cares?" he said, delivering the stupid answer. The words al-most didn't make it out of his mouth, he was laughing so hard.

A new form of torture.

"You don't think that's funny?" he asked roughly.

"Not particularly." I decided to put up a little resistance. "Why don't you just shut up and tell me where you're taking me?"

"How can I shut up and tell you at the same time?"

He burst out laughing again. His laugh was mixed with a cigarette cough.

"You really are a dumb blonde," he added.

You really are...

I stopped myself. A number of expletives were floating around in my head completing the thought.

I needed to keep my cool. For several reasons. If he provoked me much further, I'd kill him. If I provoked him much further, he might hit me. Since I was determined not to fight back, I'd prefer not to have an aching jaw or blistered cheek for the next several hours.

My satisfaction came in knowing that the man would be dead before nightfall. Before then would be a disaster. I needed him alive.

He was getting dangerously close to ruining my plan. So far, everything was going great. My kidnapping was working out. He was leading me to a rendezvous point where his partner, Willy, was to meet us. They'd load me in the vehicle and take me to a boat which would take me to Russia.

So I could rescue the girls.

I thought about them. Whatever discomfort I felt was nothing compared to what they were going through. Hopefully, by this time tomorrow, they'd be free and back in Alaska and on their way home. Thinking about them helped me to tune him out. Their images were seared into my consciousness. It helped me regain my center.

Once I calmed the rage inside of me, I thought about the journey to Russia which was pretty much worked out in my mind. It'd take us roughly six hours to drive from the *Denali National Park* to *Seward Peninsula*. I figured that's where we'd board a boat.

At the closest point possible. I assumed. Fifty-five miles. That's how far it was across the *Bering Sea* to Russia from northern Alaska. Most people didn't realize that the two countries were separated by such a short distance. You could literally see Russia from Alaska. Not that I'd ever been in that region.

It wasn't the best way to get into Russia. The CIA had other methods of infiltrating the country surreptitiously. The pipeline had been established for years.

These days we could travel by plane to Moscow on a fake passport. I wondered if I should've gone that route. I didn't because I wanted to expose the whole sex trafficking operation. Find out who was kidnapping the girls. How they took them to Russia. Who was helping them.

My plan was working to perfection.

In some ways, this hike was the least dangerous part of my trip.

Up north in the Arctic region had its own dangers. The Bering Sea was one of the most treacherous in the world. Shallow water and rough waves were almost unnavigable at times even for the most experienced seamen.

This time of year wouldn't be so bad as long as there wasn't a storm brewing. Hopefully these idiots knew what they were doing, or they had contracted with someone who lived in the region and regularly made the trip from Alaska to Russia by sea.

Theoretically, they could potentially take me to Petropavlovsk-Kamchatsky. A major city with infrastructure. If that were the case, I was dreading it. The boat ride would be longer and rougher. It might cause me to lose my patience and throw the kidnappers overboard. I wasn't looking forward to spending any more time with them than necessary.

The car ride would be bad enough. More than likely, they'd put me in the trunk. Not as bad as it sounded. There I could get some sleep and eat one of the power bars in my backpack if they put it back there with me. My stomach was growling. Curly said to eat and sleep when you can. You never knew when you'd get another chance.

He taught me how to sleep anywhere and go to sleep at a moment's notice. Alex was better at it than me, but I'd gotten pretty good at it over the years. Especially sleeping even in the most uncomfortable situations. The trunk of a car would qualify. Better than in the back seat listening to the two scum of the earth drone on and on about nothing.

Heaven forbid, I had to listen to more blonde jokes.

I'd rather listen to nails scraping against a chalkboard for six hours.

Actually, I was filled with built-in resentment for the men which was why I was already on edge. I had a disdain for sex traffickers. Even the sound of their voices made my skin scrawl. I wanted to kill every one of them the moment I laid eyes on them.

These were the hardest missions. Forcing myself to let them live for the greater good of the mission. Even if only for a few hours. They were of more use to me alive than dead. The boat would almost certainly be stopped by Russian Coast Guard authorities. I assumed the two kidnappers had all the proper paperwork. Since they had successfully made twelve other girls disappear inside Russia. Obviously with help.

The two men I was dealing with were low level amateurs. Never capable of pulling off such an operation. Someone in Russia was pulling the strings. Someone high up in government. Or an oligarch with influence.

I wanted to know who they were.

The kidnapped girls were probably taken to service men in the upper echelon of Russian oligarchy. Men who paid big dollars for American girls. Those same powerful men could hire American prostitutes easily enough and for a cheaper price. But some men preferred girls forced into the sex trade. The domination was what turned them on.

Disgusting.

I couldn't wait to get my hands on the bigger fish. I felt my hand ball into a fist. I had to be careful so the low life dead man walking didn't see me.

The righteous indignation raged inside of me again. How could these men do such a thing to women? The young girls had their whole lives taken from them. Without me, they wouldn't have a future. Would never have kids or grandkids.

The Russians would kill them and make them disappear after they were done with them. After years of inhumane treatment.

It broke my heart.

It'd caused the anger to boil inside of me like a cauldron of hot grease on an open flame.

Local law enforcement was also bugging me at that moment. Where were they in all this? If I found the two kidnappers so easily, why couldn't the local police? Because sex trafficking was low on the priority list. Lagging far behind writing speeding tickets. The main source of revenue for many small jurisdictions.

I needed to focus. Thinking about the police did me no good at the moment.

Get your mind on something else.

The hike was taking longer than I thought it would. It gave me too much time to think. Too much time to let the resentment fester. I'd do something I regretted if we didn't change the scenery soon.

I picked up the pace when we came to a hill. It made me feel good to hear my kidnapper wheezing at the strenuous activity. After we ascended the hill and started down a trail, I could see the road at the bottom. When we reached it, Willy was waiting. I let out an imperceivable groan. Not a car, but an SUV.

They did put me in the back. Not the trunk. From that vantage point, I'd be more comfortable, but could still hear them talking. The only benefit was that I might learn more about their operations.

What I really wanted to do was sleep.

Willy secured my wrists with zip ties. I put up a little bit of a fight. He raised his hand like he was going to backhand me across the face.

That'd be the last thing he did. I'd get to Russia on my own if I had to.

Fortunately, he resisted and practically threw me into the back and slammed the hatch down. Without my backpack which meant I couldn't eat my power bar or drink my water.

I flared my wrists when they secured the zip ties, so they'd be loose. Once we started moving, I freed my hands. I wasn't about to sleep for six hours with my arms behind my back. When we stopped, I'd resecure them, so they'd never notice.

Within seconds, I was sound asleep.

Jolted awake when we came to an abrupt stop. For a moment, I was disoriented. It didn't seem like we'd been driving for that long. More like twenty minutes. Not six hours.

What was going on?

20

The car doors opened and the two men got out. I quickly remembered to secure my hands behind my back but kept the zip ties loose in case I needed my hands.

Willy opened the back and ordered me out. I stepped out and looked around to get my bearings. I didn't understand why we were stopping.

A huge sign above a cabin explained a lot of things.

Two Brothers Alaskan Adventures.

A picture of a seaplane was on the sign. The two men were running a guide service business as a front for the sex trafficking.

We also weren't taking a boat. We were flying. I hadn't really considered that option, but it made sense. They'd have the proper permits to fly anywhere in Alaska and out into the Bering Sea. They obviously had the credentials necessary to travel into Russia.

Behind the cabin was an airstrip and two planes. One looked to be a ten-seater. The other a seaplane with two floats under the fuselage.

Willy gave me a push from behind. I started walking toward the airstrip. Not sure which plane we were taking. But thankful we weren't taking a boat. The ten-seater would be better. I could commandeer it and bring the girls back in the plane.

"I need to use the bathroom," I said.

Willy let out a disapproving groan.

We changed directions and he led me inside the cabin. I didn't actually have to go but figured I should anyway. Curly taught me how to hold my bladder for hours. The thought made me chuckle. Curly wasn't comfortable talking about it. I could picture his face. He could talk for hours about how to kill someone. How to sever arteries. Break bones. Puncture lungs.

Talk about a woman's private parts and Curly got as squeamish as a fish out of water.

I miss Curly.

It felt good to have a few seconds to myself in the restroom. Time to regroup. I hadn't calculated how long it'd take us to get there by plane. Much faster than a boat ride and less dangerous.

Things were looking up and I could feel it in my spirit.

I flushed the toilet and exited the restroom after Willy banged on the door and told me to hurry up. I used the opportunity to check out the inside of the cabin which was unremarkable. It had an office behind a counter. Two other rooms looked to be bedrooms. It had a messy kitchen and living area. A ham radio. A bunch of files stacked on the desks.

A sign on the wall listed services and prices. I saw a four-color brochure lying on the counter but couldn't look at it since my hands were secured again. Willy put the zip ties on again as soon as I exited the bathroom.

When we exited the cabin, Willy led me toward the seaplane. *Shoot!*

I couldn't very well tell them I wanted to go in the other plane.

The seaplane made sense. It'd be easier to land on the water and hand me off to someone in a boat or on a dock. Less scrutiny than landing at a public airstrip on land.

I was put in the back of the plane and the two men took their places in the pilot and copilot's seats. I convinced them to remove the zip ties and secure my hands in front of me and not the back. To make it more comfortable. They didn't know it made it easier for me to kill them as soon as they landed the plane on the water.

We took off shortly thereafter and I became enthralled by the view. The ride across Alaska was breathtaking. Mt. Mckinley was in my window for the longest time. Actually known as Denali now when the name of the mountain was changed a few years before. I still thought of it by the old name out of habit.

We flew over the Yukon River and were over the Bering Sea before I knew it. Fortunately, the weather was good and visibility was clear for miles. The two men seemed to be capable enough pilots which gave me time to think about my plan and not worry about crashing.

How was I going to kill them? It seemed problematic. Impossible even if they didn't exit the plane with me. I couldn't kill them in flight, since I didn't know where the rendezvous point was.

Missions were complicated.

I might have to deal with the two men later.

Those complications seemed minor, with what I saw next.

Russian warships. In the Gulf of Anadyr.

What?

Two Russian Migs appeared on the horizon. Fighter jets.

I had to blink twice to assure myself I really was seeing fighter jets streaking toward us. The men quickly veered to the north.

Were the Russians going to shoot us down? Fire warning shots? Force us back to the United States?

What was going on?

I couldn't hear the communications since I wasn't wearing headphones.

It appeared that the planes and warships were part of some sort of military operations. Brad hadn't briefed me on any activity in the area.

When the plane turned to the right I got a good look at what the Russian planes and warships were protecting.

It looked like missile installations. On the southern peninsula. We'd obviously gotten too close. I only saw one, but it was a mobile missile launcher. From the looks of the clearings, they were setting up more.

The one missile I saw was pointed to the west. Towards the United States.

This was strange. Not that missiles were pointed at the U.S. but that they were positioned so close. Clearly an act of provocation.

Surely Director Coldclaw knew about it. We had satellites taking pictures all over the world. Missiles didn't move anywhere in the world without the CIA knowing about it.

What if Ryan didn't know? Or at least didn't know the extent of it?

Nothing could take the place of on the ground intel.

It wasn't my mission.

Maybe it needed to be.

I was close. Close enough to gather information and report it back to Brad.

Rescuing the girls could wait twenty-four hours.

The decision was made.

I had to come up with a new plan.

Figure out how to get close to those missiles.

21

Somewhere in the Sea of Okhotsk

Due to circumstances beyond my control, I wasn't able to kill the two men in the seaplane. They landed us in a small cove and maneuvered the plane to a dock near the shoreline where a burly Russian met us.

Before I could do anything, I was ordered out of the plane and had no choice but to comply. The Russian opened the door and practically dragged me out. He grabbed my arm so roughly I'd likely have a bruise. He gave an all clear signal to the two pilots, and they quickly pulled away from the dock and sped across the water lifting off before my new threat and I were off the dock.

Clearly as spooked by the Russian troops in the area as I was.

I was torn.

What I'd seen had shaken me to the core. Left me certain I needed to deviate from my mission. I hated to leave the girls in the prison, but the missiles were a bigger worry. We were taught to prioritize threats. Terrorism, missiles, especially nuclear devices, took priority over almost anything else.

Decisions were made in the field based on the total number of people affected. Twelve girls were rotting away in the prison. My heart ached for them, but missiles threatened the lives of tens of thousands of people. My oath was to the citizens of the United States of America. I felt an obligation to pursue the missiles first. Then worry about the girls.

This wasn't the first time we'd had to make such a decision on the fly. A few years before, Alex was in North Korea chasing Pok. He came across a young girl named Bae Hwa who liked to steal backpacks. She unknowingly got her hands on a satchel full of nuclear codes the North Koreans sold to a group of Iranian terrorists.

While Pok was still a threat, the nuclear codes in the hands of the Iranians was a bigger one and put millions of people at risk. Alex diverted from his original mission, killed the Iranian terrorists, and got the codes safely out of the country. Then went back to deal with Pok.

The delay allowed Pok to slip through his fingers. Sometimes, it couldn't be helped. Even though Pok was still a threat. Alex did the right thing.

Now he was on his way to Vietnam to kill Pok once and for all. I wondered how he was doing. Hopefully, Alex's arch nemesis was dead or would be soon.

My mind was spinning like a carnival ride in an amusement park. Trying to decide what to do before I was forced into the waiting vehicle at the end of the dock.

So many questions.

Should I kill the Russian now or in the car?

Should I go after the missiles or the girls?

How could I take out the missiles by myself?

How would I get the girls out of Russia?

I looked back and saw the seaplane flying off in the distance.

There wasn't enough time to make all the calculations. The Russian was clearly in a hurry. I practically had to run to keep up. I was tempted to kill him at that moment, but it was too soon. I needed to assess my situation. Figure out a plan. I wasn't sure yet if I needed him alive.

We arrived at the vehicle and he forced me into the passenger seat. I preferred the back seat but didn't have a choice in the matter. He let out a flurry of Russian expletives in the process as he roughly pushed my head through the door like a cop pushing a murderer into a police car.

Within seconds, the Russian was behind the wheel, and we were on the move. He looked me up and down one time before driving off. I knew what he was thinking. After that exchange, he kept his eyes on the road concentrating on avoiding the huge ruts which bounced me around the vehicle like a rag doll. Since my hands were in zip ties, I had no way to secure a seatbelt.

Not that I wanted to. I might need the freedom of movement. Still my teeth rattled from the motion. It was all I could do to keep from slamming my head against the ceiling or the passenger side window.

The road leveled out which gave me more time to think about the missiles and why they were there. I'd decided to put the girls out of my mind for now and focus on the bigger threat.

The Russians were exercising some kind of power play. The only thing I could think of was that they had moved the missiles to the eastern shore and aimed them at US cities in an attempt to use them as leverage. To blackmail us. Possibly to get us to remove the financial sanctions.

On the way to Alaska, I'd read the CIA mission report on Russia. The sanctions were crippling the Russian economy. Despots did desperate things when backed into a corner. Like North Korea selling those nuclear codes to the Iranians. When leaders with massive egos get trapped into a corner, they fight their way out like a treed coon.

Were the Russians bluffing?

In a poker hand, you only lost money and a part of your ego if you called someone on his hand and it turned out he wasn't bluffing. In real life, missiles shot into highly populated cities could kill thousands of people.

The risks were enormous. The United States couldn't afford to get it wrong. To miscalculate. That's why I had to act. Get as much information as possible. I was close to the action. There's no way the CIA had anyone this close to the missiles.

Of course Brad knew that as well. Why didn't he contact me? Maybe he tried. My phone was in my backpack. Which was lying on the couch at the cabin. At the offices of the *Two Brothers Adventure Services*.

He had no way to contact me. Another reason I needed to kill the man sitting next to me in the car. He had a phone. I needed it.

I would call Brad and get guidance from him before I went traipsing off looking for the missiles. I could envision a scenario where I could make things worse. Things might already be happening behind the scenes. Through diplomatic channels.

Or military ones.

What if the President had already decided to take out the missiles? I might find myself on the wrong end of friendly fire. They'd never even know I was there. I'd be disintegrated along with the Russian soldiers.

Alex would never know what happened to me.

A more reserved approach seemed prudent. Not being careful. Being smart.

The President of the United States should decide what he wanted me to do. I was in a position to give him information and had a duty to do so and would offer my services. If he declined them, then I'd go back to the original mission and get the girls out of there as fast as possible.

Before missiles started raining down on Russia.

Right now, I could see that I was a liability to the President and his ability to make a decision. More than likely, he wouldn't act while I was still on the ground here.

All the more reason why I needed to call Brad.

The sooner the better.

Curly always said not to act until I was ready unless I was forced to. I needed to get my bearings and assess my current situation.

I looked the Russian up and down. In the same way he'd eyed me except for different reasons. The man was formidable. Muscular. Hardened. I'd faced down men like this before. They weren't easy to kill. He had height, weight, and reach on me. He also had a gun on his belt.

The opposite of the two men on the seaplane. This guy was as mean as a lion in the wild. My arm still hurt from his tight grip. He was also smart. He hadn't put me in the backseat. From that position, I could've wrapped my zip ties around his neck and choked him out. Struck him on the neck and knocked him unconscious.

He probably wasn't worried about that. He'd looked me over and determined I wasn't a threat. After all, if I were going to fight back, I would've done so before I got to Russia.

That was a good thing. He underestimated me. To his peril. I'd use that to my advantage.

He looked me over again then grinned. His intentions were clear. He didn't put me in the backseat because he had other plans for me in the front seat.

I thought of the other twelve girls. Who'd probably been in this same position. With no ability to defend themselves.

The thought infuriated me.

Thinking about what they had to endure. Brought over on the seaplane like me. Scared out of their wits. Thrown into the car with a Russian thug.

It had to be horrible.

Now I knew I was going to kill the Russian. Sooner rather than later. I wasn't going to wait to find out his intentions. I also needed to act before we got too far away from the missiles.

Curly said to assess your resources. The Russian had a handgun. In the backseat was an assault rifle. Another reason he didn't put me in the back seat.

He would have I.D. on him. That might be useful. His clothes were several sizes too big so I couldn't wear them and get away with being a Russian man. That thought occurred to me as a way to get close to the missiles.

The cellphone and weapon were the two things I really wanted to get my hands on. I needed to call Alex. He could help me with the missiles. He could hack into anything. He could change the software so the missiles would fall harmlessly in the Pacific Ocean if fired.

I also needed the Russian's vehicle. We were in a military looking Jeep that had seen better days. Probably once used on the battlefield. Maybe Afghanistan. Or in Russia for military training or maneuvers.

It'd have to do. It beat walking.

He had water and a snack in the vehicle. Along with a bottle of vodka. No Russian ever left home without the liquor. My throat was parched and I suddenly craved the snack and water.

He'd have Russian rubles on him. That might be useful at some point as well.

"Do you speak English?" I asked.

"Nyet."

That told me he did speak a little since he knew what I asked.

I thought about asking him how he preferred to die in Russian. That'd give him a shock.

I forced back a smile.

That wasn't the most important question.

How did I prefer to kill him?

22

Killing the Russian had to be quick. Hand to hand combat in those close quarters would not be fun. It needed to be over in one strike. A backhand karate chop to his larynx was my first choice.

He was driving though. Like a maniac. I didn't want him to wreck the vehicle. It'd be a long walk back to the missiles.

The element of surprise was on my side. I could act before he realized what had happened. I'd then have to react quickly to bring the car under control before it crashed. Curly always said to make the first strike devastating. So the person had no opportunity to fight back. That certainly applied in this situation. I couldn't give the Russian a fighting chance.

My body tensed as I prepared to strike.

The angle wasn't the best for a shot to the windpipe. However, it was the most efficient if executed properly.

I hesitated.

The road was bumpy. What if I hit him on the chin and not in the larynx? Or in the chest because he hit a bump and the blow was misdirected.

Rarely did killing a man go perfectly.

My hands were still in the zip ties which also complicated things. He was beside me, not in front of me. His neck was thick and muscular. A shot to the neck might not do the trick. To the bridge of his nose would be painful for him and for me although not deadly. I couldn't put enough force behind it.

The windpipe was vulnerable. The man could bench press five hundred pounds and his throat would not be strong enough to protect him from a well-executed strike. Minimal force would crush his windpipe and he'd be dead within a minute.

It wasn't the most pleasant of experiences for the assailant who had to watch the person die. But I was long past that. This man was part of a sex trafficking ring. It'd bring me great satisfaction to make it impossible for him to take another breath on this earth.

If I succeeded, it'd be over quickly. He wouldn't fight back. Couldn't. The only thing he'd be able to think about in that situation was grasping his throat and gasping for air. Pleading for me to help him.

It wouldn't take long for him to realize he was going to die a horrible death.

My mind said move, but I still hesitated.

Something didn't seem right.

Before I could tell myself to strike again, the Russian slowed the vehicle. My hand had already been lifted off my lap. I caught it and pulled it back down.

He veered off the road. Onto the shoulder.

Slammed the vehicle into park, turned off the ignition, and turned to look at me. His eyes were filled with a mixture of rage and lust.

His intentions were clear. He wanted to try out the new merchandise.

Before I could react, he was climbing over the center console. I let out a shriek for effect. Mostly to egg him on. Encourage him.

Sometimes killing a man did go perfectly.

He wasn't being cautious. He didn't perceive me as a threat at all.

So he led with his head. Big mistake. Although, based on his intentions, he had no other option. He had to come over to my side to get on top of me.

I put my hands up in a normal defensive response and put them on his head and resisted slightly slowing his momentum. He bullied his way forward.

His hair was oily.

His breath smelled of vodka, cigarettes, and some kind of nasty fish.

He called me a disgusting and disparaging name in Russian. The words were mixed with a spray of saliva that saturated my face.

Infuriating me.

My left hand clasped his right cheek. My right hand his left.

I tightened my grip.

And twisted.

Violently. My left hand sharply to the right. My right hand up and in the opposite direction.

His neck snapped.

I'd severed his spinal cord.

Well executed.

He collapsed onto the console.

Dead. Or he would be soon.

I pushed him off of me. Roughly. Angrily. The adrenaline was flowing through me like the white-water of the Yukon River I'd seen earlier that day.

No need to check for a pulse.

I ripped off the zip ties and took a look around in each direction. To make sure no one was coming. To get a sense of where I was. We were facing west. On what appeared to be a deserted road. Most roads in that part of Russia were sparsely traveled and in disrepair.

The winters were harsh, and the residents congregated in a handful of cities where they had water and electricity and heat for the winter. Where the food supply was brought in. Nothing was going to grow in that region and industry was nonexistent.

A perfect place to run a clandestine sex trafficking operation.

It pained me that I wasn't going to help the women right away.

I had some idea where I was, but not exactly. I got out of the car and stretched and took in the brisk air. Nighttime was just around the corner. Something I was thankful for. My intentions were best carried out in the cover of darkness.

The Russian was dragged into the woods after I relieved him of anything that might be of use to me. His wallet was filled with rubles. More than I expected. Probably not his. Given to him by his oligarch boss to use in the operations.

The keys to the vehicle were now in my possession. He had a cell phone and I tested it for a signal. We must be close to a village because the signal was strong.

I checked the location app on the phone and we were within five miles of a small village. I took a few minutes to memorize the area and determine the best route back to the missiles. Also how to get to the prison to rescue the girls when the time came to do so.

I was still standing outside the vehicle. With the weapon the Russian had on him just in case another vehicle appeared on the road.

I called Alex. It went straight to voicemail. Of course it would. He wouldn't recognize the number.

"It's me. Call me back on this number as soon as you can. I've got a bear of a problem to discuss with you."

That told him I was in Russia. Bear was a well-known symbol.

Once I hung up, I planned my next move. I considered going into town. I was starving. Instead, I decided to wait. I figured I'd come across a vacant cabin somewhere and stop there to get food and water. Better to keep out of sight for the time being.

I gulped down the snacks and water the Russian had in the car. Decided against a shot of vodka. It might calm my nerves, but also might make me sleepy.

I wasn't out of the woods yet. Literally and figuratively. I was surrounded by woods.

I used the keys to open the trunk. There I found an arsenal of weapons. Knives. A machete. Machine guns. Ammo. Grenades. Smoke bombs. Small firearms. Enough firepower to fight off a small army.

Something I might have to do.

The thought made me shudder. I had to get close to the missiles without being seen. Otherwise, I would be fighting a small army of Russians.

At that point, I decided to get moving before something went wrong as it tended to do when a mission was going too well. Sitting by the side of the road was problematic. It was only a matter of time until someone came along.

I decided to drive away from the town and back toward the missiles. Careful to stay on the back roads. All the roads in the area were back roads but some weren't capable of transporting mobile missile launchers. Those had to be moved on bigger trucks.

After I felt like I was in a secure place, I pulled off the side of the road and dialed a familiar number.

Brad would know who it was. Only two people had that number. Alex and me. Brad would assume I was in a secure place and not calling under duress. Even though he wouldn't recognize the number.

He answered on the first ring.

Why did he sound different?

I noticed it immediately after the first words came out of his mouth.

23

Swinks Mill, Virginia

Brad should be asleep but wasn't.

Such was his life. The reason he wasn't married. How could a wife be expected to put up with his job? The secrecy. Always on call. Twenty-four hours a day, seven days a week, three hundred and sixty-five days a year.

Or at least it seemed like it.

Since the CIA wasn't allowed to operate inside the United States, all missions were conducted overseas. Which meant his operatives called him at all hours of the night from every time zone imaginable. Usually with some kind of fire that needed putting out.

Making sleep too irregular and stress common. The average lifespan of men in his position was ten years below the average American's.

The only thing more nerve wracking was being on the other end of the call. If the operatives in the field lived to fifty, they were doing well. At least the ones who took their jobs seriously. The Jamie and Alex's of the world who were willing to put themselves in harm's way. Risk life and limb for the mission.

They usually died before their time. Like soldiers in a war. On the front lines of the war against the evils of the world. Brad was a strategic player in that war, but he was like the President of the United States. He sent others to do the actual fighting.

He'd sent Alex after Pok. Not that he could've stopped him. Alex's life mission was to track down and kill his nemesis. It appeared something had gone horribly wrong. Probably some kind of mechanical failure on the airplane, ironically enough. Alex had been shot at more times than any man should ever be subjected to. He had survived them all.

Like the space shuttle that blew up because of a faulty O-ring. Alex's plane probably crashed because some ten dollar part malfunctioned.

It didn't seem fair. If he had to die, it should've been in a gunfight.

Brad couldn't shake the aching in his heart. The loss he felt.

At least Alex was on a mission. Doing what he loved. Trying to make the world a better place.

Brad tossed and turned in the bed and put the pillow over his head roughly. As if he could somehow silence the voices telling him to accept it.

Alex was dead. Nothing he could do about it. He still had a job to do. He wouldn't be of any use to anybody if he didn't get some sleep.

What he wouldn't give to get one of those late night phone calls. To be awakened and hear Alex's familiar voice on the other end with some kind of convoluted explanation. How he only made it look like a plane crash to fool Pok.

He'd pretty much lost hope of that happening. The search and rescue in the Indian Ocean would soon become a search and recovery. The Navy had already completed one search of the area. A fourteen thousand square mile swath of ocean was meticulously searched by two planes. The planes created a wide circle then worked their way into the center from opposite directions. Closing the gap until they'd covered every square inch of the only logical area to search.

Spotters were on board. Looking for any evidence of a crash. Debris or an oil slick. The area was filmed so his people could look as well. In case the human eye missed something.

Nothing.

High waves and fierce winds caused them to call off the search for today. It'd resume the next morning, but the Admiral in charge wasn't hopeful. His exact words, "That plane is at the bottom of the ocean. I don't think we'll ever find it."

One more go at it and it'd be called off for good. Simply too many resources being wasted on one airplane. Even as valuable as Alex and the other men were to the CIA.

There was no time to mourn.

Russia had become a full-blown crisis.

The President received an ultimatum from Popov, the Russian President. Remove the sanctions or he would begin firing a ballistic missile at a United States city. President Kemp had forty-eight hours to comply, or the first missile would be launched. One every day until the U.S. gave in.

President Kemp took a hard line. An eye for an eye. He issued his own ultimatum. Fire a missile and the U.S. would level a Russian city. Kemp was even considering a preemptive strike but was waiting for Jamie to rescue the girls out of the Russian prison.

Director Coldclaw told Brad to get Jamie out of there as soon as possible. He would if he knew how to get in touch with her.

Pretty soon, it'd be too late. If missiles started flying out of Russia, the President would have no choice but to retaliate. He'd have to act regardless of Jamie. Protecting thousands of people in American cities would take priority.

So he tossed and turned. Sleep would be impossible tonight. Taking several years off his life in the process. A sleeping pill was not an option. He needed to have his full wits about him if he did get one of those late-night calls. A development in the search. A call from Jamie. The Director saying he was needed in the war room at the White House immediately.

Any kind of call could come tonight.

It felt like he dozed off. At least he thought he was dreaming when he heard the phone ring.

The second ring caused him to bolt straight up in bed. His heart was suddenly in the back of his throat. It wasn't his regular phone. This was a special line he always had on him. Only two people called him on that number.

Alex or Jamie.

He practically tripped over the bedspread jumping out of bed to get to his phone on a charger across the room.

Please be Alex.

Don't be Jamie.

He'd been dreading a call from Jamie. Director Coldclaw instructed him not to tell her about Alex until she completed her mission. He didn't want her distracted. Nothing she could do about Alex anyway.

Brad fumbled with the phone. Dropping it to the ground trying to get it off the dresser. He retrieved it intent on looking at the caller I.D. before answering.

His heart sank back to the bottom of his chest when he saw a Russian number.

It had to be Jamie.

She had managed to make it into Russia. Obviously, stole a cell phone. He took in a deep breath to try and control his hand that was shaking.

How could he not tell her?

Probably didn't matter. Jamie would hear it in his voice.

He'd blame it on the hour of the night if confronted. That she woke him from a deep sleep.

Jamie was smarter than that. She'd never believe it.

He steadied his hand and answered it right before it went to voice-mail.

"I take it you're in Russia," he said, with as much aloofness as he could muster. Trying to make his voice sound like he'd been asleep.

She wouldn't expect a standard greeting. He rarely answered their calls with a hello. If he did now, she'd suspect something immediately.

"I am."

It was surprisingly reassuring to hear her voice. At least he knew she was alive.

"You must've stolen some poor Russian guy's phone."

"He won't be needing it anymore. If you know what I mean."

Brad let out a perceivable groan. That meant the man was dead. Jamie was resourceful that way. If she needed something, she had an uncanny ability to get it.

"It's okay," she said. "He was one of the bad guys."

"Do you have the packages?"

The code word for the girls. Even though it was unlikely anyone was listening to their conversation, standard protocol was to be vague. They never used real names or discussed the details of a mission on an unsecured line. His end was secure but hers wasn't.

"Not yet."

"Is your Ingenue with you?"

"No."

He didn't respond.

Ingenue meant young woman. He was talking about Kaley. Jamie knew the word because they used it in the past to describe Bae Hwa. The young girl from North Korea who had inadvertently stolen a backpack full of nuclear codes from an Iranian terrorist.

Alex rescued her. Not before Bae paid a tremendous price. Her parents were killed by the terrorists. Alex brought Bae back to America where she enrolled in college even though she was only thirteen. She graduated in no time and had finished her doctorate before she was twenty-one.

Bae wanted to be a spy, but Jamie had discouraged it and Brad agreed. Bae even dropped out of school one semester and began hitchhiking across the United States pretending to be some sort of vigilante. Determined to prove her worth as an operative. That didn't go well. All she managed to do was almost get herself killed.

Jamie rescued her and some girls in Chicago who were being held as sex slaves by a gang called the Strikers. As was usually the case with Jamie, somehow everything worked out for good in the end.

The whole incident caused a schism in Jamie and Bae's relationship. The last Brad heard Bae was still on a fast track to becoming a doctor. Hopefully, she would stay on that career path.

The well-meaning girl didn't have what it took to be an operative. Too impulsive.

Brad was pinning his hopes on Kaley. He hoped Kaley was with Jamie in Russia and was disheartened to hear she wasn't.

"I left her behind," Jamie added after the silence became awkward. "No fault of her own. You'll probably hear from her soon."

Again, Brad didn't respond. He decided to keep his mouth shut. No reason to get in an argument with Jamie about it. He made it a point never to question his operative's judgment when they were in the field. If Jamie didn't take Kaley to Russia, she had a good reason for it.

"Have you talked to Alabama?" Jamie asked, out of the blue.

Brad hesitated. He wasn't prepared for the direct question. Alabama was Alex's code name.

"No. I haven't heard from him. Have you?"

"No. But I need to talk to him," she said. "We have a situation over here."

"I think I know what you mean. We are aware of the situation. You need to get out of there as soon as possible. Once you secure the packages. Hopefully, within two days."

Jamie had obviously learned about the missiles. That explained why she was calling. Her first thought had been Alex. Brad's too.

Alex was the foremost computer hacker in the world. He could hack into Russian military control and redirect the missiles. They had other hackers in the CIA, but none with Alex's skill.

Brad became choked up with emotion thinking about it.

Just hearing Jamie mention Alex sent a dagger through his heart. He bit his lip to keep from spilling his guts to her so they could mourn together.

He fought back the urge. Now was not the time. He didn't have confirmation. The girls were also still in that Russian prison.

He also had an additional worry. Somebody still needed to kill Pok. Jamie was probably the only other person in the world capable of pulling it off. When he told her, she'd drop everything and go to Vietnam. He needed her in Russia right now.

"I'm on the ground," Jamie said. "Within thirty miles of the vultures. I can check them out for you."

Brad hesitated again.

"I won't cause an international incident," she added. "Just snoop around."

He wasn't sure what to say. He didn't have authorization for her to surveille the missiles. It was an opportunity though. They could tell a lot from satellite photos but they could tell even more from eyes on the ground. If anybody could get close, it'd be Jamie.

According to the CIA Director, they did have forty-eight hours. What would it hurt to give Jamie twenty-four of those?

"Look, but don't touch," Brad said. "Report back to me as soon as you can."

"Of course," I said. "I'll use discretion. You know me."

He laughed nervously. "That's why I said it. Because I know you. Don't try to take them out on your own. We're going through the proper channels. At first, anyway. We'll take them out if the time comes."

"I understand. Remember that I'm here. Okay. I'd like to be back on safe ground before the forest fire starts. "

"I'm relieved that you're okay. It's good to hear your voice."

He realized his mistake immediately. A strange thing for him to say. She'd know something was wrong.

As if on cue, she said, "What's wrong? Did something happen to Bama?"

He hesitated. Lying wouldn't work with her. She'd see through it. So he took an indirect approach. "I don't know. I haven't heard from him."

"That's not unusual. Why would you hear from him? He should be taking care of his problem. Why are you worried about him? And me?"

"I always worry about you."

"What are you not telling me?"

"I don't want to say anything until I know for sure."

Brad winced. He'd given it away. Jamie wouldn't know what was wrong but would know it was bad.

"You need to focus on your mission. Don't get distracted."

"I'll check out the vultures tonight and get the packages tomorrow," she said, soberly. He thought he heard her voice crack.

"You have twenty-four hours."

"Understood. If you talk to Bama, have him call me ASAP," she said.

"For sure."

The line went dead.

24

Denali National Park

Willy was happy to be back in United States airspace. He'd been spooked by the Russian fighter jets intercepting the seaplane in the air even though they had permission to be there. He guessed they'd ventured too close to some military maneuvers. He took a northerly route back to Alaska, so he'd avoid any possible confrontation with the Russian Migs.

They might have to raise their price. Demand combat pay.

The thought made him smile. The men he dealt with didn't take very kindly to demands. They usually didn't negotiate. They stated their expectations and the compensation and they could take it or leave it.

So far, they had taken it. Willingly. The Russians were paying them handsomely for the girls. Surprisingly so. They had to or he never would've agreed to the plan.

It started with drugs. The Russian oligarch paid the two brothers to courier drugs to and from Russia in their planes.

Fentanyl. OxyContin. Cocaine. Methamphetamine.

The cheaper drugs like marijuana were brought across the porous Mexican border. The more expensive drugs came through the ports or were brought in by plane.

The process was practically foolproof. The brothers already owned the planes and had the tour guide business. It was barely profitable, but they were able to eke out a living. Now they were millionaires.

Without taking a lot of risk.

The drugs weren't on the ground in the United States for long. If they were intercepted in the air, they simply dropped the drugs into the Bering Sea or the wilderness of Alaska. Making them impossible to be found.

To this point, they'd never even had a close call. There's only one DEA office in all of Alaska. One office to police 586, 412 square miles. 365,000,000 acres. An impossible job.

When their Russian contract approached them about kidnapping and bringing girls to Russia, Willy was skeptical at first. Too much risk. The drug trade was going well. Why draw attention to themselves?

His brother, Benji, didn't agree. He was all for the plan. What was the risk, he argued? They'd kidnap the girls out in the wild. On the trails. Amazingly, hundreds of girls every year came to Alaska, alone for an adventure.

If they were careful, the kidnappings could never be traced back to them. They did one. It went well. So they did another one. Today was number thirteen.

Case in point. The blonde today. It didn't get any easier than that. She didn't even put up a fight. Obviously in a state of shock. Taken completely by surprise.

His only regret was not getting to keep her for himself. She was a real looker. He preferred blondes. She was model pretty. Toned and fit. Flowing hair. A shame she had to be wasted on the Russians. That's why they hadn't gone for the younger girl. The redhead. She would've been easy game as well.

Willy had considered designing his own prison cell in the wilderness. He could keep a girl there for years and no one would ever know about it. The only reason he hadn't mentioned it to his brother was because he wouldn't want to share the girl. That'd be like incest or something.

He had his standards.

They landed the seaplane on the runway shortly after dark. It'd been a long day and he was tired. Neither of them had said much on the flight back. Tomorrow, they had off. The next day they were flying a group up to see the glaciers. He dreaded those excursions.

They made more today transporting the blonde to Russia than they'd make on all the group excursions for the entire year. Had to be done, though, to keep up the front. The Russians had also started laundering money through their business, so they had to keep the guide service going.

Between the drugs, sex trafficking, and money laundering, they were building a small fortune.

"I'm glad to be home," Willy said.

Benji simply grunted and exited the plane. They secured it in case a storm came up overnight. Then headed inside.

Willy entered first and flipped on the light.

He felt it immediately.

A presence.

A person.

He looked around. What he saw didn't make sense.

The girl from the Visitor's Center. The redhead. She was sitting in his chair.

With a gun pointed at them.

25

Kaley remained seated. With her gun pointed at the two men.

Standing might be more practical. Sitting inhibited her mobility but made her a smaller target. It also gave her a persona she was going for. A tough girl who wasn't afraid of them. She could be nonchalant while threatening.

Jamie said to always come across confident when facing down a threat. You either wanted the bad guy to be terrified or underestimate you.

These two men were surprised and fearful at first. After assessing the situation, they'd clearly become emboldened and didn't see Kaley as much of a threat. She didn't see them as much of a problem either. They were at least twenty paces away. Both had handguns on their hips, but they were latched to a holster.

Stupid.

It would take too long for them to draw. She had an assault rifle. A bit of overkill for that small a space, but Jamie said always bring more firepower to a gunfight than you need if possible. The modified special forces weapon would chew the two men up faster than a woodchipper.

"I wouldn't make any sudden moves if I were you," Kaley said, with as much bravado as she could muster. The rifle was off her lap and pointed in between them. Her finger on the trigger, ready to fire at the slightest twitch of a muscle.

The only thing that didn't quite fit the persona she was going for was her voice. More on the soprano side. She wished it were deeper, gruffier.

Kathleen Turner like. A smoker's voice, although Kaley abhorred smoking and would never touch a cigarette, even if it did help deepen her voice.

"I remember you from the Visitor Center," Benji remarked. He was the one wearing the Wisconsin tee shirt. The one she encountered inside the Visitor Center. She knew his name from a brochure she found on the counter. It had his picture along with his brother Willy's.

Willy was standing to the right. Benji to her left. She hadn't determined yet which was the one more likely to do something stupid.

"Yeah. You were there," Willy said. "What are you doing here? Did you follow us? Are you trying to rob us? Why don't you lower that gun?"

"Where's the blonde-haired girl?" Kaley asked roughly.

The two men looked at each other. A clear sign of recognition.

"We don't know nothing about no blonde," Benji said. Clearly the stupid one.

"You realize you just said that you do know something about the blonde," Kaley said.

The man twisted his lips to the side and his forehead burrowed like he was confused.

"When you say you don't know nothing, it means you know something," Kaley said, with disdain in her voice. "If you knew nothing, you'd say you know nothing. Did you even graduate from high school?"

"I don't know what you're talking about," Benji said.

"Never mind," Kaley said. The ingrate obviously hadn't taken elementary English.

Willy took a step toward her. Kaley turned the gun toward him, and he stopped in his tracks.

"What do you want from us?" Willy asked, escalating the tone and the tension in the room.

"Where did you take the girl?" Kaley said, matching his tone and raising it a couple of menacing notches.

"We don't know what you're talking about."

"Don't lie to me!" she said, angrily. She was already on edge. She'd been at the house for hours, waiting. Impatiently. For them to return.

Willy raised his hands in a pose of surrender but also took two steps to the side. To his left. A smart move on his part. He put some distance between himself and his partner. It'd make it harder for Kaley to shoot both of them quickly.

Harder, but the difference was imperceivable. Kaley could kill them both before either could draw his weapon. At this point, she didn't care if that was the outcome. The only reason they were alive was the hope that she could gather more intel from them.

At this point, she didn't have a valid reason to kill the men. Even though she knew they were behind the sex trafficking operation. Jamie had given her specific instructions on when to kill the enemy on a mission.

So many rules to remember.

Kaley tried to put them out of her mind and focus on the task at hand. Jamie warned her not to try and remember them all, but to act on instinct.

In this instance, the situation was complicated by the fact that they were on U.S. soil. The men had constitutional rights. She needed a sufficient reason to kill them. More than likely, they'd give her one in time. They didn't seem like the type to give up easily.

She could defend herself which was why she had to wait for one of the men to act.

What would Jamie do? Shoot them at the slightest provocation. No doubt about it. Probably tie up the men, load them on the plane, and dump them in the *Bering Sea* on the way to Russia. Take the U.S. constitutional problem out of the equation.

"Look," Willy said. "I don't know who you are or what you want, but you need to put that gun down before somebody gets hurt."

"I want to know where you took the blonde girl."

"Like I said, I don't know anything about any blonde girl."

Kaley stood to her feet. The man kept inching his way to her right.

Like he wanted to cut off the angle. Surround her. So she decided being confined to the chair wasn't a good plan in the unlikely event that the gun jammed.

"Then who does that backpack belong to?" Kaley asked. Pointing at Jamie's backpack on the couch.

She had taken two steps to the right as well. She was closer to Willy, but the couch was now between them.

Benji let out a groan. Willy glared at his brother.

"I told you to take the SIM card out of the girl's cell phone and destroy it!"

"I did," Benji answered. "It's over there on the counter."

"Obviously you didn't. How else did she find us?"

Benji actually did destroy the SIM card. CIA phones had a built-in tracker that put out a signal even without the SIM card. Although the men could never know Kaley was with the CIA or that's how she tracked them back to that location.

When Kaley arrived back at the Visitor Center, she was still shaken from the encounter with the bear. Jamie was nowhere to be found. After going inside and using the restroom, Kaley went back to the car and pulled up the tracking device on her phone. To her surprise, Jamie was on a trail several miles away. Headed south.

Why would Jamie be in that part of the woods? In the middle of nowhere. Headed away from the Visitor Center.

It became weirder when the location blip started moving faster. On a road. Headed due south. Jamie was clearly on the move. It didn't take long to figure it out.

Jamie had been the one kidnapped. The men had gone after her. Their car was no longer at the Visitor Center.

Kaley immediately started her vehicle and sped away racing toward the signal. She was a good twenty minutes behind it.

It took a couple of minutes to get her bearings and figure out the best road to take. Even looking for a shortcut to cut them off. The blip stopped about twenty minutes later. At the cabin she was in now.

Kaley drove as fast as humanly possible, but Jamie and the two men were gone by the time she arrived at their offices.

No sign of anyone, although the men's car was parked in front of the cabin. Kaley picked the lock to the back door and entered the cabin. That's when she found Jamie's backpack and got a clearer picture of how the men were transporting the girls to Russia.

They ran a guide service with two planes. She rushed outside, sprinted down a trail to an airstrip. One of the planes was gone. The sea-plane.

They'd obviously taken Jamie to Russia in that plane. Kaley went back inside and tore through the office. Searching for anything she could find. She found the flight plan written on a log in the office.

After searching the rest of the place, all she could do was wait. For hours. Expected. The trip to Russia and back would have to take at least four hours. Probably more.

She considered calling Brad but decided against it. Jamie had been emphatic. Brad was a good guy, but he was a suit. In an office. The operatives worked in the field. They ran the missions. Brad was there for support. Morale and logistical support.

Jamie was adamant that Kaley needed to be a self-starter. With the ability to think on her own and make decisions without running back to Brad every time she faced a decision.

"You have a mission," Jamie said strongly. "Fulfill it. Do what you think is best. If you make a mistake, then own up to it."

"How will I know if I made a mistake?" Kaley asked.

"If you are dead," Jamie had added for emphasis. "That's how you'll know you made the wrong decision."

So Kaley waited for the men to return rather than call Brad. Certain they eventually would. She thought about taking the other plane and following them to Russia, but she wouldn't get into Russian airspace. She needed the men to file a flight plan for her. When they did, she intended to go to Russia and help Jamie.

26

The two brothers were still fighting. Blaming each other for the screw up.

Another thing Jamie said. "Don't analyze a mission until it's over. There'll be plenty of time for Monday morning quarterbacking. Beating yourself up in the throes of a mission is counterproductive. It'll cause you to make another mistake."

"I told you we should leave these two girls alone," Willy said. "I thought something was up with them."

"Nothing's up with them. You saw the blonde. She ain't nothing. She didn't put up a fight at all."

"None of this would've happened if you'd just handled the phone. And why did you leave her backpack lying around as evidence. What if a customer came in and saw it?"

"Aw. Shut up. You think you know it all."

"You shut up."

"No. You."

"Both of you shut up!" Kaley shouted. "You act like a couple of bratty kids."

The gun was firmly on Willy now. The closest one.

"Your brother is right about one thing," Kaley said. "You picked the wrong girls to mess with."

"We didn't take the blonde anywhere. She came back here with us voluntarily. She must've left her backpack. The last I saw her, she was on the road, hitchhiking back to the Visitor Center."

Kaley laughed.

"It doesn't matter," she said. "I already know where you took the girl. Here's what's going to happen. I'm stealing your jet. One of you is going to file a flight plan from here to Moscow."

Kaley had a plan. She couldn't fly directly to the prison. That'd raise too many red flags with the Russians. She'd file a flight plan to Moscow, then pretend to have a mechanical failure and land at the airstrip at the prison. Rescue Jamie and the girls and fly them out of Russia, back to Alaska, before anyone was wise to her plan.

"That ain't going to happen," Willy said roughly. "You're crazy if you think I'm going to let you steal an eight-million-dollar plane."

"The person with the biggest gun sets the rules. That'd be me."

"You need to put that gun down, little girl," Willy said. "Before you hurt someone."

"I'm not a little girl," Kaley said. "And don't think I won't use this."

"How do we know you even know how to use it?" Willy said.

"Yeah," Benji agreed.

"Try me and you'll find out fast that I know how to use it."

"Who do you work for? The DEA?"

"She don't work for the DEA, man," Benji said. "If she did, she'd have to identify herself."

"That's a good point. If you're with law enforcement, then I want to see some identification."

Kaley didn't say anything.

"That's what I thought," Willy said.

"She's too young, man. She don't work for nobody."

"He's right," Kaley said. "I don't work for the DEA."

She actually didn't work for anyone. Technically, she didn't work for the CIA yet. That did give her new information. The brothers were running drugs along with the sex trafficking.

"Who do you work for?" Willy asked roughly.

"I work for myself." Kaley answered.

"Do you work for Vinny?"

"I don't know Vinny."

"Is Vinny trying to muscle in on our action?"

"I already told you that I don't work for anyone," Kaley said. "You kidnapped a friend of mine."

"I told you we should've nabbed this one," Benji said.

"Shut up."

Kaley let out a huge sigh. "Both of you shut up. I'm tired of hearing your voices. Here's what's going to happen. One at a time, you are going to slowly remove the weapons from your belts. Put them on the floor and kick them over to me. Then get on the floor spread eagle. Who wants to go first?"

Neither of them said anything. They were looking at each other. Sending each other signals with their eyes. They had clearly decided to act.

Kaley waved the gun at Willy. He seemed to be the biggest threat. "Willy, I want you to slowly unlatch your weapon, take it out, and set it on the floor."

He seemed surprised that she knew his name.

He hesitated.

"Now!"

His hand started moving slowly toward his holster.

"Not your right hand," Kaley said. "Take it out with your left hand."

The gun was on his right hip. She wanted him to take it out from across his body.

"Slowly!"

Benji suddenly reached for his gun.

Kaley let out a shout.

With unexpected calmness, Kaley fired her rifle, hitting Benji in the chest. Before the gun could even be drawn. The force knocked him backward. Before he hit the floor, Kaley had the gun pointed at Willy who stood in disbelief. He held his hands out.

Willy's jaw was clenched. His fists were balled now. His eyes were filled with burning coals of fire.

"You killed my brother."

"I told you I would. I'll kill you too if you make one wrong move."

That wasn't actually true. She would have to wound him. She needed him to file the flight plan. Maybe she could do it herself, but she needed to make sure everything was done properly so she could get into Russia without a problem. If she had to, she'd take Willy with her.

"On your knees," she ordered.

Willy hesitated.

"I'm not going to ask twice."

He fell to his knees.

"Lock your hands behind your head."

He complied. Kaley walked behind him and took his gun out of the holster. Emptied the cartridge. The bullets clanged on the floor. She tossed it on the couch. Then patted him down.

"Stand to your feet," she said.

He stood. Looked over at his brother. Kaley didn't even bother checking on Benji. He was dead. His chest had exploded from the round.

"Go file a flight plan to Moscow. Wheels up in ten minutes."

He didn't hesitate. Probably feeling as much shock as Kaley was at the moment. She'd just killed her first man. The emotions began churning inside of her like butter inside an old plunge churner.

She thought she'd be numb. Emotionless. She had no idea it'd hit her like this. One second Benji was breathing; the next second he was on his way to meet God. Right before he was redirected to hell.

Kaley grew up a person of deep faith. She believed in an afterlife. The battle of good versus evil. A satisfaction came over her knowing she had done her part in the battle.

Jamie called it a righteous kill.

Then a wave of doubt hit her. Did she really have to kill him? She could've tied them up sooner.

Jamie was suddenly in her head. The instructions came flooding back to her mind. All of them all at once.

If they intended to harm you and you know for sure they are bad guys, then kill them before they kill you. Now or later. Doesn't matter. Don't hesitate. Afterwards, don't feel the least bit of remorse or regret. Know you did the right thing.

One instruction came to the forefront of her mind. *Never dwell on the past. Not while on a mission. You can't undo what you've already done. Don't let it affect your ability to complete your mission.*

There was still a lot to do. Rescue Jamie and the girls in Russia being the primary focus.

Kaley pushed Willy in the back with the barrel of her rifle. "Get moving," she said.

"Are you going to kill me, too?" he asked, clearly humbled and afraid.

"I haven't decided yet."

27

Kaley wasn't sure exactly what to do.

Technically, she had broken several laws that could get her thrown in jail for decades. Breaking and entering into the offices of the *Two Brothers Adventure Guide Services* for one. Holding them at gunpoint. Which could bring charges of false imprisonment. Kidnapping now that she had Willy tied up in the back of his plane.

Which she stole. So, add theft to the list of felony charges.

Killing his brother Benji might be considered self-defense. Might not. Alaska had a stand your ground law meaning an individual had the right to protect his property. Which she had encroached upon. Threatened him with bodily harm.

The multitude of laws Benji had broken aside, he was well within his rights to pull his weapon on her. Maybe a jury would be sympathetic.

When she dumped his body out of the plane over the Bering Sea, she certainly was guilty of the improper disposing of a body. Not reporting an incident which resulted in a death. Obstruction of justice. Tampering with evidence. Perjury when she lied about it, which she'd be forced to do.

A dozen more charges could probably be added to her rap sheet if she had time to think about it.

This was not how CIA missions were supposed to work. Operating inside the United States was a crime for an operative. In a foreign country, the CIA had cleaning squads that could take care of such situations. Not in the U.S.

Calling Brad would be the last thing she would want to do.

So she was making decisions on the fly.

Literally. She was speeding across the Bering Sea toward Russia and the prison where Jamie and the girls were being held.

As soon as she entered Russian airspace, she'd break a number of Russian laws. That she wasn't concerned about. Her job was to act with subterfuge in other countries. Jamie made it clear that foreign laws didn't apply to them.

The CIA, as the police of the world, served a higher law. Protecting the interests of the United States of America. Within the confines of a moral code of behavior given to our great country by God. With a responsibility to rid the world of bad actors, terrorists and the like.

Benji and his brother certainly fit into that category. But the CIA didn't act inside the United States for a reason. The men had rights. The right to an attorney. Right to a trial by peers. The right to remain silent. Willy had spilled his guts at the barrel of her gun.

In a way, Kaley was bypassing stepping all over those rights and executing her own form of justice.

Complicated.

She wasn't sure what she was going to do with Willy. The only reason he was still alive was because he'd been helpful. Practically whimpering like a hurt puppy. Pleading for his life. He'd warned her to take a northerly route in her flight plan. Apparently, the Russian military was conducting operations in the Sea of Okhotsk.

What was that all about?

She didn't have a clue, but didn't want to mix it up with Russian Migs. Like the proverbial saying, don't crash into a semi-truck hauling a load. He will always win. Don't bring a water gun to a shootout. And don't fly a ten-seater passenger plane into a war zone.

Willy had also spilled the beans about the sex trafficking operation. Given her his contacts. The location of the prison, even though Kaley already had it. She had names and phone numbers of the other players in the organization. Actionable intelligence for the drug trade as well.

Maybe Kaley hadn't handled things by the book, but she'd done a great service to the mission. Hopefully, rescuing the girls and Jamie from prison would cover a multitude of sins.

Wishful thinking.

She didn't have enough experience to know how to handle it.

Would Jamie have done the same thing? Kaley was dreading that conversation. She didn't know if Jamie would be furious or complimentary. Maybe if she saved Jamie's life that might swing things more to the latter.

She'll find out soon enough. Jamie wasn't shy about telling her what she'd done wrong. If her CIA career ended before it started, then so be it. As Jamie always said, the past is the past. Nothing she could do about it now. Benji was dead. Willy was in the plane. She needed to focus on completing her mission.

A plan was formulating in her mind. Bringing Willy along might work in her favor.

She kind of felt sorry for the man. Another mistake in her judgment. Jamie told her never to feel those emotions.

She could hear Jamie berating her now. "Benji and Willy didn't feel bad about those twelve girls they kidnapped and forced into a life of slavery. Or the drugs they trafficked that ended up on school playgrounds."

That empathy was supposed to be forced out of her in the training. She couldn't help it. Up to this point in her short life, she'd always tried to find the good in people.

I know.

Inside her head, she could hear Jamie yelling at her.

What are you crazy? These men are pure evil. Save your sympathy for the victims. I was right about you. You aren't cut out for this line of work.

Not that Jamie would ever know the thoughts for that very reason. Her mentor already doubted her ability to do the job. If Jamie knew that she had the least bit of sympathy for Willy, she'd kick her out of the CIA on her keester. So fast, it'd make her head swim. Something her mother used to say when she was younger.

So she rationalized her actions. To this point, she could justify keeping Willy alive. He might be useful in Russia. And he wasn't going anywhere. Jamie showed her how to tie up bad guys in the most uncomfortable positions. The worst being a hogtie. With wrists attached to ankles from behind. Nothing short of torture.

She had resisted the temptation to tie Willy up in that manner since he was cooperating. If he gave her any trouble, she wouldn't hesitate to do so.

Still.

It seemed cruel.

Was she going soft already?

She kept reminding herself what kind of man he was. Willy admitted they'd seriously considered kidnapping her instead of Jamie. Both he and his brother would've killed her if given the chance. Willy still would. If the roles were reversed, there's no way he'd show her the least bit of consideration. He wouldn't show her the kind of mercy she was showing him.

Didn't matter. She was better than him. That's the whole justification for doing what she did. Good versus evil. She was on the right side of things. She refused to stoop to his level, even if Jamie insisted on it.

Maybe she wasn't cut out for this kind of work. Not if she had to lose her humanity. Her sense of decency.

She'd kill a bad guy if she had to. Already had. Benji was deader than a doorknob. Shark bait now. She didn't feel bad about it at all. What she did feel bad about was the thought of pushing Willy out of the plane while he was still alive.

That'd solve her problem. Take care of the evidence. He might even deserve it. But Kaley didn't have it in her. If it meant she wasn't suited for this line of work, then so be it. At least she'd still keep her soul intact.

If Jamie thought she was too soft, then that's how it was. Nothing she could do about. At least she'd be able to live with herself.

Actually, she wasn't entirely sure that Jamie would push Willy out of the plane either. In training, Jamie was emphatic.

"'Vengeance is mine,'" says the Lord. We aren't in the revenge business. We also aren't in the punishment business. That's up to God and the authorities."

Kaley had been confused. "I don't understand the difference."

"You will. Once you are forced into those decisions. Your job is to find the bad guys and stop them from hurting innocent people. Kill them if necessary so they don't ever hurt anyone again."

"It seems like semantics."

Jamie had been patient with her and tried to explain. "Hate the sin, not the sinner. Abhor what these men do. Don't abhor them. If you do, you won't be able to live with yourself. The hatred and bitterness will eat you alive. You don't kill them because you despise them. It's for a greater good. Use your head not your emotions when you make those decisions. Otherwise, you may kill someone out of anger."

"I thought anger was good."

"Righteous indignation. That's when the anger is justified. Otherwise, anger is toxic."

"How do I shut off those emotions?"

"You'll learn. If you don't, you won't be able to do this for very long. Most people burn out anyway. Either that or they cover up the emotions with sex and alcohol. You have to learn to compartmentalize. Bury the emotions. Put them in a box."

"I don't know. I'm not a robot."

Jamie got harsher with her. "You have to do it. Emotions will get you killed. Fear will cause you to go backwards when you should go forward. To be careful when you should take risks. Use your mind. That's why God gave it to you. You know evil when you see it. Justify once and for all in your own mind that your job is to fight evil at every turn. Do whatever it takes."

Maybe it was starting to make sense. Now that she was in the field. She'd killed her first man. She had to decide about the other one. Willy's fate was in her hands. Whether he lived or died was her decision.

She still wasn't sure what she was going to do.

28

Somewhere over Russia

Kaley made it into Russia airspace without incident. She was twenty minutes out from the prison. Time to execute step one of her plan.

"Mayday. Mayday. Mayday," Kaley said over the radio. She knew how to speak Russian but pilots from the U.S. spoke English when in flight in other countries.

"What is your emergency?" air traffic control responded.

"I'm having engine trouble. One engine is out. I'm losing altitude fast. Requesting emergency landing at the nearest airport."

A momentary silence.

"Roger that. You've been cleared to land at Obraztsov Regional Airport."

"Confirmed. I'll try. I don't know if I can make it. I may be bringing this plane down sooner than that."

Kaley began descending quickly so the air traffic controller would see what she was describing from the air. Obraztsov was about thirty minutes away which would work perfectly. She could make it look like she was heading in that direction, but would land at the prison instead.

From her intelligence briefing, the prison was used for years to hold political prisoners. It was secluded in a valley which was perfect. She could disappear between the mountains and no one would ever know. The air traffic controller would assume she had crashed. It'd take them hours to organize a search party. She'd be in and out within twenty minutes. Hopefully. If things went well.

She went on the intercom to let Willy know she was landing.

"All passengers prepare for landing. Be sure your seatback is upright and in its most uncomfortable position. Also make sure your tray tables are secured. If you took out any luggage on the flight, please return it to the overhead bins. A flight attendant will be by shortly to gather your trash. Thank you for flying with us. I hope it has been memorable and that you don't consider flying with us again."

Kaley laughed out loud, amusing herself.

Willy was already in a most uncomfortable position. Upright. Secured to his seat. His legs and arms were totally secured. He couldn't move if he tried. He was probably back there cursing her. Wondering what she intended to do with him. He probably didn't see her throw his brother's body off the plane, but no doubt had a good idea that's what happened.

He was likely thankful he was still alive but wondering how much longer that would be the case.

Kaley prepared to land. She sent one more message to air traffic control.

"I'm not going to make it to the airport. I see an abandoned airstrip. I'm going to try and land there."

"Copy that."

Kaley maneuvered the plane carefully between the mountains. Her father flew in the Air Force and taught her how to fly shortly after she learned how to walk. At least it seemed like it. She couldn't fly large commercial craft but was fairly proficient with small airplanes like this one. During her CIA training, she learned to fly other craft including helicopters, seaplanes, and single and twin engine private sized jets.

She brought the plane to a smooth landing, half expecting to do so under gunfire. Several of the runway lights were out, but she managed. She taxied to a spot as close to the prison entrance as possible. Lights were on inside and it looked like people were there. According to satellite photos, the place had between two to four guards at any one time.

That's assuming Jamie hadn't taken any of them out. This mission might even be unnecessary. It's possible Jamie already got the girls out. Something she considered while flying over.

A soldier with a rifle came out of the prison almost immediately and took up a position at the bottom of where the door would open and the stairs would meet the ground. His rifle was pointed down, but he was definitely on high alert.

Willy had said they never brought this plane to the prison. They'd always used the seaplane and met the contact at a dock in the bay.

Kaley shut off the engines and said a quick prayer that the plane would start up again when necessary. She went into the back and untied Willy but left his arms tied in front of him. He was coming with her. For effect.

"If you so much as open your mouth, I'll put a bullet in your head. Do you understand?"

He shook his head nervously.

Kaley already had a gun on her hip. She secured her own assault rifle and led Willy to the front where she opened the cabin door. Then ordered him down the stairs.

She followed him down.

As soon as the soldier saw what was happening, he raised his weapon. Kaley didn't respond. Only acted like she expected it.

"I'm here to pick up the girls," Kaley said, once she had descended the stairs and was next to the soldier. Taking a page out of Jamie's playbook.

Kaley positioned herself close enough to the soldier that she could attack him if necessary. But remained calm and casual in a non threatening stance.

She spoke to him in Russian. Kaley's father was stationed in Germany. That's where she grew up. He took her everywhere with him. Consequently, she was fluent in a number of languages. German. Dutch. French. Italian. She also learned Polish and picked up a lot of Russian.

When she signed on with the CIA, they gave her a crash course on Russian and she became fluent easily enough.

Clearly she was American, but the Russian soldier seemed to relax when she spoke to him in her native language. At least the gun was no longer pointed at her.

She grabbed Willy and jerked him forward. Roughly.

"This man is a traitor. He told the Americans about the girls. I've been ordered to move them to another location."

"How come I wasn't told?"

"Not enough time. We just captured him. I have my orders. General Yuri sent me here to move the girls. Time is of the essence. Can you take me to them?"

Surprisingly, he turned and walked toward the prison. Jamie said in Russia, the soldiers followed orders or they died. He seemed to be buying it. He turned his back to Kaley. A dumb move and a perfect opportunity for her to take him out. She resisted. If the ruse worked, she might get out of there without firing a shot. He was clearly taking her inside.

She pushed Willy from behind and told him to follow the soldier. She wasn't sure if Willy spoke Russian and knew what she said. He didn't react if he did.

"I'll stay here with the prisoner," Kaley said once inside. "Go and get the girls and bring them to me."

The guard disappeared behind a door. While he was gone, a second man appeared and began questioning her. Kaley answered him and he seemed satisfied.

"What do you want us to do with him?" the second soldier asked.

"Whatever you want to do," Kaley said. "He's your prisoner now. Kill him. Put him away for years of hard labor. I don't care. I'm sure General Yuri has something planned for him."

"I don't know General Yuri."

"You're not supposed to know him. He's in intelligence. I'd clear out of here as soon as we're gone. I suspect the Americans are already planning on sending armed men to try and rescue the girls. That's why we have to get them out of here right away."

The door suddenly opened and the girls appeared. Kaley had to fight back a gasp.

Jamie had warned her about what to expect from sex trafficked girls. One by one the ladies filed into the room. Physically, they seemed to be in good shape. That was to be expected. Even though they were housed in a prison, they were prostitutes expected to service men. Their hair was done. They were bathed. They had clothes on. Some still had makeup on their faces.

What caused the emotional reaction in Kaley were the sunken eyes. The look of despair. Their eyes were vacant. Distant. Shallow. Without hope. Almost like death. It sent a chill down her spine.

Like Jamie said, "Save your empathy for the girls."

They were in this situation because of Willy. Now she despised him. No longer felt the least bit of sympathy. Pushing him out of the plane would've been the least he deserved.

Kaley had to fight back a gasp. Jamie wasn't with the girls.

"There are only twelve," Kaley said. "I was told there were thirteen."

"No. We only have twelve. One of our men is missing. Have you heard that? He went to get one of the girls but hasn't returned."

Kaley nodded.

"Yes. I did hear. I don't know where he is."

A more important question.

Where is Jamie?

29

Kremlin Moscow

President Popov called a meeting of his military advisers.

Not that they did much in the way of advising. What the President said was the final word in anything. Few were willing to cross him for fear of banishment to Siberia. Or worse.

Only one ever expressed an opinion that might remotely be considered contrarian. Alexi Sergov was a moderate. He'd been in his position as Minister of Private Forces for so long most people didn't even know when he rose to power. The private military was more powerful than the official government forces and were involved in conflict zones throughout the world. He was arguably the second most powerful man in Russia.

"Do we really want to awaken a sleeping dog?" Sergov said with authority. "Why rattle the cage of a cur who could kill us with one bite?"

"President Kemp is more bark than bite," Popov argued. "He will give in when backed into a corner."

Sergov shook his head.

"I might've said that about his predecessor. He was weak. He kept drawing lines in the sand. We'd cross them and he'd move the line. In essence, he was afraid to act. We don't know enough about this President to say that."

"The American people don't have the stomach for a protracted war," Popov argued.

"That's what I'm afraid of," Sergov said, basically interrupting President Popov.

A couple of the men in the room audibly gasped.

"What are you afraid of, dear friend?" Popov said. "We are Russia. I intend to restore us to our previous glory."

"I'm afraid that the Americans don't want a long war. Like Afghanistan or our war in Crimea. President Kemp will want to end any conflict quickly. I'm afraid that is not to our favor. We can't start a war we can't win."

Popov took a big swig of his vodka, then refilled his glass along with Sergov's. The conversation was mostly between them. No one else was likely to interject anything.

"What would you have me do?" Popov asked. "The sanctions are untenable. We can't back down or we will be the ones who appear weak."

"Shoot off a missile, but aim it into the ocean. Don't give President Kemp a reason to fire at one of our cities. If you hit an American city, he will retaliate."

"We can withstand an attack. Better than President Kemp. But I will take your advice. Because I appreciate it."

He turned to his military advisor who was in charge of the government forces. The one who had moved the mobile missiles to Eastern Russia.

"Fire two rockets. One that lands in the ocean. The second one at San Francisco. That will send a message. The President will think that the second one will be like the first and not take any action until it's too late. Then they'll know that we are serious."

Even Sergov knew the conversation was over evidenced by his silence. The President had spoken and more rebuttal was futile.

"Let us drink to a great victory," Popov said, raising his glass.

The men in the room raised their glasses in unison.

"To Russia."

* * *

At the Russian Prison

I called Brad immediately upon arriving.

"The girls aren't here," I said to him. Exasperated. I'd traveled to the prison where the girls were being held. The entire facility had been abandoned. Even the lights along the runway were off.

"I don't know what to tell you," Brad said. "We had good intelligence that the girls were there. Satellite photos as of yesterday showed soldiers still guarding the compound."

"The girls were here. I found evidence. They were moved in a hurry."

"That happens."

"It may be my fault."

"How so?"

Brad still sounded weird. Something related to Alex, but I couldn't put my finger on it. Curly said not to speculate about things you didn't know. It's a waste of mental energy. Especially on a mission. If your mind was somewhere else, your body soon would be as well. In other words, distractions get you killed.

Especially when it came to the suits. Talking to men like Brad. He's a good guy but don't read between the lines. He might be constipated.

Thinking about Curly brought a smile to my face, regardless of the dilemma I was now facing. Curly was right. Worrying about Alex was a distraction. If Brad knew something he'd tell me at the right time. I couldn't worry about it now. I had a bigger worry. Where were the girls? More importantly, how could I find them?

I couldn't. That's why I was as frustrated as a farmer with a broken tractor.

"The phone I'm calling you on belonged to one of the men in the sex trafficking organization," I explained.

"I assumed as much."

"When he didn't show up at the prison to turn me over to them, I suspect they got spooked. They tried to call his phone several times, but I didn't answer it. So they assumed the worst and moved the girls. Like I said, my fault."

A despondent sigh was added to the words for effect. I was no longer in the compound in case someone came. I was in my car, hidden in the shadows on the runway. Ready to make a quick getaway if someone did come.

"Things happen," Brad said.

"I could've come right away, but I felt like the missiles were a priority."

"You did the right thing. What did you find?"

"Probably nothing you don't already know."

"We know a lot."

Brad's responses had always been terse. The last two conversations, he'd been downright rude. Almost dismissive, if I didn't know him better.

Something was clearly wrong. Not related to his bowels.

"Ten mobile missile launchers," I said, starting a rundown of what little I knew. "Still on the trucks that move them. In pairs. About two miles apart. They are pointed in our direction. Minimal guards. Only two armed men with each. I noticed a lot of activity around two missiles. I think they are preparing to fire them."

"That makes sense. The Russians aren't worried about us attacking the missiles by land which is why they are lightly guarded. The Bering Sea, on the other hand, is where they focused their protection. Two battleships and several squadrons of Migs. You'd think they believe war is inevitable."

"We encountered some of those Migs flying over. Which reminds me. There are two men in Alaska who are the ones kidnapping the girls. They run the *Two Brothers Adventure Guide Services*. About forty minutes from the Denali Visitor Center. It shouldn't be hard to find. It's a front for drug running along with the sex trafficking."

"Any reason why I shouldn't send the FBI in?"

"None at all. We're good. I didn't do anything other than let them kidnap me. My backpack is there, but nothing that ties me to you know what."

We weren't being as careful in our conversation, but I still wasn't going to use names or mention the CIA. Too much trouble, considering I'd be out of Russia soon.

That thought caused my heart to sink a couple of notches. I had no choice. The girls could be anywhere. It didn't seem prudent to run off looking for them. I wouldn't even know where to begin. All I could do was go back to the States and wait for more intelligence to surface.

The missiles also complicated things. I wanted to be out of Dodge when they started flying.

Brad was thinking the same thing. "That's good. I'll make a call and have them picked up and questioned. You need to come home. Home home. Let me know if you need help. Don't go back to Alaska to deal with the men. I'll take care of them."

I wanted to take care of them myself, but it wasn't a smart move. Even though I wasn't technically in the CIA, and could operate inside the United States, it didn't make sense to do so. Law enforcement would have to deal with them. That meant building a case against them. Obtaining search warrants. Taking evidence to a grand jury.

It probably meant the men would make bail. Hire lawyers. They might get off. In the meantime, at least the sex trafficking operations were shut down. They wouldn't be kidnapping any more girls any time soon. Hopefully, the cabin and the planes contained DNA evidence that would nail the two men.

I didn't have any evidence to assist in the investigation. Other than the fact that they kidnapped me. I would never be involved. For obvious reasons. My kidnapping was one that would never be charged.

The reason I didn't want to operate within the United States.

The wheels of justice moved too slowly. I didn't disagree with it. Those safeguards were there to protect the innocent. While I knew beyond a shadow of a doubt that the men were guilty, they had the protection of the Constitution.

Which I had taken a vow to protect.

If the two men were in Russia right now, those protections didn't apply and I'd kill them in a second. If they somehow got off on a technicality in the U.S. court system, I might try to figure out how to take them out myself if they resumed operating again.

"Willy and Benji Cantrell," Brad said. "That's their name."

He must've looked it up on the internet. They might even have an FBI file.

"That's them. I heard them mention Willy's name, anyway."

"I'm on it. I've already notified the FBI."

I could hear keys typing in the background. Brad did almost everything with a sense of urgency, which I appreciated.

"They are armed," I added. "Not too dangerous."

Brad laughed. The first sign of warmth.

"You're one of the few people I know who thinks that an armed man isn't dangerous."

"Me and Alex."

Brad didn't take the bait. If he was going to tell me something about Alex, he would've done so with that prompting.

For now, I had to drop it. Whatever was going on with Alex, would have to wait. I needed to figure out how to get out of Russia.

30

Brad had not been off the phone with Jamie for ten minutes when his phone rang. A different line. It could be any number of his operatives. The one line was for Alex and Jamie to use. His main line was for everyone else.

Kaley.

He answered it. He was in his office and would be late into the night. Regretting the conversation with Jamie. He should've told her about her husband.

There had been a development. The search in the Indian Ocean had been called off. No sign of Alex's plane. It would probably never be recovered. He'd have to tell Jamie soon or face her wrath.

It was beyond time. He would tell her. Once she was out of harm's way.

"Brad. It's me," the young sounding voice on the other end of the line said. Her high pitched not fully developed voice certainly didn't match her toughness.

"I've been expecting your call," Brad said. "Where are you?"

He'd been racking his brain trying to figure out why she hadn't called. He couldn't think of a good reason.

"I just left Russia," she said excitedly.

The last thing he expected her to say. He heard airplane engines in the background.

"I have the girls," she added. "You know the ones from the prison."

Brad almost fell out of his chair. A lot of things had surprised him over the years. None more than this news.

"Explain, please."

Kaley began talking a mile a minute. Brad had a hard time keeping up.

"I was the one supposed to be kidnapped. But they took Jamie. I tracked her phone. *Two Brothers Adventure Guide Services*. They're behind the kidnappings."

Kaley took her first breath. Brad had a thousand questions, but refrained from asking them. At this rate, Kaley would get through all of them in no time.

"I tracked Jamie's phone. They took her to Russia. By plane. I stole one of their planes and went to the prison. To rescue Jamie and the girls."

Alarm bells started ringing inside of Brad's head. Kaley stole the plane from a U.S. company. And flew it to a foreign country.

What did you do, Kaley?

"Jamie wasn't there. I don't know where she is. We've got to find her. She's in danger. I left Russia without her. I had to. You know. I had the twelve girls to consider. You know. Jamie said to do what's best for the victims first. I hope I did the right thing. I didn't know where Jamie was anyway."

Kaley's voice was cracking. Like she was tearing up. It almost felt like a confessional. She needed reassurance from him that she had done the right thing.

"Jamie is fine. I just got off the phone with her."

"Whew. That's a relief."

"Where is she?"

"She's at the prison."

"I just left there an hour or so ago. She wasn't there."

"She wasn't there an hour ago. But she's there now."

"Do you want me to go back and get her? How would I do that? I pretended that I was having a mechanical problem. That's how I was able to land at the prison. I told the air traffic controller that I fixed it, but I needed to return to the United States to get it repaired properly. I don't think I could turn around and fly right back without them being suspicious."

"Kaley, take a deep breath," Brad said. "Don't go back to Russia. Jamie can get out on her own."

"I'm just glad she's okay. Why wasn't she at the prison?"

"She's running a side mission."

"What is it?"

"Need to know basis."

"Does it have to do with the Russian military maneuvers? You should know there's a lot of activity in the area. Something's up."

Kaley was a lot like Jamie already. Inquisitive. Kept pushing the envelope. Brad liked the passion he was seeing in her. He was also impressed by the initiative. She found where the men took Jamie. Took it upon herself to fly to Russia and free the girls. Thinking she was going after Jamie as well.

It explained why Jamie didn't find the girls. He should feel relieved but didn't.

Brad had two burning questions in his mind. How did Kaley rescue the girls without firing a shot? Jamie didn't mention any dead Russian soldiers. An even more pressing question. How did she steal the plane? What happened to the two brothers?

Brad was almost afraid to ask. A case of déjà vu struck him. This conversation seemed all too familiar. He'd had it a dozen times over the years with Jamie. Not sure how in the world she pulled off some of her stunts. Almost always leaving him with some kind of mess to clean up.

Kaley was still prattling on. Talking so fast, Brad's head was spinning. Jamie had learned to temper her enthusiasm with him over the years. Be more precise in explaining things to him. Hopefully, Kaley would learn the same sooner rather than later.

"Slow down for a second," Brad said. "I have some questions. Just answer with yes or no. Can you do that?"

"Yes."

"Do you have all twelve girls?"

"Yes."

"Are they okay?"

"As good as could be expected. Oops. Sorry. That wasn't a yes or no answer. Yes. They are okay. I think."

"Where are you right now?"

"That's not a yes or no question."

A smile formed on Brad's face. Like Jamie. Sassy. He still needed to be firm with her or this conversation would take an hour.

"Kaley! Answer the question."

"Sorry. I'm over international waters. Headed for Alaska."

"In Willy and Benji's plane?"

"How do you know their names?"

"It's my job to know these things."

"Yes. They have two planes. A seaplane and a ten-seater. I couldn't take the seaplane. The girls wouldn't fit. So I took the ten-seater. Actually, two of the girls have to sit in the stewardess chairs. I mean flight attendants. But we're making do."

Brad was going to have to get used to this if he continued to work with Kaley. He reminded himself of the big picture. This girl was incredibly resourceful. She rescued the twelve girls. He would put up with a lot for those kind of results.

"What happened to Willy and Benji?" Brad asked.

He was dreading the answer.

"Benji is dead."

Brad's heart skipped a beat.

"Please tell me his body is not at the guide service location."

Brad wondered if it was too late to call off the FBI. Probably. They were likely already on their way to the premises. They'd enter as soon as they secured a search warrant. If they found a dead body, it'd be a disaster. Maybe a bigger mess than he could actually clean up.

"It's not."

"Where is it? Actually, don't answer that question."

"It will never be found."

"Okay. That's good."

"His blood is all over the place, though."

"Dang it!"

"So are my fingerprints and DNA."

"Your fingerprints and DNA are not in any databases anywhere. Nothing can be traced back to you."

"It was self-defense, if that makes you feel any better."

Brad ignored the comment. It didn't matter to him. He couldn't care less that the bad guy was dead. He was only concerned about the fallout to the CIA. And to Kaley. And to him. Since she worked for him. For all practical purposes.

"You said Benji was dead. What about his brother?"

She started rambling again.

"I took him with me to Russia. He helped me get the flight plan. I left him there. I told the Russian soldiers he had betrayed our organization. I don't know what they did with him after that."

Brad was starting to get a good picture of what happened in Russia. It sounded like something Jamie would do. Waltz into the place like she owned it. Fool the Russians into thinking she was there to pick up the girls. Remarkable that Kaley used one of the brothers as a ruse to get into Russia and into the prison.

Knowing the Russians, Willy was on his way to Moscow. To be questioned by the KGB. Questioned was the wrong characterization. Tortured would be a better description. Willy would give them some convoluted story that he was not a traitor, but they wouldn't believe it. They believed what they wanted to believe.

Eventually, Willy would confess and tell them whatever they wanted to hear, thinking the torture would stop. It would momentarily. Then he'd be hanged or taken to a prison where he'd spend the rest of his life in harsh conditions.

Brad felt better. The two men were out of the picture. The FBI wouldn't know what happened to the two men. The plane was the only thing he was concerned about at the moment.

He had to figure out where to have Kaley land the plane. Alex could change the transponder number and then she could land anywhere. Except Alex couldn't. A fiery dart shot through his heart.

Then a thought through his head with the same intensity.

Could Alex have changed the transponder number on his plane? Made it look like it crashed in the ocean.

No.

Not possible.

The plane was tracked on radar. No way to make that happen. As much as he wished Alex was alive, it just was wishful thinking.

"Here's what I want you to do," Brad said. "Land the plane at *Clear Air Force Station Base* in Alaska."

"I can do that."

"I'll have someone there to meet the plane and fly the girls to a hospital in Anchorage."

"That sounds good."

He wasn't sure what he would do with the plane. His first thought was to give it to AJAX. Would there even be an AJAX now that Alex was gone?

Brad rubbed his eyes roughly. He'd think about that later.

"After I drop off the girls, I'm going back to Russia to get Jamie," Kaley blurted out.

That sounded like something Jamie would say.

This girl was just like her.

31

Russian prison

It took some effort, but Kaley finally convinced Brad to let her go back to Russia to pick up Jamie. Mostly because of the missile threat. Jamie could find any number of ways to get out of Russia and back to the States including a commercial flight out of Moscow. However, with the rising tension between the two countries, air travel could shut down at a moment's notice and she'd be stranded.

It seemed like the most practical way to get her out safely.

Kaley was fully briefed on the missile threat. Apparently, flying into harm's way put her in the need-to-know-basis category. It felt good. Made her feel more a part of the team.

She was able to file a flight plan easily enough back into Russia including a stop at the prison. Under the guise that they had left some things there when they had to make an emergency landing the day before.

Kaley took the northerly route again and arrived at the prison without incident and taxied to a stop in broad daylight. Jamie emerged from where she'd been hiding to meet the plane. Before Kaley could leave the cockpit to open the cabin door, Jamie motioned for her to exit.

That wasn't the plan. Brad had given Kaley the cell phone number Jamie took off the Russian and they had gone over the logistics on the phone. Kaley was to taxi to a stop, open the cabin door, and Jamie would board right away so they could get out of there as quickly as possible.

Instead, Jamie made a slashing motion across her neck which could only be interpreted as kill the engines. Kaley did and scurried to the back where she lowered the cabin door. Jamie was at the bottom of the stairs and motioned for Kaley to come down to meet her.

Kaley exited the plane as Jamie waited at the bottom nervously. She kept looking around for any threats. Jamie was well armed. Kaley wasn't sure if she needed to take a weapon but did anyway. Not willing to risk Jamie yelling at her for not doing so.

She also gathered up some supplies. Food and water. Jamie mentioned on the phone that she was looking forward to the plane ride. That she was starving. The food and water left in the prison was nasty.

Kaley brought extra in case they weren't coming back to the plane anytime soon. She had no idea what they were doing. When she got to the bottom of the stairs, Kaley noticed an immediate change in Jamie's demeanor. Her mentor was warm and friendly. Even gave her a slight hug.

"What are we doing?" Kaley asked, half expecting a dismissive "none of your business" kind of response. Instead, Jamie answered right away.

"Change in plans. We have a new mission. I'll explain on the way."

"What about the plane?"

"Leave it like it is. In case we need to make a quick getaway."

Kaley looked around the prison yard as well and didn't see anyone. It seemed strange to leave the plane on the runway with the cabin door open, but she wasn't about to argue with Jamie who had already started walking briskly away from the plane toward a vehicle sitting at the end of the runway. It looked to be a military rig. Similar to an American Jeep only an Army green color.

"Get in," Jamie said. Not dismissively or brusquely like what Kaley was used to in the training. Jamie was clearly still the boss and making that clear. Her words had authority behind them, but she was treating Kaley like her equal.

It felt strange.

It continued after they were in the car. Before anything was said, Jamie attacked the food and water like a ravenous lion. She seemed genuinely appreciative and thanked Kaley for the thoughtfulness.

"You're welcome."

She'd never seen this kind of warmth from her mentor. Maybe Jamie felt like she needed to play the part of bad cop during training and had switched to good cop. Kaley liked it and wasn't complaining.

Several times during training, she had hated Jamie. Couldn't imagine anyone being so harsh and cruel. It must've all been an act, because the person in front of her now was as pleasant and nice as could be. She'd been more cordial in Alaska, but not like this.

Kaley still felt the eggshells under her feet and chose her words and questions carefully so as not to ruin things. For the most part, she kept quiet and took her cues from Jamie.

Even though she was as curious as a dozen cats, she resisted asking any questions. She didn't have to ask where they were going. When Jamie finished scarfing down the food, she volunteered it.

"As you know, Russia has positioned mobile missile launchers on the eastern shore of Russia, presumably pointed at the western cities of the United States."

Kaley nodded.

Even though Jamie had a different tone to her words, Kaley still knew better than to interrupt her. The vehicle was started, but Jamie hadn't put it in motion yet. Another thing that seemed strange.

"President Kemp received a call from Russian President Popov earlier this morning. On the red-hot line. Normally reserved for nuclear warnings. Apparently, that conversation did not go well. Popov demanded the U.S. end the financial sanctions and the President refused. Popov responded by saying he was ordering two missiles launched at the United States."

Kaley let out a gasp.

"I know. The President has eight hours to comply, or fire will rain down on our cities. Those were Popov's words."

"Why would Popov signal what he's going to do? It takes the element of surprise out of it and gives us time to prepare a response."

"The President asked the same question. Popov said it was a courtesy. From one world leader to another. That he wanted to give Kemp a chance to evacuate San Francisco. Apparently, that's where the missiles are headed. If Popov is to be believed."

"Thank you very much for the courtesy," Kaley said sarcastically.

"Exactly."

"What does that have to do with us? Sounds like we need to get on the plane and get out of here as soon as possible. I can't imagine President Kemp won't retaliate. I suppose he could aim the missiles away from us. Russia is a big land mass. Still, it seems dangerous to be in the country right now."

"And you're free to leave if you want. I'm staying. I'm going to go and take out those missiles."

"Does Brad know?"

"No."

"He didn't tell you to do it?"

"No."

Jamie stared deep into Kaley's eyes. She felt like her soul had been violated. Jamie's tone was terse. Almost condescending. Perhaps with a hint of disappointment behind them. Kaley wasn't sure how to read Jamie's demeanor.

So she backtracked. "Of course, I'm staying, if you are. I'm only asking."

"All I'm saying is that you don't have to stay. We're on our own here. You can get back on that plane and get out of Russia. In fact, you probably should. It could get extremely dangerous where I'm going."

"That's what we do. I'm not afraid."

Jamie's serious facial expression lightened. As did her tone. "I know you're not. Good job by the way. Rescuing the girls. That showed ingenuity and nerves. I can't wait to hear how it all went down."

Kaley started to say something.

Jamie put her hand up to stop her. "Not right now. We need to focus on this mission. I'll fill you in on the way."

She put the vehicle in drive and sped off. Heading east. It seemed like she knew where she was going and talked as she drove.

"I've seen the missiles," Jamie said. "That's why I didn't come to the prison to save the girls. Couldn't be helped. Keep that in mind in the future. It's called mission priorities. Sometimes things come up that are more important than the original mission."

"How is that determined?"

Kaley was feeling a little more comfortable interjecting questions. Jamie didn't seem bothered by this one.

"Usually by how many people are affected. In this case, the missiles potentially could affect millions of people. With all due respect to the twelve girls in prison, who my heart breaks for by the way, I still had to focus on what might save the most lives."

"That makes sense."

"I appreciate you stepping up and rescuing them. That was a brave thing to do. Very resourceful stealing the brother's plane."

"You're welcome. I thought I was rescuing you as well. I was shocked when you weren't there."

"Like I said, couldn't be helped. Thanks though. I wasn't sure how I was going to get the girls out of Russia. Using the brother's plane was a stroke of genius."

Kaley's heart felt suddenly warm from the compliment. She'd never seen this side of Jamie. The bigger than life CIA hero was almost human.

"Anyway... there are ten missiles," Jamie said. "In groups of two. Two miles apart or so. Each set of missiles is guarded by two guards."

"That's a lot of twos."

Jamie frowned. She clearly didn't like the frivolous interruption.

Shut up Kaley.

"I think I know which two missiles will be the first ones launched. We're going to take out the two guards. Hopefully, we'll get there in time."

"How are we going to sabotage two huge missiles? I wouldn't even know where to begin."

A sly smile formed on Jamie's face.

"These are mobile missile launchers. In other words, they're on trucks. We're going to turn them around, so they are facing toward Russia."

Kaley's mouth gaped open.

Jamie let out a full-throated laugh. Which seemed strange considering the seriousness of the moment.

"When they launch, those missiles are going to land somewhere in Russia," Jamie said.

She had a huge grin on her face when she said it.

"That's brilliant."

Jamie pounded her hand on the steering wheel and rocked back and forth. Clearly pleased with her plan.

"Let's go have some fun," she said.

"I'm ready."

Jamie stepped on the gas and was flying down the road. As fast as the old crate would take them.

It did sound like a great plan in the confines of the car.

As soon as Kaley saw the two massive tube like missiles sitting on the trucks, she began to have her doubts.

32

Later that night

A cold rain and fog had moved into eastern Russia. The low cloud ceiling was particularly helpful when we arrived at the missile launch sites. Fortunately, I was able to make my way through the thick soup and find the missiles I suspected were the two that were to be launched first. Without being spotted by any Russian troops. A gunfight would spoil my plan.

The fog allowed us to get within a stone's throw of the two guards who were busy at work presumably preparing the missiles for launch. They were clearly acting with a greater sense of urgency than when I'd seen them before.

We couldn't do anything until they were finished. If we took them out too soon, the missiles might not be ready to launch, and I didn't know what needed to be done to fire them. All I could do was guess when they were finished based on their demeanors. I suspected that when the countdown started, the men would obviously take cover and it'd be obvious they were about to launch the missiles.

Timing was critical. Too late would be as bad as too early.

The missiles were massive. Right now, they lay passively on the truck beds. Perfectly flat tubes. I guessed they'd take up a third of a football field.

The trucks that hauled them were humongous as well. Especially the oversized tires. I'd never seen anything quite like them. If I remembered right, they used pneumatic air-filled tires. Special tires that could carry that much weight off-road.

I did know a little bit about how the trucks operated. They obviously couldn't fire the missiles in their current position. When ready for launch, the missiles would begin to rise in the air. The bottom structure attached to the missiles would go all the way to the ground behind the truck and become a base of support.

That'd be our cue to move.

Kaley was directly to my left. The two trucks sat next to each other. One guard working on each. The cabs were facing toward the east.

Kaley would be responsible for taking out the truck furthest away from me. She was actually closer to her target. Within ten feet of the soldier. So close she could probably hear him breathe. The closer the better. We needed to take them out without firing a shot. Even though the other soldiers were a couple of miles away, they'd still be able to hear the sound of gunfire and would come running.

The last thing we needed was to alert them of a threat. Have them prevent us from sabotaging the missiles. Or block the roads and make us fight our way back to the prison.

The rain was coming down harder now. Chilling me to the bone. I should've had Kaley bring me some clothes but didn't think of it. I was dressed for a hike in Alaska. Not for hiding in the bushes in the boonies of Russia.

I had expected to be in the comfort of the private jet. Not standing in the icy rain. Waiting for hours at the prison had given me a long time to think about the missiles. That's when the plan came to me. By the time the plan had formulated in my mind, it was too late to tell Kaley to go back to Alaska.

It actually worked out better. Two was better than one. Hopefully. As long as she did her part.

I shivered from the cold. Careful not to make a noise and alert the soldier to my presence. Curly taught me to block it out and I needed to do that now. I wondered if Kaley could as well. I had experience in difficult situations like this. I'd been in much worse environments. I put her through some tough situations in training but simulating these conditions with all the tension associated with it was impossible in a controlled setting.

I had to hope and pray she was up to the task. If not, I was prepared to take out both guards myself. No way these missiles were getting off these launch pads heading towards the United States.

Not on my watch.

My hair was soaked. My shirt was drenched. The only reason I let myself think about it was because it might affect my actions. The ground was starting to soften. The plan was to move the huge trucks, so that the missiles faced the opposite directions. Towards Russia.

They had to weigh several tons. Would the trucks bog down in the mud? We wouldn't know until we tried to move them. Thankfully, the vehicles were running. Another thing I didn't have to worry about. I could see the whole mission falling apart because we didn't have the keys or didn't know how to start them or get them in drive.

I'd never been in the cab of a missile launcher, so I had no idea how to drive it.

First things first. The bigger worry right now was my footing. I envisioned in my mind how I was going to take out the guard without firing a shot. I had a knife on my belt, but that wasn't the best tactic. Knives caused blood. I'd just as soon not have blood on my hands or clothes. Curly taught me any number of ways to kill a man with my hands. Always preferable to knives if a gun couldn't be used.

Kaley knew those techniques as well. I wasn't worried about her ability to carry out the moves. I only worried about how well she would do under pressure.

I warned her about making sure she had good footing when she launched her attack.

We had the element of surprise on our side. The men had handguns on their hips. But their rifles were out of the rain and in their vehicles. Their hands needed to be free to work on the launchers. The last thing they would be expecting was for two girls to spring out of the fog and put them to sleep.

If done properly, they might not even see the blows coming.

The men suddenly stopped what they were doing.

I caught myself holding my breath and reminded myself to let it out and breathe normally.

The men were through with their preparations. They were no longer working with the launchers. Both soldiers were on their phones now. I could hear them confirming what I already suspected.

"The missiles are in position," they both said almost in unison.

"Stay cool, Kaley," I muttered under my breath.

A loud bang pierced the fog.

Then a screeching sound.

So loud it hurt my ears. The massive missiles began to move upward. Groaned in unison as they defied gravity and began lifting toward the sky.

Without hesitation, I sprung into action.

Now. Kaley.

I couldn't see her and had no way of knowing if she was on the move as well.

My soldier was at the back of the launcher facing away from me. My footing held and I was on him in a flash. He either heard me coming or saw me out of the corner of his eye because he turned toward me. I brought the palm of my right hand directly under his chin. With such force that it jerked his head backwards. Violently. Severing his spinal cord. He collapsed in a heap.

I heard another thud. An exhale of air. Then something hit the ground.

It had to be Kaley taking out the other guard. She was impressing me more and more by the minute.

Especially when I saw that she was in the cab of the other mobile truck before me. Whoever was first wasn't to wait on the other. The missiles were still rising in the air. Moving the trucks wouldn't stop that process. But we had to get the trucks moved before the base of the launchers touched the ground. Otherwise, they'd be impossible to move. Or they might cause the missiles to malfunction. Not the worst outcome in the world, but I had my heart set on launching the missiles toward Russia.

I thought it'd be funny.

I somehow managed to get my truck into gear. I had to wait on Kaley. She backed her rig out and drove past me then backed it in next to me so the cab was facing west.

Between the sound of the missile pivot mechanism and the diesel engine on my truck, my ears were ringing from the deafening roar.

Once Kaley cleared my truck I pulled out. Almost stalling it, but somehow managing to keep it moving. I drove the truck into the spot Kaley had vacated only with the cab facing the opposite direction.

We both bounded out of the cabs at the same time. The missiles continued to rise until the bases were on the ground. It seemed like everything was in order.

"Let's get out of here," I said.

Kaley and I took off running.

I heard the missiles igniting.

Then an exploding sound.

A burst of light.

Then a swoosh.

I had to turn and look. In time to see the first missile leave its base and go off into the horizon, disappearing in the fog.

I high fived Kaley.

We did a little dance in a circle.

We had pulled it off.

Ten minutes later, the second missile launched.

I felt an exuberance come over me.

We laughed all the way back to the prison.

33

Kremlin

Minister of Private Forces, Alexi Sergov, did not expect the day to end well. The team of military advisors had been brought to the Kremlin war room to watch the launch of the two missiles and to advise President Popov on how to respond to the certain retaliation from the United States.

The plan was ill conceived. A knee jerk reaction to the financial sanctions. What Russia needed was a long-term strategy. President Popov was foolish to believe he could restore Russia to its former glory by the use of military might. The country simply could not compete with the United States and NATO and was irresponsible to try.

America was superior in every way. It had more nuclear weapons. Conventional forces outnumbered Russian forces two to one. America had more battleships and airplanes. Better technology. Money to build and replenish.

It was also basically untouchable. Protected on both sides by large oceans. A missile could cause damage, but in a limited space. Russia had nothing in its arsenal other than nuclear weapons that could cause significant damage. Nothing more than a mosquito biting an elephant.

America's economy dwarfed Russia's. Russia's GDP was 1.3 trillion dollars. America's was more than twenty trillion. It had vast natural resources and a well-developed infrastructure. Up until a few decades before, it had a strong manufacturing base and could produce vast amounts of steel, iron, and bronze.

A war might resurrect those industries which would be detrimental to Russia's interests. Much better to have those things outsourced so that other countries could build up their strength.

As a student of military history, General Sergov knew never to start a war you couldn't win. By every matrix, Russia would be considered the underdog. The only thing Russia wasn't lacking was nationalistic pride. Its people had endured years of suffering and never quit. They'd fight to the end. From that standpoint, they might be able to outlast the Americans in terms of resolve.

But that wasn't the most prudent strategy. The leaders of the past had been smarter. Knowing they couldn't compete with the Americans in most areas, they matched them step for step in one area. Nuclear weapons. Russia could build as many as they needed and did so. As long as they had enough nuclear weapons, the Americans would never enter into a war with Russia.

A mutual deterrent.

A last resort.

Neither side could ever consider using those nukes. The purpose was simply to neutralize the American advantage. Nothing more than that.

The Bay of Pigs fiasco aside, Russian military experts knew that's all they needed to maintain the status quo. Spout off as much as they wanted about Russian superiority, but when push came to shove, Russia needed to avoid a confrontation with the United States at all cost.

Unfortunately, current President Popov was an idealist. Blinded by his love for the Motherland and his belief in Russia's ability to overcome the odds and defeat the weak Americans. Somewhat like the religious fanatics in the middle east who somehow believed their god would help them win a war, even if winning by conventional means was impossible.

Too many civilizations were crushed into oblivion by such misguided ideology. The battlefields of the past were littered with armies annihilated because their military leaders refused to accept reality and cut their losses when they had the chance. Or act rationally before the losses began to mount.

The better strategy was to wait for America to implode from the inside. Something they were almost certain to do. Every empire eventually crumbled. The forces within America were leading the country down a road of destruction.

Out of control spending and high taxes would eventually cripple the U.S. economy even more than the financial sanctions imposed on the Russians. The Russian people were used to hardship. They could endure it longer than the fat and lazy Americans who weren't used to bread lines or going months in the wintertime without electricity or heat.

America was on a course that wasn't sustainable. Declining moral values and the breakdown of the nuclear family were eroding the foundation that had made America great over the years. All Russia needed to do was get out of the way and let it happen. It would've happened sooner if not for men who foolishly challenged America militarily.

The Great Depression and stock market crash of the 1920's crippled the United States economy. The only thing that saved it, in Sergov's mind, was the rise of a madman. Hitler. Who thought he could take over the world. Had he used restraint, his regime might still be the major power of Europe.

But he overplayed his hand. His greed and avarice led him to cross a line. America wasn't going to stop him. Not until he became too powerful. They remained on the sidelines until they could no longer sit back and let him take more territory.

When they did act, Hitler was no match for the resourcefulness of the American machine. The best thing for a capitalistic society was a war. It created jobs. Put people to work. Restored nationalistic pride. Gave the people a common cause to rally around. Which was why United States Presidents kept getting the country into foolish wars through the years.

Popov was in danger of making the same mistake. Awakening a sleeping dog. Better to let the sleeping dog lie.

Eventually, America would destroy itself and Russia would be left standing. Stronger for showing restraint. America was a shell of its former self. The independent free spirit that formed the country had given way to a bloated government that was now powerful enough to impose its will over the wishes of the people.

Capitalism would never work in the long-term. Sergov was convinced of it. All democracies eventually reverted back to a central government. It was in the nature of man to want a king. A dictator. To be told what to do. America was becoming socialist. The government was grabbing more and more power. Taking away the people's individual rights.

Ironically enough, America was becoming more like Russia and Russia was becoming more like America.

Sergov was afraid a war with the United States would shift the tide. Slow the decline. Help America make a comeback.

Not that Russia was in a good condition. Communism didn't work any better than capitalism. History books were filled with accounts of failed despots who were once the most powerful men in the world.

So what should Russia do? Pull back. Stop the aggression in the region. The imperialists would end the financial sanctions and Russia could adopt a new strategy. An economic rather than military expansion.

Expand drilling for oil and natural gas. Russia had plenty of untapped resources. If Sergov was suddenly made ruler of the world, he'd fill the Russian coffers with money. Cause the other countries to become energy dependent on them. Then share the wealth with the Russian people.

Something that would never happen.

The reason why communism and socialism would never work was the same problem America would eventually succumb to. Men in power shared a common trait. They lusted for more power. It didn't really matter how much money and power they had, they wanted more. It's never enough.

When money begins pouring into the public coffers, the leaders can't help themselves. They become richer and richer. Spend lavishly. Build monuments and castles for themselves.

While the people starve.

Neither system of government would work in the long run. The oppressed would eventually become more powerful than the oppressors and the governments would inevitably collapse.

Sergov was a student of government history as well. He'd seen the same scenario play out hundreds of times. No one kept their power forever. Because fools ran countries. If men weren't fools when they took power, they eventually became ones. Drunk with power.

Sergov looked around the room. He loved the men there. He'd known them all of his life. Even President Popov. Sergov grew up with him. They were boys of privilege. Scaling the mountain of political power together.

At some point, their synergies changed. Sergov grew more pragmatic. More sober. The richer Popov became the crazier his thinking.

The financial sanctions had destroyed the Russian economy. No doubt about it. But Sergov had more riches now than he had before the financial sanctions were put in place. The sanctions didn't affect him. The burden was carried by the Russian people. They were the ones who suffered.

The men in the room didn't know hardship. Evidenced by the huge bellies around the table and the daily drunkenness.

Fools.

Foolish leadership had never been more on display than right now. The men in the room were taking their cues from President Popov who was practically giddy. All thinking firing those missiles was a good idea.

The room was abuzz with excitement. President Popov was almost coming out of his pants with so much anticipation.

It'd be short-lived.

Firing missiles at the United States may be the dumbest thing any Russian leader had ever done. America would retaliate. Russia would fire the other eight missiles. Or America would take them out.

Russia would launch more. We could launch hundreds. America would launch ten for every one of Russia's.

Popov wouldn't care how many Russian people died. He'd be safe. The men in the room would be holed up in a bunker somewhere.

Fortunately, Sergov's private forces weren't involved in this fiasco. They'd be kept out of harm's way. At least initially.

If this war escalated, no one would be able to escape the horror.

The only thing that brought Sergov from total despair was knowing that Popov would eventually give in. He'd have no choice. The Russian people would protest over the unnecessary war.

Popov would play all of his cards until he had only one left in the deck. Nuclear weapons. Even Popov wasn't stupid enough to consider using them. Everyone would be destroyed in that case.

Sergov didn't want power, but this might be his opportunity. Which was why he hadn't protested more than he had. When the dust settled, literally, he might be able to seize the Presidency. He didn't want it. He was perfectly content. Popov might force his hand.

Starting in ten minutes.

A countdown clock was on the wall.

That's when the missiles would launch.

34

The Kremlin war room had state-of-the art capabilities. A large screen took up an entire wall. Superimposed in the background was a map of Eastern Russia, the Pacific Ocean, Alaska, and the western coastline of the United States.

When the missiles launched, radar would pick them up, and track them all the way to their destinations. They'd be able to watch them in real time.

Sergov wished they controlled the missiles from that room. They didn't. Mobile missile launchers had to be programmed on site. These weren't the most sophisticated missiles in their arsenal. Rather than entering coordinates, they had to enter speed and trajectory. Once fired, the destination couldn't be altered.

The more sophisticated missiles were controlled by computers. They could be changed in mid flight, disarmed, or turned in a different direction. Destroyed even. Which meant they could stop them in midair. Something Popov was unlikely to do, but it'd be prudent to at least have the capability to do so.

Once these were fired, there was no turning back.

The thought sent a shiver down Sergov's spine.

He was trying to be optimistic but was having a hard time doing so. The only good thing that might come out of this would be to gauge the capabilities of the U.S. missile defense system. Sergov's hope was that the Americans were successful in blowing the missile's out of the sky and that they never landed on U.S. soil.

TERRY TOLER

As a military man, it seemed strange rooting against his own military. He couldn't help it. He didn't want a missile to hit an American city. No one knew what would happen at that point. It was an act of war. America would declare war against Russia.

Kind of like the Japanese bombing Pearl Harbor. America was hesitant to enter the war. Once they were bombed, they were fully involved. They dropped nuclear bombs on Japan and the rest was history.

An epic strategic military blunder by the Japanese leader. The beginning of the end for him. Japan was never the same. It never became a military force again. America saw to that.

Sergov wondered if Popov was making a similar mistake. Was about to thrust Russia into World War III.

Let's hope not.

The clock on the wall continued its countdown.

Three minutes to launch.

President Popov quieted the room.

He lifted a glass. No military operation could ever begin without the military leaders first drinking and toasting.

Popov could go one of two ways with this first toast. Under most circumstances, the first toast was a blessing or sacrament. Something like "Budem Zdorovy." Which meant "Let's be healthy."

Popov went with more in keeping with the moment. "To Stalin," he said. One of the greatest military leaders the world had ever seen. The men let out a cheer of agreement, then raised their glasses and drank. Even Sergov toasted with fervor.

The next toasts followed tradition.

The second was for success in the mission. Literally, "to the success of the scheduled tasks."

The third was always for soldiers who had died.

The fourth was always a hope that no one in the room would ever drink the third toast for anyone sitting at the table.

The countdown clock was at two minutes.

There'd likely be ten toasts.

Toast five was delayed as new bottles of vodka had to be opened to refill the glasses.

The doomsday clock was at one minute. Popov would have to hurry to get all ten toasts in.

"To the defenders of the Motherland," Popov said. Toast five.

Thirty seconds.

The next five came in rapid fire and were all to women.

As the clock was already on zero, Popov delivered the tenth. "Ask your wife for advice and do the opposite. Let us drink to women who always help us make the best decisions."

The toast almost seemed fortuitous. Popov almost certainly didn't ask his wife for advice in this instance. He should've. She'd tell him not to do it. Sergov knew Popov's wife. She despised her husband. Thought he was a fool.

She wasn't wrong.

The group was feeling the spirits. The cheering got louder with each toast. Popov added a last one before turning his attention to the radar screen. Sergov was already eyeing it with trepidation.

"Here's to those who wish us well," Popov said. "All the rest can go to hell."

"Hoorah!"

The loudest cheer was saved for the last.

The room got suddenly quiet as Popov stood and faced the screen.

A cheer erupted when the missile was finally spotted.

"There it is!" Popov said.

He raised his hand to toast the missile even though he didn't have a drink in his hand.

The first missile was supposed to fall harmlessly into the ocean. But Popov didn't care. He was exhilarated by seeing the missile.

Something was wrong.

Sergov noticed it first.

The missile was on the wrong trajectory.

It wasn't traveling out and over the ocean. It seemed to be traveling inland.

Popov turned and glared at General Vagin. The man in charge of the missiles.

"It must be a blip on the radar," Vagin said. "Give it time to correct itself."

A minute later, it was clear the missile was heading in the wrong direction. Toward Russia.

The entire room let out a collective gasp.

"What is the meaning of this?" Popov said, angrily.

General Vagin didn't answer. He was already on the phone.

A few seconds later, he said, "I'm not getting an answer."

"I demand to know what is happening!" Popov shouted. His booming voice practically shook the room.

"It must've malfunctioned," Vagin said. "Or the imbeciles entered the wrong coordinates."

"Stop the second missile," Popov demanded.

"I'm trying. No one is answering their phones."

Popov slammed his fist on the conference table.

Sergov knew what happened. The Americans had somehow sabotaged the launch. He wondered where it would land. Hopefully, not in a major city.

Popov was furious. He had come to the same conclusion.

"The Americans did this!"

"It's the only explanation," Vagin said. "That's why I can't get in touch with my men."

Sergov fought back the grin on his face. He couldn't let his relief show.

The relief turned to horror when he heard the next words out of Popov's mouth.

"Prepare the nuclear weapons."

35

CIA Headquarters

Brad was busy doing what he did best. Cleaning up one of his operative's messes. Namely Jamie Austen's disaster in Alaska. Technically, Kaley's issue. Killing a man on U.S. soil while working a CIA mission.

He didn't blame either of them. They uncovered the organization, rescued the girls, and lived to tell about it. An added bonus was that Kaley had grown up right in front of their eyes. Proven her worth as an operative. His instincts about her had been correct.

Did he wish she hadn't killed the guy on U.S. soil? Not really. As long as it couldn't be tied to her. One less bad guy on this earth was a good thing. She'd actually cleverly put both of the brothers out of commission. The only thing he wished was that he had known about it. Then he wouldn't have called the FBI. They could've covered it up, and the mission file would be closed as a success.

As it were, the FBI was at the scene at that very moment. Investigating. Brad needed to act before they began to piece things together.

He dialed the number for Larry Peay, the special agent in charge of the investigation. He answered on the first ring. Brad could hear activity in the background. As he suspected, Larry was still at the scene.

"What a mess you dropped in my lap." Peay said after the minimal amount of pleasantries.

"What ya finding?" Brad asked.

He'd fish for information before interjecting. How he proceeded would depend in part on how much Peay knew or didn't know.

"You were right," Peay said. "The two brothers are dirty. I got evidence they were into drug running."

"That's what my sources are telling me."

"The problem is that the two brothers are nowhere to be found. One of their planes is missing. And I've got blood here at the scene. I don't know if the brothers were tipped off and fled the country on their plane. Did they take an injured hostage with them? Was one of them wounded somehow in a shootout? I have more questions than I can pray over."

"I think I can shed some light on the situation," Brad said.

"You'll be my next best friend."

"I think you can close down your investigation. I'm about to solve the case for you."

"Not only are you my best friend, you can be the best man at my wedding."

"I didn't know you were getting married."

"I'm not. But I will someday. You'll be the first person I call."

Brad chuckled. "I won't hold my breath. No girl is ever going to marry you."

"Nah. Somebody will marry me for the money."

Brad laughed even harder. "That's the funniest thing I've heard in a long time."

"I know. Right. On my salary, I can barely afford to take a girl on a date. Much less pay for a marriage."

"Then pay for a divorce a few years later."

"Exactly."

"Anyway. . . I didn't call to talk about your love life."

"Or lack thereof."

"Like I said. I'm going to wrap this thing into a nice bow for you so you can get home early."

"I like the sound of that."

"The two brothers are dead."

"Really. Who killed them?"

"The Russians. Willy and Benji Cantrell were running drugs for the Russians. I have it on good information that they were skimming off the top."

"Not a smart move."

"Right. The Russians came to Alaska and killed them. Then stole their plane. I have evidence that the plane flew to Russia earlier today. I'll send you the proof."

Brad already had the information documented. Of course, Kaley was the one who flew the plane to Russia, but Peay would never know that fact. She flew the girls back to Russia in that plane, but landed at the Air Force base. Peay would put the information in the file and close it. He'd never have a reason to pursue it any further.

"I've got an APB out on the plane," Peay said. "The tail number is in the system."

That's what Brad was afraid of. He had hoped he'd get to Peay before that happened. That complicated things. Kaley went to Russia to pick up Jamie. That meant she couldn't fly back into American airspace, or the plane tail number would be flagged, Peay would be called, Jamie and Kaley would be detained for questioning, and all sorts of problems would arise.

"I don't think the plane is coming back to America," Brad said.

"Well, if it does, I'll be notified, and we'll be on it."

"Sorry you don't get to arrest the two brothers," Brad said. "I know you were looking forward to it."

"No worries. It makes my job easier. Like you said, I can sleep in my own bed tonight."

"I hope it's not alone."

Peay laughed.

"My bed will be cold when I get it in tonight."

"My bed is cold when I get it in. Even colder back in the day when my ex wife was in it."

"That's funny, right there."

"At least you have the satisfaction of knowing you are making the world a safer place. At the expense of your love life."

"That doesn't make it any easier."

"It makes the world a safer place for the women of Alaska as well," Brad quipped. "I'm not one to talk. I'm saving the women of northern Virginia a lot of heartache by working every night until all hours."

The whole subject was depressing, and Brad was ready to get off the phone. Satisfied he'd successfully covered his tracks. This would probably be the last he heard of the two brothers.

"Thanks for the heads up," Peay said. "We'll wrap this thing up and shut it down. How sure are you about your information?"

"One hundred percent."

"That's good enough for me."

"Stay safe."

Brad hung up the phone and immediately dialed Jamie. He actually called Kaley's cell phone which was a secured CIA line. More than likely, Jamie had already ditched the Russian cell phone she stole off the dead guy.

Jamie answered on the first ring. He could hear the sound of airplane engines in the background. He could feel tension leave his shoulders. The Alaska problem was handled. It looked like Jamie was on the plane and headed out of Russia. The only problem was where to land the stolen plane but that was manageable.

"Are you out of Russia?" Brad asked. "Please say yes."

"Leaving as we speak," Jamie said. "We just left Russian airspace. We're somewhere over the Bering Sea."

"Excellent."

Brad hit a few keystrokes on his computer and their location came up on his screen. He was able to track them by satellite. The plane was over the Bering Sea and in international waters.

He felt some of the tension return to his shoulders. Time was of the essence. Before long, the plane would be picked up by an American air traffic controller and the FBI would be notified.

"Change of plans," Brad said.

The phone on his desk rang. Director Coldclaw was calling.

"Hang on Jamie. Ryan's calling me. I'll call you back."

He hung up the line not waiting for a response. As much as he needed to deal with the plane issue, a call from the Director took priority. Especially given the rising tensions in Russia.

"Hello, Ryan."

"There's been a development."

Brad felt the tension return with a vengeance. Not so much from the words but from the seriousness of the tone.

"What kind of development?" Brad asked.

"In Russia."

"I already assumed as much."

Brad tamped down any panic he was feeling. It could be anything.

"Russia fired the two missiles," Ryan said.

Brad was confused. He hadn't seen any alerts come on his phone or his computer. If two missiles hit the United States, his electronic devices would be lighting up like the city of Las Vegas at night.

"No surprise there," Brad said. "They said they were going to launch them. Where did they land?"

Brad could hear the flurry of activity in the background. Something had clearly set the room Ryan was in on fire. Ryan was in the war room at the White House. With the President, his chief of staff, his military advisers, and members of his cabinet. Brad wasn't invited but was to remain by his phone in case Ryan needed him.

Which he obviously did, although the reason wasn't so obvious.

Ryan chuckled nervously. "The two missiles landed in Russia."

"How did that happen?"

"You tell me."

"I don't know. Did they malfunction?"

"We think the mobile missile launchers were turned so they were facing Russia. One landed harmlessly in a field somewhere. The other landed in Moscow. In a business district."

"Are you serious?"

"As serious as a heart attack. Any chance Jamie Austen is behind this?"

The thought hadn't even occurred to Brad. "It does sound like something she would do."

36

When Brad talked to Jamie seconds before, she sounded as cool as an ice cube. Of course, that was Jamie. She didn't mention sabotaging the Russian missiles.

"I take it you didn't know anything about it?" Ryan asked next. More of a question than a statement.

"Of course not. I would've told you. If Jamie did it, she acted on her own."

Ryan's tone mellowed some. "Anyway… be that as it may, she did us a favor. Based on the trajectory and distance, one of the missiles would've reached America had it been launched towards us."

"What's the President going to do to retaliate?"

"That's why I'm calling. He wants to take out the other eight missiles. But not if Jamie is still there."

"She's not. She's on a plane out of Russia. Kaley picked her up at the prison and they just left Russian airspace."

"Excellent. That makes me feel better. It means the President can act right away."

"Sounds like a prudent thing to do."

"Maybe Jamie didn't have anything to do with it after all. Not if she's on an airplane."

"The next time I talk to her, I'll ask."

He actually couldn't wait to get off the phone and talk to Jamie and ask her about it. Now that he'd had time to think about it, he was certain she was behind it.

The Russians weren't stupid enough to fire the missiles in the wrong direction.

He hoped Jamie was behind it. Especially since Ryan wasn't upset about it. How brilliant an idea to turn the missile launchers, so they were facing the opposite direction. He wished he'd thought of it.

"I'll be back in touch if I need you," Ryan said.

Brad hung up and called Jamie back.

"What did Ryan say?" she asked when she answered on the first ring again. Brad could almost envision Jamie smirking as she said it.

"What do you think he said?"

"He wanted to thank you for making sure those missiles landed in Russia."

She was behind it!

"Where did they hit?" Jamie asked.

"One landed in a field. The other in the business district of Moscow."

"Ooh."

Kaley was giggling in the background. Jamie was clearly trying to keep from laughing.

"I hope no civilians were injured," Jamie said in a more serious tone.

A good point. He needed to find out right away. Ryan would want an assessment report as soon as possible. The news networks were probably already reporting on the story. The CIA and their disinformation apparatus needed to get to work right away.

Some would wonder where the missiles came from. Did the United States fire them? Was it a terrorist attack? The best thing might be to tell the world the truth. Russia threatened the United States and the missiles malfunctioned. Of course, the Russians would deny it. Claim the U.S. was the one who sabotaged the missiles.

Once the President bombed the other eight, then there'd be no denying the U.S.'s involvement. It was going to be a late night.

"I don't have any information as to civilian casualties. Too early."

"I didn't know where they would land."

"If you hadn't acted, one would've landed in the ocean. The other was headed for the west coast."

"There are eight more missiles. I couldn't take those out."

"I know. That's why Ryan was calling. To make sure you were out of harm's way before they lit them up."

"That warms my heart to know he was concerned about my welfare."

"Not you. Kaley. She's the future. You're old and washed up."

Brad laughed so she'd know he was kidding. He didn't joke with his operatives that often but tried to when they were finally out of danger. It seemed appropriate to help them relax as well.

Jamie retorted, "It feels good to be working with you again. I'd forgotten about your horrible sense of humor."

"Ditto. I mean, it's good to be working with you again. Good job on this mission. The girls are safe. The two brothers are dead. The FBI is handled. You saved the day with the missiles. At least for now. That's a good day at the office."

"You said there's a change of plans."

"Right. You can't land in the United States."

"I was wondering about that."

"The FBI has registered the tail number. If you show up on U.S. soil, you'll be arrested. That's a complication, I don't want to have to deal with."

Jamie let out an audible sigh.

"I'm sure you don't have enough fuel to make it to the Midway Islands," Brad said.

"No. We didn't have time to stop and get fuel in Russia."

"Greenland is even further," Brad said. "If you go south to Canada, you'll get picked up by U.S. air traffic controllers. You might even be close now. I don't want your tail number coming up on their radar. I've got the situation handled. That'll open it up again to questions I can't answer."

He heard Jamie talking in the background. Giving Kaley instructions to turn south.

"Stay far enough east," Jamie said, "so you don't attract the attention of the MIGS, but don't get close enough to Alaska to get picked up by air traffic control. I'll explain why later."

"Good idea to steer clear of Russia." Brad said. "I would imagine those MIGS have orders to shoot first and ask questions later."

"Tensions will be running high over there. I'm glad we got out when we did."

An alarm sounded on Brad's computer. He pulled it up to see what it was.

"I just got an alert," Brad said to Jamie. "All air traffic into Russia from the United States and their allies has been halted."

"What about Savoonga?" Jamie asked. "Kaley suggested it."

Brad hesitated. Savoonga Airport was on St. Lawrence Island. Technically, in the United States, but closer to Russia than it was to Alaska. He wondered if the FBI alert would make it to that location.

Maybe, maybe not.

"I think you can stop long enough for fuel," Brad said. "Then head to Midway Island."

"Why can't we just ditch the plane? We can land on Savoonga and then disappear."

"It might raise some red flags. Besides, do you want the plane?"

This time Jamie was the one who hesitated.

"I don't know. I haven't thought about it. It's pretty nice."

"The CIA doesn't want it. I figured AJAX could have it after the dust settles."

"Sure. We'll take it. I'm sure Alex will find a use for it. Speaking of Alex."

Brad's heart skipped a beat. Then took several laps around his chest.

"Why not call Alex and have him change the tail number and then we can land in Alaska? It won't take him but a few minutes to do."

Brad hesitated. Then bit his lip. Was now the time to tell her?

"I can't call Alex," he said, then winced.

"Why not?"

"Because Alex is dead."

37

It felt like I'd been punched in the gut.

I always knew this day might come. Was likely even. That didn't lessen the shock.

Brad told me Alex was dead. I almost didn't believe the words coming through the speaker of the cell phone. Kaley was in the pilot's seat and immediately turned with her mouth agape. Confirming I'd heard the words right.

My cheeks suddenly felt wet as tears began to flow uncontrollably down my face. I didn't even bother brushing them away.

How was this possible?

What a stupid question to pop into my head.

Of course, it was possible. Considering what we did for a living. I never thought Alex was invincible and couldn't be killed. It just never occurred to me that Pok would be the one to get the better of him.

When I dropped Alex off at the airport to go to Vietnam, I wasn't worried at all. Every mission was dangerous, but Pok was a lightweight. A computer hacker.

How could Alex be dead?

Something must've gone horribly wrong.

Guilt rushed in and flooded my soul. Regrets that avalanched into a mountain.

It was my fault.

I could've killed Pok any number of times. In Hong Kong, he was my prisoner. I kept him alive on purpose. Convinced Alex to let Pok into our inner circle and come work for us. Pok betrayed Alex. Stole our three billion dollars then conspired with CIA Director Neal Fuller to bring us down.

Fuller tried to kill us. Almost did. We nearly lost everything. None of this would've happened if I had killed Pok when I had the chance.

We had another chance. Alex found Pok and we had him in our crosshairs. A rifle aimed at his head. Alex didn't pull the trigger because a woman and young girl were standing next to Pok. Alex didn't want the little girl to see her father killed in front of her.

Turned out Pok wasn't married and didn't have any children. He hired the woman and little girl as a ruse.

It saved his life.

Pok was evil to his core. I should've known better than to trust him. I thought we could control him and use him in AJAX. It worked for a long time, until he turned on us.

Alex was dead because of me.

I realized Brad was still hanging on the line and the silence had become awkward. My thoughts raged like an out-of-control forest fire. I wanted to speak but couldn't find the words.

What would I say? Everything I thought of seemed so shallow.

How did he die?

An obvious question. But did I really want to know? That might make the guilt worse. Especially if Alex suffered a horrifying death.

A nausea came over me. I swallowed hard several times to beat it back.

Curly would be mad at me. He'd say I should've pulled it together by now. I tried. From the notable silence on the other end of the phone, Brad was obviously giving me a moment to do so.

Where was Alex?

Another question I was afraid to ask. I didn't want to picture him dead in a morgue somewhere. Or in a casket on a plane on his way home. A panic darted through me. I wanted to be there to meet him.

Was his body back home?

Oh my word! I have to plan a funeral.

I didn't even know where to begin. We never talked about funeral arrangements. Alex thought it was bad luck. When the time came, he said to do whatever I wanted. It didn't matter to him. He wouldn't be there.

Would he be buried at Arlington National Cemetery? He was killed in the line of duty.

No. Alex was an undercover CIA operative. There'd be no public notice. No funeral. If he had a gravestone, the marker wouldn't have his name on it. He could be cremated and his ashes spread somewhere privately.

That's what we did for Curly.

The three most important men in my life were gone. Curly. Alex. Only God knew where in the universe my father was. He could be alive or dead. I'd never know his fate. At least I knew Alex's. As if that were any consolation.

The Memorial Wall.

I looked at it the other day. Stared at it for a good five minutes. On the north wall of the lobby of the original CIA headquarters, were stars etched in the stone by a carver. One for each person who had died in the line of service. Below it in a steel frame was a black book, called the Book of Honor. With the dates each CIA employee died over the years while serving the country. Some had names beside them, some didn't.

Alex's name would not be in it.

We didn't have kids. His parents were dead. There wasn't anyone left to remember him other than me. The hundreds of people whose lives he'd saved, would want to pay their respects, if they knew who he was.

How could I have possibly known that Alex's name would be there before mine?

Standing in front of the Memorial Wall that day, I'd actually wondered if a star would ever be in that book for me. Probably. I took so many chances. I was never careful. Curly told me not to be. Which meant a bullet would eventually catch up to me.

An anger rose up inside of me. I had to search my heart to see who it was directed toward. Pok for sure. If he was still alive, I resolved to go after him. I also realized I was angry at Brad. Which might've been why I hadn't said anything.

How long had Brad known? My instinct was right. I could tell something was wrong when we talked a couple of days before.

Why didn't he tell me sooner?

He waited until I finished my mission. Obviously. In the CIA nothing was more important than the mission. Not even our lives.

Anger turned to rage. I'm the wife. Didn't I have a right to know right away that my husband was dead?

I wanted to yell at him but resisted. My emotions were getting the best of me. This wasn't Brad's fault.

It was the right thing to do from his perspective. What could I have done about it if he had told me? I might've left Alaska seeking revenge. Then the twelve girls might not have been rescued. The missiles might've hit the United States.

The anger toward Brad dissipated like a puff of smoke in the wind. Whatever emotions I was understandably feeling, I shouldn't take them out on him.

Kaley looked over at me and shrugged her shoulders. The exact response I needed. It reminded me I still had the phone in my hand.

I need to say something.

"What happened?" I finally blurted out between muted sobs.

"Plane crash."

A plane crash. Strange.

Not what I expected to hear. Alex always said if he died on a mission, he hoped he went out in a blaze of gunfire.

Where did he crash? I thought I had asked, but the question was in my head. I was kind of numb. Also busy answering it myself as I considered all the ramifications. If he crashed on the way to Vietnam, Alex never completed his mission. That meant Pok was still alive.

I could only hope Alex died on the way home. Then Pok was dead and at least some good would've come out of it.

Although, I needed a target. Someone to focus my rage on.

Then it hit me.

A-Rad. Bond. Colonel.

They were all on the plane with Alex. My worst nightmare had suddenly become worse.

"An . . . y . . . survivors?"

My voice cracked and I could barely get the words out of my mouth which suddenly felt parched. Like I'd spent ten days in a desert with no water.

"I'm sorry," Brad said. "They're all gone. A horrible loss for all of us."

Not one star on the wall. The carver would have to put four on there.

Unimaginable.

38

Brad showed no emotion. I didn't read anything into it other than that he was the consummate professional. Alex was like a brother to him. He was torn up about it as well but was holding it together better than I was.

The sobbing stopped as quickly as it had come upon me. The tears dried up and I wiped them away with my arm.

For whatever reason, learning that they were all dead caused me to gain my composure. Surprisingly, a strength came over me. A somber reality. At least momentarily, I had the composure to think and speak clearly.

"At least they were together," I said. "Doing what they loved."

I could take some comfort in that.

"They were the finest men I've ever had the privilege of working with," Brad said.

"No doubt. I already miss them terribly."

The emotion returned. It took all my strength to fight it off.

I took a deep breath. I had so many questions. I couldn't ask them if I was a blubbering idiot. The Bible says there's a time to mourn. A time for war and a time for peace. I wouldn't mourn until I knew if Pok was dead.

I had to ask. "Did they finish the mission? Is Pok dead?"

"Unfortunately, no. Pok's still alive."

"Not for long," I said. "Was Pok behind the plane crash? Did he have some kind of missile that hit the plane?"

"No. I don't think Pok is behind it. We don't know all the details, but we believe it was a mechanical failure."

"I wouldn't jump to conclusions. Pok might've sabotaged the plane on the ground."

"I don't think so. Colonel is so careful. He wouldn't get in a plane unless he inspected it first. Same with A-Rad."

"He might've missed something."

"Anything's possible."

"The black box and inspecting the debris should tell us. If it was a bomb, there'd be residue."

"We haven't recovered the plane."

My heart jumped to the back of my throat.

"What are you talking about? Are you telling me that you haven't recovered the black box or any of the bodies?"

"It crashed in the Indian Ocean."

"Then there'd be a debris field. An oil slick."

"We didn't find anything. And we searched. The plane is at the bottom of the ocean. Probably still intact. Apparently, it didn't break apart when it hit the water. It wasn't going that fast."

A glimmer of hope overwhelmed the darkness in my soul.

"If you don't have a body, then how do you know Alex is dead?"

"I watched the plane go into the ocean on radar."

"Whoa! Hold on for a minute. Start at the beginning and tell me what happened."

"Everything was normal. The plane passed by India at cruising altitude. It suddenly veered right and started heading south. Out of the Bay of Bengal over the Indian Ocean."

"Why did it veer right?"

"We don't know. But it did. I saw it on radar. It began losing altitude. It descended until it disappeared off the radar screen and into the ocean."

My grief had turned into nervous energy. Something didn't sound right to me.

"You know Alex," I said. "He's the master at sleight of hand. Sleight of computer. He can make it look like he crashed."

"I don't think so."

"Alex might've created a diversion to make Pok think he was dead."

"I thought about that. But it's not possible."

"Why not?"

"It's not a matter of changing a tail number or the transponder signal. The radar is an actual image of an actual object that shows up on the radar screen."

"Maybe Alex hacked into the radar and made it look like a plane."

"It was seen on four different radars. Vietnam, Malaysia, Australia, and India. I watched it myself by satellite."

"But did anyone actually have eyes on the plane? Did any of those countries scramble jets and actually see the plane hit the water?"

"Well no, but the radar is clear. You don't have to see the plane visually to know it's there."

"I need more proof."

"I know you want to believe Alex is alive. I'd give anything if that were true. But it's not."

"I'm not going to believe Alex is dead until I see his body for myself!"

"I don't think we'll ever be able to recover the plane. The Indian Ocean is too deep."

"I'm not saying Alex didn't die on that plane. I'm just saying that I'm not going to believe it until I investigate it further."

"I have more proof."

"What?"

"Pok is still alive. That's all the proof you need. If Alex did only make it look like he crashed, then where is he? Why didn't he go to Vietnam and kill Pok?"

"I don't know. But I'm going to Vietnam to find out."

"I'm going, too," Kaley said.

"It's okay, Kaley. This is my battle to fight."

"I'm going with you. You need someone to fly you there."

"Did you hear that?" I said to Brad.

"I heard it. I'm fine with it."

"I'm going to Vietnam to kill Pok."

"I couldn't stop you even if I wanted to. And I don't."

"Send me the complete file."

"It's Alex's mission and you aren't with the CIA anymore."

"I don't care. Send me what you can. I still have my security clearances."

"It'll be in your inbox."

"We're going to need help. All our supplies are back in Alaska."

"Tell me what you need, and I'll get it for you."

"We need fake identities. Passports. I need a secured cell phone."

"Done."

"We'll need weapons."

"You got it."

"This also solves the problem with the plane we're in. We're going to Vietnam. Not the U.S. That'll give us time to change the tail number."

I heard shuffling in the background. Then the sound of Brad typing on his computer.

"Stop in Savoonga and refuel," he said. "Then instead of flying to Midway Islands, fly to Okinawa. You can land at the Marine base there."

"No. I don't want to do that. Pok will be able to track this plane. At this moment, he doesn't know anything about it. We aren't on his radar, no pun intended."

I was feeling better. In my mind, Alex was still alive. I was drawing energy from that hope.

"If we land at a Marine base, then fly to Vietnam, Pok will suspect something. We'll land in Thailand. We'll stop for fuel somewhere along the way. I've been there dozens of times on a mission to rescue girls. I know the area and speak the language. I have all kinds of contacts who will help me."

"Go to the safe house in Bangkok and you can get your weapons there. And a vehicle. You already know the route into Vietnam."

"I do. We can get in with no trouble."

"Excellent."

"We'll be in touch."

I hung up the phone. Excitement was bubbling inside of me like the jets of a whirlpool.

"Did you think to bring my backpack from the guide service offices?" I asked Kaley. The two brothers had taken it from me. The last I saw it, it was on the couch in their offices.

"I did. It's in the back."

"You are awesome." I was starting to love her.

I touched her shoulder, then got out of my seat, went to the back, and found the backpack stored in a luggage bin. I pulled out my laptop and charger cord and went back to the cockpit.

"Do you think Alex is still alive?" Kaley asked.

"I don't know."

I powered it up and waited for the screen to come to life. Trying to will it to come on faster.

Alex and I had a secret email account. Brad didn't even know about it. It was for these circumstances. We didn't actually send emails from that account, otherwise it'd be traceable. What we did was go on the site and write draft emails. That way either one of us could log in and read the draft as if it had been sent. Then delete it so the other knew it was read.

I typed in the url for the website.

Praying.

Hoping against hope that I had a message from Alex. Explaining what had happened. I didn't think he would fake his own death without telling me.

Fear suddenly engulfed me. Alex would tell me. He didn't. What if there wasn't a message? Brad was right. Alex was probably dead. The radar couldn't be wrong.

I was afraid to look.

I took a deep breath, then exhaled loudly. Kaley looked at me funny but didn't say anything. We were getting close to Savoonga and she was busy with her landing checklist. She was working off of memory. I was impressed by her flying skills.

Everything about her, really.

The site opened.

My jaw was so tense, my teeth hurt.

Drafts had a one beside it.

My heart did a complete somersault in my chest. That meant there was a message.

That didn't mean Alex sent it. It could be old.

No. Old drafts would be deleted by now.

It had to be a new message.

I clicked on it.

The draft came up. The message was from Alex.

My heart was beating so loud I could hear it in my ears.

I blinked twice when I saw the date.

I couldn't believe it.

The date on the message was today.

Alex was alive!

39

I could barely contain my excitement.

I'd gone from the lowest of lows to the highest of highs. All in less than an hour's time frame. I'd walked through the valley of the shadow of death. Now I was walking on the proverbial cloud nine. Above it, considering we were cruising at an altitude of 20,000 feet. I could look out the window and see the clouds below us which made the analogy even more visual in my mind.

Kaley was on the radio with the air traffic controllers at Savoonga, so I had to tamper my enthusiasm. I couldn't wait to tell her the news. Amazing how close we'd gotten in such a short time. It felt like we'd survived a fox hole together.

I wasn't sure if I completely trusted her in a difficult situation, but I was getting there. I genuinely liked her and was impressed with her skills. My first reaction about her had been wrong. I was glad Alex talked me into giving her another chance. She might very well have what it took to grab the mantle from me when I was ready to pass it on.

Based on how tired I was feeling, it might be sooner rather than later. I hadn't slept except for the twenty minutes in the back of the SUV in Alaska. Not only was I physically tired, but also emotionally drained from the roller coaster. In my younger days, I could endure it more easily.

When Brad told me Alex was dead, it had sent an adrenaline jolt to my system. I still hadn't come down from it. When I did, I expected to crash, emotionally. Before we landed in Thailand, I needed to eat and get some sleep or I wouldn't be at my best to figure out how to take out Pok.

When Kaley finished with air traffic control, she said, "You'd better buckle up. We're cleared for landing. In about ten."

Kaley wouldn't look me in the eye. Obviously feeling awkward about the Alex situation. If she had looked at me, she'd have seen a huge smile on my face and wondered if I had found a bag of drugs in the back cargo hole and taken some.

I was feeling euphoric. Like I was on a high. It wouldn't take her long to notice. Considering the news I'd just received, she was going to think I was crazy.

"My husband is a horse's behind," I said, jokingly. At the right moment. I tried to be serious, but not possible with the huge smile on my face.

Kaley looked over at me, clearly stunned. "Are you talking about Alex?"

"Yeah. Alex. He's poo on a stick."

"What are you talking about?"

She was probably thinking, "Is that a good way to talk about your dead husband?"

The thought caused me to laugh, drunkenly, which caused her eyes to widen even further.

"Alex is not dead. He's alive."

For the third or fourth time in the last half hour, Kaley's eyes got as wide as quarters and her mouth gaped open so far, a swarm of bees could've made a nest.

"Alex is alive?" she asked. Like me, barely able to believe it.

"Not for long," I quipped. "As soon as I see him, I'm going to kill him myself."

"What's going on?"

"Alex faked his death. And he didn't tell me! I'm going to wring his neck."

"How do you know he's alive?"

"He sent me an email message. Dated today."

"Shut the front door!"

"I'm serious. I had a feeling. It's just like Alex to pull a magician's trick out of his hat."

"You need to tell Brad."

"No," I said as strongly as I could. "You can't say anything to Brad. Or anybody for that matter. It's part of the ruse. Alex wants Brad to think he's dead and that his plane is at the bottom of the ocean."

"Why wouldn't Alex want Brad to know?"

"He wanted Brad to order a search to make it believable."

"Why didn't he tell you?"

"Apparently, he didn't even trust me to keep the secret. Like I said. He's jerk water."

"What's jerk water?"

"It's something I made up. In place of curse words. My mom washed my mouth out with soap when I was a little girl for saying a bad word. She said damn and hell were in the Bible so I could say those. Anything else was off limits. So I came up with alternative words. Like jerk water. Fudge nugget. Son of a biscuit eater. Horse pucky, to name a few."

"You're weird."

"I know."

"I guess Alex's plan worked," Kaley said. "Everybody thinks he's dead."

"The plan didn't really work. That's how missions are sometimes. Alex faked his death so he could sneak up on Pok. Kill him when he least expected it. But that didn't happen. Pok is still alive."

"Why didn't Alex kill him?"

"He explained why in the email."

A silence ensued as Kaley waited for me to tell her the reason. I hesitated. Thought through the email in my mind to make sure there was nothing in it considered classified. Satisfied there wasn't, I said, "I'll read it to you."

I opened my laptop and found the draft email. I hadn't deleted it. Alex would know I read it because it didn't show one unread email in drafts anymore.

"Hello Lover," I said, reading the first line.

"Aww. That's sweet."

I let out a deep throated guffaw. "Oh no. Alex isn't getting any for a while. I promise you that. He won't be able to sweet talk his way out of this. He put me through hell."

Kaley laughed. Her schoolgirl giggle I'd heard several times.

"The moment you see him, you'll forget all about it."

She was right. As soon as I saw Alex's face, I'd give him a hard time, but all would be forgiven. Deep down, I was relieved beyond belief that he was still alive.

"We're landing now," Kaley said, as she touched something and I heard the landing gear start to deploy. We emerged out of the clouds into a bright glaring sun and saw the island for the first time. I'd never been to Savoonga before. It was stunningly gorgeous.

"You focus on landing the plane safely," I said. "I'll tell you what Alex said when we're on the ground."

40

It took nearly an hour to get the plane refueled. I was worried the whole time. We still had to be concerned about the FBI alert. I half expected the local authorities to show up and arrest us on the spot. We didn't have time to go over the email and I couldn't relax anyway. Always looking out the window. Trying to figure out if there was a way to talk ourselves out of a difficult situation.

Once we were cleared to leave, Kaley got us out of there as soon as possible. She put the plane on autopilot, and we went in the back to eat something. The plane had a few supplies already in it, but we restocked at the airport. Enough to last us a week. We weren't sure how long this mission was going to take.

After we'd both eaten until we were stuffed, I read Kaley the rest of the email.

"What does it mean?" she asked.

Alex had been intentionally vague about some things related to Pok.

"I had to read between the lines," I said. "But I think it means Alex has no way to get to Pok. Pok has built a fortress around himself and his operations. He's leasing a building in an industrial complex outside of Hanoi. That's in northern Vietnam. Close to China in case he needs to disappear again."

"He's leasing it? If he has so much money, why doesn't he buy it?"

"That's how things work in Vietnam. The government owns all the land. I mean, technically the people own the land, but it's controlled and managed by the government."

"So residents can't buy property and own it?"

"No. The state leases the property to individuals, but they can't own the land on it. If you build a house on the land, you own the structure, but not the land under it. Once the lease is up, the government takes over the house and you lose it. Unless you get the lease renewed."

"That doesn't seem fair."

"It's not. But that's how these socialist governments work. They take as much control from the people as possible."

"Sounds like it. I hope America never gets like that."

"It could happen. Anyway, to complicate matters, Pok is a foreigner. So he doesn't even own the building he's in. A Vietnamese national owns it. He leases from the government and then subleases it to Pok's foreign corporation."

"Sounds complicated."

"It is complicated. Anyway, Pok made a lot of improvements to the building. He put in bullet-proof windows. Reinforced doors. An advanced security system. He lives in one section of the building. That's where he works out of. His cyber lab operation is in another part of the building."

"It seems like Alex and his men could still storm the building and take Pok out."

"Maybe. But it's not as simple as that. Keep that in mind when you're operating in a foreign country. Whatever you do, you have to make sure you can get out of the country without getting caught and without it being tied to the CIA. You also don't want to act if there's a high degree of risk to innocent civilians."

"The innocents being the people who work in the building?"

"Alex was hoping that Pok would come out of hiding if he thought Alex was dead."

"So Alex faked his death."

"Yes. And the ruse worked. Pok believed it. But he hasn't come out yet. So Alex came up with a plan to smoke him out."

"How?"

"That's where I come in."

Kaley's lips contorted to the side in a confused look. "Let's back up. How did Alex fake his death? Remember what Brad said. The radar doesn't lie. It shows an actual object on the radar screen."

"It was an actual object."

"Alex crashed his own plane?"

"No."

"Alex crashed someone else's plane?"

"No. After they took off, Colonel unhooked the transponder and attached it to a drone. While they were flying over the Bay of Bengal, they released the drone. Alex preprogrammed it to slowly lose altitude and fall harmlessly in the ocean. He made it look like it was his plane, but it wasn't. His plane continued on to Vietnam under a different transponder signal. Actually, he probably landed in Thailand like we're going to do."

"That's brilliant," Kaley said with emphasis.

"I know. I probably should let Alex live a little longer. He can be extremely resourceful."

I smiled so she knew I was kidding.

"Alex taught me how to change the tail number and transponder signal on the FAA website," Kaley blurted.

"I didn't know that. When did he do that?"

"That time he came to The Farm. During my training."

"Where was I?"

"You were gone somewhere."

"Oh yeah. I remember. I had to go to Langley to give Brad an update on your training. Alex tried to surprise me and showed up out of the blue. But I was gone. I don't like surprises. That's one of the reasons why."

"You guys just missed each other. While we waited for you to get back, Alex told me all about computer hacking. I asked him a bunch of questions. He asked me if I wanted to learn the basics. Of course

I did. That's when he showed me how to hack into the FAA website and change a tail number and transponder number. It's not that hard."

"That's why it was so difficult for Alex to fake his own death. Pok knows how to hack into the site as well. Alex changed the tail number and transponder signal on our AJAX plane. But he knew Pok would know he did it. So Alex attached the transponder information to the drone and fooled Pok. Made him think the plane crashed. Even Brad believed it."

"I can change the tail number and transponder signal to this plane."

"Good. That'll be helpful."

"What else did Alex say?"

"Get this. Pok had plastic surgery on his face. Total reconstruction. He changed his entire look. Alex sent me a picture of the new Pok."

I turned the computer screen around so she could see it.

"Ooh. Yeah."

Kaley had never seen a picture of Pok before, so she had no frame of reference. If I looked closely, I could see a slight resemblance. Mostly in the eyes. A plastic surgeon couldn't change the evil in someone's eyes.

"I can't tell he's had plastic surgery," Kaley said. "Not like some of those Hollywood actresses who get all that work done. They look like freaks." Kaley contorted her face for effect.

"I know. Pok had a good surgeon. Maybe I can get his name."

"What are you talking about? You're gorgeous."

"I'm finding new lines and wrinkles every day."

"You don't need plastic surgery."

"I wouldn't get it even if I needed it. This is how God made me and I'm happy with it."

"You should be."

"You're sweet. Anyway, I need to give you some of the back story. Pok stole three billion dollars from Alex and me."

"I know. I heard."

"How did you hear?"

"It's common knowledge around the CIA."

"Really?"

"I didn't know the amount. But I knew it was a lot of money."

"Well, Alex found it. Now it's grown to five billion."

Kaley's mouth flew open again. "Five billion dollars!"

"Yep. And Alex knows where it is."

I turned the screen around a second time.

"This is the link Alex sent me. All I have to do is hit this link and all the money will be transferred out of Pok's accounts and into our accounts."

"Wow. That's great. Why don't you do it? I'd hit that link in a nanosecond."

"I can't. Not yet. Not until I have a plan."

"Why did Alex send it to you? Why didn't he steal the money himself? I don't understand."

I noticed something. Kaley didn't say "like" after every other word, like so many girls her age. One of my pet peeves. I appreciated that about her.

"Alex can't. Pok would know he was alive. That's why he wanted me to do it."

"Won't Pok know it's you?"

"He will. But he'd expect it. Since Alex is dead, Pok knows I'll step in and try to steal our money back."

"Sounds good."

"There's a problem."

"What kind of problem?"

"Once I hit the link, I have seventy-two hours to do something with the money."

"Why seventy-two hours?"

"That's how long it'll take Pok to find the money and transfer it back."

"Can't you hide it from him?"

"It's not that simple. Alex and Pok are the two best hackers in the world. Alex is better but Pok is right there with him. The two of them can hack into any financial website. There is literally nowhere in the world they can hide the money from each other."

"Not even a bank?"

"Especially not a bank."

Kaley let out a huge breath. "Seventy-two hours? That's not a long time."

"I have to either spend the money on an asset that Pok can't touch, or I have to kill him within seventy-two hours. Killing him is unlikely or Alex would've already done so. That leaves spending the money."

"How are we going to spend five billion dollars in three days?"

I laughed. "We?"

Kaley rubbed her hands together. "I'm going to help you."

"Do you have any suggestions?"

"We could buy shoes and purses."

This time I laughed. I knew she was kidding, but it was still funny.

"We'd have to buy all the purses and shoes in Thailand. I don't think we have enough time to go shopping."

"What about real estate? You could buy the Empire State Building. I heard it's for sale."

"Real estate takes a month or more to close."

"What about crypto currency? You know, Bitcoins. Things like that."

"That's all digital. Anything that's online, Pok can take back."

"Mmmm. What about giving it to charity?"

"I thought about that, but Pok can still take it from their account. He'll follow the money trail and steal it back."

"If Pok can steal money so easily, why doesn't he just take all the money in the world?"

"That's a good question. Here's the answer. He has to be careful who he steals from. It can't be governments or other bad guys. Terrorists, Oligarchs and the like. He doesn't want to make enemies out there. He's already got Alex trying to kill him. He pays off the bad guys so they leave him alone."

"And he still has five billion left over. So he's kind of a reverse Robin Hood. He steals from the good guys and then gives to the bad."

"Exactly."

"So what are you going to do?"

"I don't have a clue. Pok will see me coming a mile away."

"There must be a way to get inside that building. What if I go there? Pok doesn't know me. He's never seen my face. I'll knock on the door. Maybe we'll get lucky and he'll let me in."

"He wouldn't let you in. He'd be suspicious. I appreciate the offer though."

"I'm trying to help."

An idea came to me.

"Not so fast," I said. "I know a way you can get inside that building."

"How? You said Pok wouldn't let me in."

"What if he didn't have a choice?" I asked.

"You mean, if I pull my gun and force him to open the door?"

"That wouldn't work. You'd need a key."

"How am I going to get a key?"

"We're going to buy the building from the owner."

I paused to let that sink in. For my benefit as well as hers.

It could work.

Brad sent me the file. I studied it while we were on the ground in Savoonga. I had the name and contact information for the owner of the building Pok was leasing. Alex had even hacked into the man's computer and gotten a copy of the lease agreement.

The term was for fifty years. If at any time in the fifty years, Vietnam allowed ownership of the land, then Pok had the option of purchasing the land and the building. He'd get a credit for rental payments made over the years.

Pok didn't care about losing money on the lease. The lease was a drop in the bucket compared to what he made every year.

"How much would you offer the owner for the building?" Kaley asked.

"Whatever it takes. It doesn't matter. The building is probably worth half a million U.S. dollars. I could offer him a billion dollars for all I care."

"A billion dollars?"

"I'll be buying it with Pok's money."

"And yours."

"He stole three billion from us. We'd still have four billion left. Sounds like a good deal to me."

"You said Pok's in a fifty year lease. The landlord can't break the contract simply because he's offered more money."

"Normally, that'd be true. But there's a clause in the agreement that says Pok can't operate any illegal activities out of that building. If he does, the lease can be terminated effective immediately."

"He's definitely doing that. What's the next step?"

"First I need to get that money transferred over. Then I can pay the landlord a visit."

"We can."

"Right."

Pok might have a surveillance camera at the landlord's office or residence. I might have to send Kaley to buy the building and infiltrate it.

I still had the laptop open to the draft email. Once I touched the link, Pok would be able to find the website. Couldn't be helped. We'd set up another one.

"Can I touch the link?" Kaley said, with a mischievous smile on her face, like she'd be doing something wrong. "That's the closest I'll ever get to five billion dollars."

I turned the computer around so it faced her.

"Sure. Go ahead. You can hit the link."

"Are you serious?"

"Have at it?"

"What if I do it wrong?"

"You can't. Just hit the button. That'll put everything in motion."

Kaley put out her finger to touch the screen, then pulled it back and clutched her chest.

"Are you sure?"

"Absolutely."

"Okay. Here goes."

She put out her finger, hit the button, then squealed like a college girl at a frat house.

"It's done. I can't believe I did that."

I checked to be sure. The link was active. I suspected I'd see the money in our accounts within minutes.

"What happens now?" Kaley asked.

"Go get some sleep. We're going to Hanoi. You're going to kill Pok."

She squealed again. "I can't wait."

Neither could I.

41

General Sergov's worst nightmare was coming to pass. He'd spent his entire career helping build up Russia's arsenal of nuclear weapons, so they'd never have to use them.

President Popov was acting like a madman. Spewing out all kinds of ominous threats. His advisors sat in their chairs silent. Unable or unwilling to speak. If Popov was to be stopped, it'd be up to Sergov to stop him. All he could do was try to reason with the man. That'd be like reasoning with a treed bobcat.

Sergov wasn't afraid to anger the President. He was sixty-seven-years old and not in the best of health. Popov knew better than to try and replace him anyway. Sergov's men would run off a cliff for him. They'd never follow Popov if Sergov told them not to.

Treasonous thoughts. The kind that would get most men hanged.

They might turn into treasonous words if Popov continued on the present course. Sergov wasn't worried. If he was arrested for treason, his men would have him freed before the jail door clanged shut.

His fear was what he might be forced to do. Overthrow Popov. Have him arrested, then exiled. A last resort. Someone would have to fill the power vacuum. Sergov didn't want the job. A replacement might be worse. The last thing he wanted to do was throw the country into chaos or have someone like Vladimir Gagarin take the helm.

Popov's chosen predecessor. That could never happen.

Sergov might not have a choice but to take the job. The people would support him. Popov was despised in his country by everyone except those he handsomely paid. Soldiers. Oligarchs. Titans of business. Those who got wealthy off the public treasury.

The common folks wouldn't give two rubles for Popov. He lost the last election by a wide margin. To Fedor Ilyin. That'd be the best choice to replace Popov. Except he was dead. Mysteriously poisoned in his hotel room. Although the official word was that he died of natural causes. No one believed that to be the case. Even Popov's most ardent supporters knew he was behind it.

The people took to the streets to protest, but the rebellion was quickly crushed. Sergov's private forces sat on the sidelines and could only watch.

In reality, Popov only got about thirty percent of the vote, Sergov estimated. A percentage equal to the number of people he propped up and kept in power.

Ilyin probably got close to seventy percent. But the election was rigged. The ballot boxes were stuffed with votes that couldn't be verified. Machine totals were changed via the internet. Sergov saw the actual room where the tallies were changed.

Popov won by a massive landslide, and the rest was history.

Most impartial observers didn't believe it. Including the United States, but what could they do? Popov controlled the elections. He controlled the judges. Legal challenges were quickly thwarted. The media only reported what he told them to report. Social media was highly regulated in Russia. The truth was quickly extinguished and called disinformation.

Ilyin was even accused of a crime and arrested. For election interference. He was released after the world outcry. He was deported out of the country to England where he mysteriously died in his hotel room.

Sergov was too old for such corruption. The older he got, the more he sympathized with the people. Feeling somewhat hypocritical since he'd played his part in keeping the elite in power. Getting rich in the process and feasting on the spoils while the people suffered.

How much longer could he do it? Where would he draw the line? He'd turned a blind's eye so many times. Nuclear destruction was a line he couldn't let be crossed.

But could he stop it?

Maybe, maybe not. Popov was powerful as all Russian Presidents were. Once they got their power, they cemented it. Wrestling it away would not be easy. Even with the people's support and Sergov's army which could hold its own with the government forces.

Which was how the Communist Party stayed in power. When one party controlled every institution of government, corruption will abound. The will of the people will be disregarded and trampled on at every turn.

Revolution would be the only recourse. The people had to rise up and take their country back. By force. In most cases, that wasn't possible since the despot greased the hands of the men who kept him in power. Especially the men with guns. The government soldiers. The KGB.

The people were not allowed to own weapons. They could be arrested and executed on the spot if found in their possession. So the communist regime persisted for generations. Unfettered.

Popov was about to destroy his own power. He was thinking irrationally. Initiating a nuclear war was about the only way he could actually lose power.

A spirited argument suddenly broke out. Sergov could be silent no longer.

"You can't deploy nuclear weapons," Sergov said. "That'd be suicide."

"I can and I will!" Popov said.

He sat at the head of the table. Sergov at the other end. A dozen or so military advisers sat between them. Too afraid to express how they really felt.

"The Americans will not hesitate to do the same," Sergov argued. Refusing to back down.

"America is weak. President Kemp will acquiesce."

"What if he doesn't? Then what?"

"He will. He doesn't have the fortitude to stand up to me."

"Don't kid yourself. If you back the President of the United States into a corner, he'll be as stubborn as you are."

Popov's eyes burned like black coals of fire. His jaw was tensed, and his fists were clenched. He was a stocky and imposing figure. Sergov matched him in size and exceeded him in battle tested resolve.

"One nuke hits America and Kemp will lose his support," Popov added. "The American people will crumble. They've never been attacked on their own soil. It's time they knew what it feels like."

"Ten nukes will hit Russia for every one you launch at America. You think our economy is bad now, wait until that happens and the entire country is shut down."

"Kemp doesn't have the nerve. He'll fold like a cheap fedora."

"I've met him. He does have the will."

"I've met him, too. He's all talk and no action."

"That's a risk you cannot take."

"I have to do something. He made me look like a fool when he sabotaged our missiles."

Sergov turned to his new chief military advisor who had replaced the general in charge of the botched missile launch. "Did you find the people who did this?"

"Not yet,"

"I want them found!"

"They're out of the country by now," Sergov said. "If not, what if they do the same thing to our nuclear weapons? What would happen if you launched a nuclear weapon at one of our cities? You feel like a fool now, you'd be the laughingstock of the world."

"It won't happen," the advisor said. "Our nuclear weapons are well guarded."

"Better to be thought of as a fool, than to act and prove it's so," Sergov grumbled.

He could practically see the steam coming out of Popov's ears.

"Enough!" Popov said. "I've made my decision. I want thirty nukes armed and each one aimed at an American city."

Sergov grimaced and let out a moan.

Popov noticed and was furious.

"Whose side are you on?" he demanded.

"I'm on the side of Russia!"

Sergov decided he needed to match the President's anger.

"Russia will be destroyed," Sergov shouted from across the table. "It cannot happen."

"We will rebuild her," Popov said. "We've done it in the past and we can do it again."

The tension was as thick inside as the fog outside.

"I will not stand by and let you lead us down the road to destruction," Sergov said.

Popov's eyes widened at the threat. "What are you going to do to stop me?"

Sergov considered pulling his weapon on the spot. Shoot the man and end his miserable existence. That might not be the best approach. Sergov wasn't prepared to fire his weapon. Popov's lackeys weren't willing to get in the middle of the debate, but they'd likely pull their own weapons if Sergov threatened Popov with more than words.

A wise man once told Sergov not to aim a gun unless he intended to use it. The same could be true about nuclear weapons. Don't arm them if you didn't intend to use them.

He couldn't stop that from happening. They would be armed. What happened next was still up in the air.

Despite the bravado, Popov didn't want nuclear war. He didn't want to fire the weapons. He thought Kemp would be the one who backed down when the time came. Not a risk worth taking. Sergov had to keep making his case. Hoping against hope that Popov listened to reason.

"Listen to me, my friend," Sergov said, trying to lower the volume in the room. "Remember Cuba."

"I too am a student of history, my friend," Popov said, matching his tone. "Khrushchev was an idiot. He never should've given in to Kennedy's demands."

The general consensus in Russia was that the Americans got the best of Russians in that situation. Khrushchev never fully recovered. That might be why Sergov was so adamant now. He didn't want to go down the same path of humiliation.

"He averted war," Sergov said.

"Had those missiles remained in Cuba we wouldn't have the problems we're having now. The cold war would've never happened."

"America is no threat to us. It will never attack us unless provoked. Why provoke them?"

"The financial sanctions are a provocation."

"A response to your aggression in the Crimean Region."

"I only want to take back what's rightfully ours."

The tension was rising again.

"The world belongs to the mightiest."

"America is more powerful."

"No one is mightier than the Motherland."

"I agree with you. That's true in spirit. Not in weapons."

"I intend to bring America to its knees. It's the only way," Popov said. "Prepare the missiles. I will give Kemp an ultimatum. He knows now that I'm serious. I fired the two missiles, so he knows I will fire the nukes."

"He won't give in."

"You watch and see. He will."

"And if he doesn't?"

"I will rain fire down on America. I will put it in its place, once and for all."

Sergov stood to his feet and walked out of the room.

He had some hard decisions to make.

42

White House War Room

A spirited debate had broken out.

Ryan delivered the news to the President that Russia was arming their nuclear warheads and preparing for a launch.

President Kemp believed Sergov was bluffing.

"What if he's not?" Ryan said. "Then what?"

"We'll cross that bridge when we come to it," President Kemp replied.

"Once a missile is launched, you have thirty minutes," Ryan argued. "That's how long it takes for it to travel to the U.S. Ten to fifteen minutes if it's launched from a nuclear submarine closer to our shore."

"Sergov won't do it. He doesn't have the guts."

"Are you willing to risk the lives of fifty million Americans?"

The President had asked for a damage assessment. That's the best estimate Ryan could give him.

"John F. Kennedy didn't back down in the Cuban Missile Crisis. The Russians did."

"After he negotiated with them."

"I don't negotiate with terrorists."

"Kennedy made concessions. He removed our missiles from Cuba and Turkey. After he reached an agreement with Khrushchev to remove the missiles from Cuba."

"Kennedy set up the blockade. And he risked nuclear war to do it. What if the Russians hadn't given in? Those missiles might still be pointed at us. Eighty miles from our shoreline."

"That's my point. It didn't really matter. The missiles are pointed at us now. They were then. The only difference was that they would take longer to get to our shore. The destruction would be the same either way."

"Are you saying that Kennedy shouldn't have demanded that the Russians remove their missiles?"

"I'm not saying that. Kennedy did the right thing by drawing a line in the sand. All I'm saying is that he gave Khrushchev a way to save face. A way to back down without it seeming like he was defeated."

"He was defeated. He lost that battle. Russia lost the Cold War. They cannot afford to go to war with the United States."

"That's true. But you have to consider the stakes. You can't play games with nuclear weapons like they are a hand of Texas hold 'em."

President Kemp frowned like he was annoyed at Ryan. He usually didn't mind dissent, but Ryan could tell he was pushing the President's buttons. If he continued to press him, he was in danger of forcing the President to dig in his heels.

"I've looked Popov in the eye and he's weak," Kemp said. "He doesn't have the backbone. He knows we can annihilate him off the face of the earth."

"Yeah but fifty million Americans won't be around to see it."

Ryan wanted to keep throwing that number out. Hopefully, cooler heads would prevail when they considered the actual cost. Too often, world leaders saw the world as a chess board. With pieces to play. That's fine when it doesn't involve nuclear weapons.

"I've already decided. The buck stops with me. It's my decision."

"I'm not saying it's not," Ryan said. "But why not take the prudent approach and negotiate an end to the sanctions."

"I told Popov I'd remove the sanctions if he moved his troops out of the Crimean region and stops his aggression."

"He's not going to do that."

"Then I'm not going to remove the sanctions."

"That's a mistake."

"Noted."

Ryan knew he had lost the argument. Not that you can win an argument with the President of the United States. He was the Commander in Chief. The buck did stop with him. The fate of the American people was in his hands.

This was dangerous stuff. Not like a couple of school high schoolers playing chicken on a drag strip. This was real life. Real nuclear weapons. A wrong decision and people died.

Ryan stared at the briefcase full of nuclear codes. The football as it was called. The codes were changed daily. To launch an attack, the President would first confirm his identity by verifying the codes. He carried with him at all times a plastic card with the codes on it. The card was nicknamed the biscuit.

The launch codes to the missiles were not what people thought they were. They were actually there for one purpose. To confirm the President's identity. When he notified his commanders with orders to launch, they verified the day's codes, so they'd know it was a legitimate order from the actual Commander in Chief.

Someone somewhere envisioned a scenario where a hacker could impersonate the President and order a launch. Unlikely, but one more safeguard in place.

Once the codes were confirmed an EAM, Emergency Action Message, was sent through the system. With launch plan, targets, and timing of the launch specified. ICBM crews could launch within sixty seconds. Submarines within twelve minutes.

Time was of the essence in a nuclear confrontation. Our missiles needed to land in Russia before theirs landed in the U.S. Only a slight advantage in Ryan's mind.

The red phone rang causing everyone in the room to jump, including the President. The direct line between Russia and the U.S had been activated. That could only mean one thing. Popov was calling the President.

Kemp answered the phone in a confrontive tone.

"You need to disarm those nukes and I mean now."

Not how Ryan would've started the conversation. Diplomacy would've been a better strategy rather than raising the rhetoric right from the start.

"Ah. I see your intelligence community is serving you well," Popov said. The call was on speaker so all the advisors could hear it. "Have they told you how many I have armed?"

Kemp didn't answer.

"I didn't think so," Popov said mockingly. "Thirty. That's how many I'll start with."

"Why are you telling me this?"

"So you'll know I am serious. I intend to launch thirty missiles at the United States at a time and place of my choosing."

Ryan felt chills go all the way down his spine to his toes.

"You'll never do it," Kemp said.

"Don't test me. You will regret it. Remove the sanctions or I will do it."

"Remove your troops from Crimea and the surrounding regions and I will lift the financial sanctions."

"Who made you the ruler of the world? What do you care? You're thousands of miles away from Crimea. What business is it of yours? What's a few hundred thousand acres of deplorable land to you?"

"What is it to you?"

"It belongs to me."

"Are you Russia now? Are you so drunk with power that you think everything belongs to you?"

Popov sounded slightly drunk and slurred his words. That made Ryan feel even worse. If that was possible. Nuclear weapons in the hands of a madman was bad enough. A drunken despot was America's worst nightmare.

"Do not provoke me," Popov said. "I might wipe out your cities just for the fun of it." He laughed heartily.

"I'm not lifting the sanctions."

"Then America will burn like hell."

President Kemp hung up the phone. He pulled out the biscuit and handed it to his joint chief of staff.

"Prepare to launch our nuclear weapons. We need to talk about whether or not to do it preemptively."

"Are you sure you want to do this?" Ryan said.

"Confirm the codes," Kemp said.

The briefcase was opened and the codes on the card confirmed what we already knew. The President was who he said he was. Given the power over life and death by the American people and the Constitution.

Even if he was wrong.

"He said he was launching thirty nukes," President Kemp said, "prepare to launch ninety."

"We should get everyone to a bunker," someone said.

They stood and left the room.

Ryan stayed behind. He'd join them later. He picked up the phone and called Brad to fill him in on what was happening with instructions on what to do. Then called his wife and told her to get the kids and go somewhere safe. Not that there was such a place.

This really is happening.

43

Hanoi, Vietnam

Kaley sensed something was off the moment she walked into the offices of Nguyen Ai, the man who leased the building to Pok. The offices were opulent. Extravagant even. Not what she expected in a country where the average worker made the equivalent of $750.00 a month and nearly half the population made $135.00 a month or less.

Nguyen Ai owned a building, so Kaley expected him to be wealthier, but the offices were something she might see in Manhattan. Small, but extravagantly furnished. On the modern and expensive desk was a large coffee mug with the middle finger staring at her along with a saying, *I am a big deal.*

The mug that was his face was as smug as the mug on the table.

Kaley fought back a smile for coming up with the play on words in her head.

She didn't want to smile. What she really wanted to do was lean across the table and slap the smirk off his face. Which also had a lustful look occasionally, which sickened her.

Jamie looked it up and found that the surname Ai meant mugwort and originated in China. That's what they'd been calling him for the last twenty-four hours.

That's about all they found out about the man. They'd tried to research him but found that forty percent of the people in Vietnam were named Nguyen. Either first name or last. Trying to sort through and find this Nguyen Ai would've taken too much time and effort.

Kaley made a conscious effort not to call him Mugwort to his face.

Focus.

She had a job to do. Jamie was counting on her, and she wasn't going to screw it up. She was there to buy the building. Get in and out without Mugwort getting suspicious. Under no circumstances was she to walk out of there without a deal. Even if she had to pay a billion dollars.

Kaley wanted to show Jamie her negotiating prowess by offering him fair market value. Five hundred thousand U.S. dollars. She studied him carefully to see his reaction. Mugwort was as stone faced as a professional poker player sitting at a card table.

"I already have a lease with a tenant," Mugwort said.

"Ah yes. Mr. Pok," Kaley said for the shock effect.

Mugwort didn't flinch. Nothing in his face confirmed or denied Pok was the person leasing the building. The man obviously intended to play things close to the vest. Not unexpected. Kaley was an American calling out of the blue. He'd obviously be curious if not suspicious.

"I can't break my lease for many years," Mugwort said. "Even if I wanted to. Which I don't."

Time to throw a figurative grenade into the negotiations.

"I have reason to believe that Pok is running illegal activities out of that building. The lease states that you can cancel it at any time for cause."

Mugwort's eyes widened slightly. Probably because he was wondering how Kaley knew about the terms of the lease.

"I'm not aware of any illegal activities."

"I have proof."

"I'm not interested."

"Perhaps the authorities will be."

"I doubt it."

If Mugwort was concerned about the threat, he didn't show it in his demeanor. That tactic obviously wasn't going to go anywhere.

So Kaley got back to discussing price where she had unlimited leverage. "Like I said, I'm willing to pay you fair market value for the building."

"The building is worth twice what you are offering."

Kaley wasn't sure whether or not to take that as a negotiation or dismissiveness.

"I'm authorized to pay that price."

"The building is not for sale."

"Okay. Let's cut to the chase. You name your price."

"I'm sorry you wasted a trip. I'm not interested in selling at any price."

That's when it hit her. The fancy offices. The expensive diamond ring on Mugwort's hand. The expensive painting on the wall. The smugness. Pok was paying him more than fair market value for the lease. A kickback under the table. Likely in the millions to look the other way.

Mugwort didn't flinch when she mentioned the illegal activities because he was involved in them as well.

Even then, everybody had a price. She'd have to offer him an outrageous sum. Something she knew was more than Pok was paying him.

"I'll give you one hundred million American dollars for it," Kaley blurted. "Payable upon signing the lease."

He laughed. "You don't have a hundred million dollars."

"If we agree on the price, the money will be in your account this afternoon."

"Where does a little girl like you get that kind of money?"

You won't think I'm a little girl when I smack you across the side of your head.

Kaley bit her lip to keep from saying the words. Jamie said not to resort to violence unless she had no other choice. She also had authority to go up to a billion dollars. Two billion even, which seemed outrageous.

Jamie had verified the five billion dollars was in their accounts. Not for long which was why time was of the essence.

If Mugwort accepted the offer of a hundred million, it might score some points with Jamie. Maybe not. The amount was two hundred times the fair market value. Kaley suddenly felt foolish that she had to go that high.

Not that it mattered. As soon as Pok was out of the building, Alex could take the money out of Mugwort's account and give him back his building, if the amount was clearly outrageous. If it was reasonable, Jamie said she'd let him keep it.

At the moment, it didn't look like any amount of money, outrageous or not, was going to get Mugwort to sell the building. He was either afraid of Pok or was his best friend. Impossible to say at this point.

"A hundred million dollars is a lot of money," Kaley said. "You didn't get to be the successful businessman you are by turning down free money."

She thought she'd appeal to his ego. Nothing else was working.

"Like I said, the building is not for sale at any price."

Kaley was convinced Mugwort was into his own illegal activities. He couldn't sell. She didn't know what they were, but he was as dirty as Pok.

"Make it two hundred million."

"Not interested."

The middle finger on the cup seemed larger by the minute. Mugwort might as well have been making the gesture himself.

Jamie would not be happy with her.

"Why do you want the building so badly?" Mugwort asked out of the blue.

"I have a business. The building is ideal for what I have in mind."

"What kind of business?"

"Why does it matter? I thought the building wasn't available."

"Only curious. If I were to sell to you, I wouldn't want any illegal activities going on in one of my buildings."

Mugwort smirked as he said it. Clearly pleased at having the opportunity to jerk her chain.

"So will you accept my price?"

"No."

"Five hundred million."

Mugwort looked away disinterested. Why would a man turn down half a billion dollars for a building worth five hundred thousand?

Because he knew he'd never see it. Pok had warned him. Maybe offered him more than whatever we offered. Or told him not to take our money because we'd steal it back. Whatever the reason, Mugwort was definitely not interested. Kaley was wasting her time.

"Fine," Kaley said, angrily. "We could've done this the easy way. Instead, we'll do it the hard way. Give me the password to the security system and the key to the front door."

Mugwort looked over at a filing cabinet. Then caught himself. That's where he kept the information and he realized he'd given it away.

Kaley looked that way as well to see if there was a lock on the cabinet. When she looked back, Mugwort had reached under the table and pulled a gun out from under it. It was now pointed right at her.

A satisfied grin on his face was also intended for her.

44

"You're making a big mistake," Kaley said to Mugwort. He had a gun pointed at her. "You should've taken the money. Now I'm going to have to kill you."

"Mr. Pok called me yesterday and warned me about you."

Bingo. Her instinct was right. Pok had been a step ahead of them. After the money went missing from his accounts, he covered all the bases. He had to know Jamie would be coming after him. Kaley wondered what other preparations he'd made.

"What did Pok say?"

"He told me to kill you."

"That's not a good idea. My associate is right outside the door. You fire that gun and she'll kill you before you can blink twice."

"Ahh... The blonde woman. Mr. Pok said you'd have blonde hair. That's why I was confused. That's why I haven't killed you yet. I was curious. I wasn't sure who you were."

"If Pok told you about the blonde woman, he probably told you how dangerous she is."

He nodded. "He called her the most lethal female assassin on the planet."

"And I'm the second most lethal. So I'd suggest you put down that gun and accept my hundred million dollar offer before I put a bullet in your head."

He laughed again. "Strong words coming from someone with a gun pointed at them. You make so much as a twitch of a muscle, and I'll open fire and you'll be dead."

Kaley wondered why he hadn't already done so. There had to be a reason. Maybe a continuation of the negotiation. Mugwort could've shut it down earlier. But he kept it going for the sport of it. Like he was enjoying it. He seemed to be relishing in what he thought was the upper hand.

Clearly thinking he had the advantage. Which he did. He could kill her in one second. It'd take her at least three seconds to reach for her gun, draw it, aim, and fire.

Kaley tried to keep a cool and confident manner, even though her heart was beating out of her chest. This was what it felt like to have a gun pointed at her. She'd been wondering since she began her CIA training.

She thought it'd be exhilarating. Fun even. It was neither of those things. Her life and career could end before it ever started. The only consolation was that he hadn't shot her yet. As long as they were talking it meant she was still breathing.

Kaley was kicking herself for not noticing his hands and not considering the possibility that he might have a gun and the will to use it. Whether he had the will or not was still to be determined. She wasn't convinced he'd pull the trigger unless provoked. She could roll to the ground and out of the line of fire, but he'd still have the advantage. The best thing to do was let it play out.

Then Mugwort made a mistake.

"Here's what we're going to do," he said. "You're going to slowly take out your gun and put it on the desk."

Kaley couldn't believe her luck. The odds tilted in her favor by a considerable margin. Once the gun was in her hand, she could maneuver it and shoot within one second.

Probably.

If she performed the maneuver Jamie taught her correctly. Simply a matter of lifting the gun by the palm of her hand and not by the handle. Flipping it so her finger was on the trigger. Then firing.

She'd practiced it dozens of times at the Farm. The more she was in the field, the more she appreciated Jamie's attention to detail. Making her perform the move over and over again until she had perfected it.

It might save her life.

The gun was in the front of her pants. Another training point. *Never keep your gun in the back of your pants. Too hard to reach and bring around to the front of your body in time to aim and fire quickly.* Jamie's instructions were clear.

"Slowly," Mugwort said as Kaley's hand lifted her shirt. She palmed the gun and began to lift it forward. Gripping it from the top. The barrel pointed at herself. Mugwort couldn't see her finger sliding toward the trigger.

With the barrel facing away from him, he wouldn't be concerned. He had no clue what was coming.

"Put it on the desk," he said.

Perfect.

She could lean forward. The movement caused a distraction. Too many things happening at once for Mugwort to notice all of them. He stared at the gun and not her eyes. Another mistake.

Kaley knew now why Jamie said to always keep your focus on the enemy's eyes. They'd give away his intentions. You'd see when he was going to fire before he did.

This slowed down the process for him. He'd have to shift his eyes to fire. A natural tendency. To zero in on the target first.

Kaley took in an imperceivable breath to steady her nerves. Envisioned things in her mind.

Then acted.

With lightning speed.

She flipped the gun so it was pointed at Mugwort. His eyes widened in surprise when he looked up at her.

Too late.

One shot.

To the forehead. Mugwort slumped in his chair and the gun fell harmlessly to the floor.

The exhilaration did come. It felt good. She executed the maneuver exactly like Jamie taught her.

Kaley was to her feet in a flash and walked over to the file cabinet. She hadn't lied. Jamie was right outside the door. As expected, Jamie burst through the door seconds later. With her gun drawn.

"All clear," Kaley said.

Jamie looked at Mugwort and his lifeless body, then at Kaley, then at Mugwort again. Assessing the situation.

A frown came over her face, but she didn't say anything.

Jamie walked over to the window and looked out clearly to see if anyone was out there who might've heard the gunshot. She closed the curtains. Then went back to the door and looked down the hallway. Probably for the same reason. If she saw anyone she didn't mention it.

Once back inside the office she looked around the room. First the ceilings, then around Mugwort's desk and bookcase.

"What are you doing?"

"Looking for hidden cameras. I wouldn't put it past Pok to bug the place."

"Oh. I didn't see cameras."

"They could be as small as a pencil head."

Kaley didn't respond. She had the file in her hand now and confirmed it had the spare key and password to the security system in it.

"What happened?" Jamie asked, still obviously nervous.

"He didn't agree to our price."

"So you killed him?"

Kaley didn't like her accusatory tone.

"I didn't have a choice. He had a gun pointed at me. Right over there."

Kaley pointed to a spot next to the body where the gun had fallen to the floor.

Jamie walked around the desk and looked at it, as if she wasn't going to take Kaley's word for it.

"He was as dirty as Pok," Kaley said.

"I figured by the looks of this office."

Kaley knew what Jamie was thinking and decided to set her mind at ease.

"Don't worry, Jamie. I have the key and the password to the security camera. Right here." She waved the file in the air.

"Hopefully, those are them."

"They are."

"Unless Pok changed the locks and the security code."

"I don't think he has."

"Tell me everything the man said."

"Pok warned him that a blonde girl might come. Mugwort was expecting you."

"I'm not surprised. That's what I mean. Pok knew I would come after stealing the money. He'll be ready for us."

"I'll figure a way in."

"Let's get out of here before someone comes," Jamie said.

She still watched the door nervously. We surveilled the area before Kaley went inside the offices and determined no one else was around but that didn't mean someone couldn't show up.

"Did you touch anything?" Jamie was wiping down the doorknob with a handkerchief.

"Only this file cabinet."

She cleaned it off as well.

"Let's go."

They drove over to Pok's building and scoped it out. Waited until dark to act. The computer operation center closed down at dusk as well and Jamie wanted the building cleared before Kaley attempted to enter it.

While they were waiting, Jamie said, "Don't get used to killing people."

"I won't."

"I'm serious. Sometimes it's easier to kill somebody than to work the problem."

"I was working the problem. But he had a gun."

Jamie held up her hand.

"I'm not saying you did anything wrong. You always have the right to defend yourself. But what if we couldn't find the key and passcode? Then what would we have done? Mugwort was dead. Keeping him alive would've been better if at all possible."

"I thought the same thing. That's what I would've done if I thought it were possible."

"Okay. I'll take your word for it."

"I hear you. Don't get used to killing people. I'll keep that in mind the next time."

"No. Forget what I said for the next few minutes."

"What do you mean?"

Jamie had a mischievous smile on her face.

"The next person you kill is going to be Pok. Don't hesitate. If you see him, put a bullet somewhere in his body. Don't ask questions. Don't negotiate. Don't try to take him prisoner. I want him dead."

"You got it."

"Are you ready?"

The building was clear, and the sun was down.

Kaley was ready.

"Don't be careful," Jamie said as Kaley walked away and emerged from the shadows.

"I won't."

45

Kaley memorized the layout of Pok's building and knew where to go once she was inside. Jamie spent the last two hours going through various scenarios, so Kaley was as prepared as she was going to be.

The walkway leading up to the building was well lit. It didn't matter. Pok knew she was coming. He might've thought Jamie would be the one approaching the door and be temporarily confused. That'd give Kaley an ever-so-slight advantage.

He may not know she had the key and password to the security system, but he might think something was up if he tried to contact Mugwort and he didn't answer. Pok should've left then. They didn't know for sure he hadn't, other than the lights going on and off in his suite.

If Pok was still in the building, he must feel pretty good about his security situation and believe Jamie had no way to penetrate it. He was in for a big surprise if the key worked.

A big if. The scumbag still had the advantage. He might've had time to change the locks and security codes. If he did, then Kaley wasn't sure what they'd do. Jamie didn't know either. Probably try to make contact with Alex and regroup. Even if Kaley did get inside the building, it didn't mean she could get inside his living quarters.

Pok had a safe room. Rather, a safe suite. His entire living area was behind a secured set of double doors. Presumed to be fortified with steel although they hadn't seen them. He would've been better off constructing one large steel door which gave Jamie and Kaley a ray of hope. She carried a small explosive device strong enough to break open the two doors at their weakest point.

It had to work. The explosives weren't strong enough to break through the six inch thick concrete walls.

Kaley smiled for the camera as she walked up to the door.

Getting in the building surreptitiously wasn't possible. A hundred security cameras and motion detectors were attached at strategic locations around the building. At least it seemed like a hundred. Probably more like a dozen, although they hadn't counted them. The roof might've been a possible source of entry, but they had no way to get on top of it without being seen.

"Fort Knox wasn't any stronger fortified than this place," Jamie had quipped. She'd been surprised Pok didn't have armed guards out front. That's how confident he was in the structure.

Once Kaley had given Pok an ample opportunity to see her approach the door, she aimed her gun and put a bullet through the lens of the security camera. Only for effect. Pok would already be nervous. That might shake him to his core and cause him to do something stupid. Like try to escape through a side door. Jamie was guarding the only other exit. Along the side wall.

If Pok so much as stuck his head out that door, she intended to shoot it off.

Kaley hoped that didn't happen. It'd be safer for her if it did, but she wanted to prove something to Jamie. Even to herself. This was a high level mission to kill a high value target. Pok had caused Alex and Jamie a lot of heartache over the years.

Kaley would like nothing more than to be the one who put the bullet between his eyes. She could already feel the satisfaction of the kill. Like a trophy hunter bagging his first big game on a safari.

For the first time, Kaley felt like a real CIA operative. In a foreign country. In a dangerous situation. Rescuing the girls from the prison in Russia and sabotaging the missiles were technically her first missions. But those happened so fast. She hardly had time to process it all.

She'd had nearly forty-eight hours to think about this moment.

Panic came over her when she inserted the key in the lock, and it didn't work. She jiggled it slightly and let out a huge exhale when it opened. Pok didn't change the locks. Either didn't know to, or didn't have time.

Kaley stepped two steps away from the open door in case it was booby trapped.

She put the key in her pocket and raised her weapon, holding it out in front of her with both hands. Using her foot, she kicked the door open.

Then waited. For what, she didn't know.

Once she was satisfied the coast was clear, she entered the building cautiously. Pointing the gun in every direction, prepared to pull the trigger at the slightest sign of trouble.

The door opened into a set of hallways. The one to her right led to the computer building. To the left was the hallway that led to the double doors and Pok's personal residence.

Both hallways were well lit. Several security cameras were attached to the walls in both directions. Kaley put bullets in each of them.

Feeling more confident, she made her way to the two double doors and put a bullet through the camera attached to the doorbell. After pushing it a couple of times.

"I have a delivery for Mr. Pok," Kaley said mockingly, figuring it also had an intercom and Pok could hear her.

She wrapped her hand with her shirt and touched the doorknob to see if it might be booby trapped in some way. Satisfied it wasn't, she turned the handle. As expected, it was locked.

She took a couple of minutes to examine the door. Fabricated from sixteen to twenty-two-gauge steel. Armored multi-point locking system. Drill resistant. Something like what you might see in a bank vault.

Jamie was trained to pick it, but it'd take her thirty minutes or longer. Jamie had estimated it had twenty or more locking points. Kaley could pick normal locks but nothing this sophisticated.

So she took out the explosives and attached them to the door. Once attached, she scurried down the hall and took shelter around the corner and put her fingers in her ears after pushing the detonation button.

Her feet vibrated from the explosion even though she was several feet away. Rather than wait until the smoke cleared, she was down the hall and through the open door, which swung by its hinges, like a cat being chased by a dog.

Even though she had covered her ears, they were still ringing from the concussion.

All the lights in the suite suddenly went off. The only light came from the hallway. Those went off shortly after she entered the suite leaving her in complete darkness. The windows were all covered. It was dark out anyway.

Kaley pulled out her phone and turned on the flashlight and began to clear each room.

No sign of Pok.

The suite was roughly three thousand square feet. Modestly furnished, considering the amount of money Pok had at his disposal.

Still no Pok after going through the entire suite.

Kaley stomped her feet in disgust. He must've left. Maybe the lights were on a timer to fool them into thinking he was there.

A sound came from the other room.

Kaley stopped to listen. All she could hear was her heavy breathing. Was Pok still there? Had Mugwort warned him in time for him to flee? It seemed like he wasn't.

Another noise.

Some kind of door opening and closing.

Faint, but discernible.

Kaley moved cautiously toward the room where she'd heard the sound. The flashlight in one hand, her gun in the other. The sound came from the laundry room. She entered cautiously. Pok wasn't there the first time she looked. But she definitely heard a sound. He had been hiding somewhere.

There had to be some kind of hidden door in the room. Kaley ran her hands along the wall. Finding nothing, she pulled the laundry cabinet out from against the wall which was hard to do since it was attached.

Her heart skipped a beat.

As she suspected. There was a hidden door behind it.

He can't get away.

She couldn't face Jamie and tell her.

The other side of the door led to a stairwell. Going down. That surprised her. The building was on the ground level. The plans didn't show an underground structure.

The clear sound of footsteps on the metal stairs caused her to spring into action. Kaley bounded down the steps taking two at a time. After four levels, she reached the bottom and found another locked door.

Pok had obviously taken tremendous precautions. She didn't have any more explosives, but several bullets disintegrated the lock and the door swung open. She saved a few bullets for Pok. She had another magazine on her but didn't want to take the time to reload.

Kaley pushed through the door and found herself in a dark tunnel. Fortified by walls on the side but not lit. It had lights but they weren't on. Pok had obviously turned off the power to his suite and to the tunnel. So he could escape.

She held her breath and listened. Nothing.

She took a couple of steps down the tunnel. Without the flashlight on her phone, she wouldn't have been able to see her hand in front of her face. Even with the phone, she could only see a few steps ahead of her.

What was at the end? She didn't have a clue but had a bad feeling about it.

Was it a trap?

Did Pok have a gun? Of course he did. He had the advantage. He could have night vision goggles. He could simply wait at the end of the tunnel and fill her with lead when she rounded a corner.

Did she have enough time to clear the tunnel properly? Probably not. If she wanted to have any chance of catching Pok, she had to sprint down the tunnel. If she was too cautious, it'd take her too long to get to the end. Not that she knew where the end was or how long it'd take her to find it.

Should she go back?

Jamie's words rang in her ears which were still throbbing from the gunshots bouncing off the walls in the close quarters and the earlier explosion.

Don't be careful, Jamie said to her, in no uncertain terms.

Kaley still didn't understand the saying. It didn't make sense and she didn't have time to analyze it.

What she did know was that capturing Pok was a priority. So was getting out of this alive. She shouldn't go running into the dark not knowing what lay ahead.

Indecision struck her.

Hesitation will get you killed as well, Jamie said.

Kaley's first instinct was to go back to the entrance and tell Jamie about the tunnel. The safest thing to do. They could track Pok on the outside. He was in the open. Unprotected. They could find him. The goal was to get him out of his lair. Kaley had done that.

But it still felt like a failure.

Her job was to kill Pok. He got away. Not yet, but was about to. If she continued down the tunnel, maybe she could still catch him.

Maybe she could die.

46

Don't be careful, Jamie shouted in her head. *How many times do I have to tell you?*

The words were so loud, it sounded like Jamie was standing right behind her.

The impetus she needed.

Kaley sprinted down the tunnel with no regard for her safety. The floor was uneven, and she prayed she wouldn't break an ankle.

The tunnel took several turns. Fortunately, it had no forks to choose from. It led her to the end where she found a ladder attached to the wall, going up to what looked like a manhole cover at the top.

Not a good situation.

Not when the enemy had the high ground.

Hesitation struck her again. Pok could be at the top ready to blast her with gunfire. The cover could be locked. She'd lose valuable time having to backtrack.

He already had time to get away. If she'd gone back when she first thought of it, they might've had time to catch Pok. Now he had a head start.

Don't be careful, Jamie said in her head for the umpteenth time.

Enough already. I heard you the first time.

Apparently not. Since you're still doing it.

"Oh for heaven's sake," Kaley said and started climbing the ladder. When she got to the top, she pushed on the manhole cover, and it moved. It had a lock dangling from the inside. She pushed it all the way open. Then stuck her head out to get a feel for the surroundings.

She heard another noise.

Pok?

She pulled herself out of the hole. In a precarious situation for several seconds as she needed her hands for balance. If Pok was hiding with a gun, she was dead.

Once Kaley was standing, she blinked several times to get her bearings. The moon provided some light. It cast eerie shadows in every direction. Ahead was a cluster of trees. Kaley looked right, then left. Didn't see anything. The noise probably came from the trees.

Pok couldn't be far. He didn't have as big a head start as she had imagined. But if he'd gone to all the trouble to build a tunnel, he likely had a vehicle hidden somewhere. She had to get there first.

Kaley sprinted toward the trees which were thirty or so yards away from the tunnel exit.

She came to a sliding halt when a dark figure emerged from the shadows.

Kaley raised her weapon, but couldn't fire until she identified the person.

He was taller. Definitely not Pok. She could be pointing her gun at an innocent man who happened to be in the wrong place at the wrong time.

She still couldn't see his face.

A familiar voice said, "Kaley, don't shoot! It's Alex."

What is Alex doing here?

She lowered her weapon and walked toward him. As she got closer, his face came into focus. While she was thrilled to see him, there was no time for pleasantries.

"Pok got away," she said, breathing hard. "I'm not sure which direction he went. We have to find him, or Jamie will kill me."

Kaley turned back toward the building.

"There's a tunnel," she added, pointing in that direction "Pok came out of the building and I assume he ran into the woods."

"Pok didn't get away," Alex said. "We caught him."

Kaley felt her mouth fly open.

"You knew about the tunnel?"

"Yep. We knew. That's why I needed you and Jamie. To flush him out. I figured if you didn't get him on the inside, we'd get him out here. That's how it turned out. Good job."

"Jamie's guarding the front entrance."

"I know. We've been in touch. I'll call her and tell her it's all clear and that Pok is in our custody."

At that moment, the earth trembled.

A flash brightened the sky.

Alex grabbed Kaley and threw her to the ground, then fell on top of her as an explosion shook the ground beneath them. Alex was a big man and was crushing her.

An explosion.

Debris rained down along with burning embers. Kaley stuck her head up. It looked like a fireworks display. Alex pushed her head back down.

He took the brunt of the fallout and let out a yelp.

A few seconds later, he pulled her to her feet.

"Run," he said. "For the woods."

When she got to the safety of the treeline, Kaley looked back. The building was engulfed in flames. A series of explosions caused the entire building to collapse.

"Pok boobytrapped it," Alex said, shaking his head from side to side as they observed the destruction. "He got rid of all the evidence."

"Yes he did. What a lowlife? I could've been killed. Thank you."

"I need to let Jamie know you're okay," Alex said. "That you weren't in the building when the explosion happened."

Kaley nodded.

Then it hit her. She put her hand to her forehead.

Alex didn't notice. He was on his phone. Calling Jamie.

Don't be careful. Careful will get you killed.

Jamie's words were seared into her psyche.

Had Kaley turned back when she was thinking about it, instead of going forward, she *would've* been in the explosion.

Careful would've gotten her killed.

It suddenly made sense.

Epilogue

Preeda Regional Airport
Thailand

We arrived in Thailand without incident. A-Rad, Bond, Kaley, Alex, and me. With Pok in tow. We thought about killing Pok a dozen times on the way from Vietnam to the Thai airport, but Brad talked Alex into bringing him to America where he'd be put on trial and placed in a maximum-security prison for the rest of his life.

With no access to a computer.

The closest thing to hell on earth for a man like Pok who lived and breathed computer hacking. Codes. Firewalls and how to breach them. Brad's argument for keeping Pok alive was that his knowledge might someday be useful to the CIA as they continued to fight the ongoing threat in North Korea, where Pok was born and raised.

After Brad personally assured Alex that Pok would never see the outside of a prison cell, he reluctantly agreed to bring Pok back with us.

Our trip to the U.S. was delayed a couple of days because of the Russian Missile Crisis which had put a halt to most of the travel in the world. So we holed up in a hotel while we waited for Brad to tell us it was safe to come home.

The call finally came. According to Brad, Russia and America were within fifteen minutes of launching nukes at each other. We'd been watching it on the news, and Brad had been giving us behind the scenes information we weren't getting on the networks.

Cooler heads prevailed and a twenty-four hour ceasefire was called. Ironically enough, Russian President Popov passed away during that time. Supposedly from natural causes, although Brad believed he was likely poisoned.

Whether providence or a subversive act, Ryan and Brad were beyond relieved that a tragedy of global proportions had been averted. As were we. I couldn't imagine living in a world where nuclear weapons had been launched en masse.

We were given the all-clear to return home and a spirited discussion had broken out at the airport. Between A-Rad and Bond. They were arguing about who was going to fly back on the smaller jet with Kaley.

"I'll go," Bond said.

He flashed a lustful smile at her. He'd been hitting on her nonstop for the last two days. Typical Bond. I was used to it. Kaley seemed to be holding her own, so I didn't get in the middle of it.

She'd have to get used to it as well.

I recommended to Brad that he bring Kaley into the CIA. I was all in on her. She was going to be a terrific operative. Better than me in time.

Kaley and I talked about her experience in the building. How she finally understood the whole "Don't Be Careful," mantra. I was seeing her grow up in front of my eyes. It warmed my heart. Brad said he intended to use her on a lot of AJAX missions. If that was the case, she needed to get a thick skin as soon as possible. She'd be working with A-Rad and Bond alot. So I was letting her fight her own battles.

"Oh no!" A-Rad said emphatically. "I'm not going to leave you alone with Kaley for eighteen hours."

"Bollocks," Bond said. "It's not up to you. She should be able to decide who she wants to go with her."

A-Rad turned to Kaley. Bond tried to shove him away. They jostled for position.

"Kaley, who do you want to come with you?" A-Rad said. "Me or this idiot? Pick me. Pick me."

"I have an accent," Bond said in his most British drawl. "Every woman finds Brits irresistible."

Kaley looked my way and our eyes met. I rolled my eyes and she smiled. The tension made her uncomfortable, but she was clearly finding the whole spectacle amusing as well.

The two men were acting like a couple of teenagers in heat. I'd seen this rodeo many times. The guys fought all the time. It was endearing, although it'd never been over a girl.

A-Rad was clearly being protective of Kaley. Bond was being his usual obnoxious self.

I really didn't care. Alex and I were flying back on the big jet. Where we had our own room. Colonel would fly us. A-Rad could as well. Kaley wasn't licensed for the big jet. Bond could easily help Kaley. Or Colonel for that matter.

In reality, everyone was tired and ready to get home. We'd all probably sleep most of the way. It had been my idea to split up, so we had two pilots in each plane. I should've just told them who was in each plane, but hadn't realized it'd be a problem. A-Rad would've been my choice. They were closer to the same age.

I didn't want to fly home with Kaley, which was probably the best thing for her. I was looking forward to being alone with Alex. The hotel only had two available rooms. So the guys were in one, and the girls in the other. I hadn't had a moment alone with Alex since I saw him for the first time at Pok's building. After the explosion.

I intended on giving him a lot of mile-high pleasure. Thinking he was dead had sent desire pulsing through my body like someone had turned on a firehose.

Before that could happen, I needed to resolve the argument between A-Rad and Bond. Before it became even more heated.

Kaley's cheeks were bright red. She was embarrassed. They were both in her face. Pressuring her.

"I don't know," she said, hemming and hawing. Rocking back and forth on her feet. Not making eye contact with either of them. "I can't decide. I don't want to have to choose. Please don't make me."

Kaley looked over at me for help. I knew what she was thinking. She was trying to fit in with the team. Afraid she was going to offend one of them. Privately, I'd tell her to toughen up. Speak her mind or her opinions would get trampled on and dismissed. She needed to assert herself at the very beginning. So they'd respect her.

"A-Rad you go with Kaley," I said.

"Yes!" He slapped his hands together. Then began taunting Bond. Playfully sparring with him. Trying to slap him in the face.

"Why does he get to go with her?" Bond said to me with pleading eyes.

"Because he can help her fly the plane," I said.

"I can fly it too. Besides, it'll be on autopilot most of the time. Right Kaley?"

I shook my head in disbelief that he'd actually say something that lewd.

Bond was all talk. He was a big harmless flirt. He hit on me all the time because he knew nothing would ever come of it. I loved him like a brother. But we'd never had another female member of the team. I didn't know if he was being serious or not.

"A-Rad is right," I said. "No woman should ever be forced to be alone with you for eighteen hours in a confined space. I've had to endure it way too many times."

I flashed him a smile to know I was kidding, even though I wasn't. No way I'd make Kaley endure Bond for eighteen hours unless she gave me an indication that that's what she wanted.

"Ouch," Bond said. He put both hands over his heart. Twisted his face into a grimace. Like I'd stabbed him in the heart with a dagger.

"Trust me, I'd rather you go with her," I said. "So you won't be bugging me."

"You're killing me."

"I'm only kidding."

"How bout we both go with Kaley?" Bond said.

"No way," A-Rad said. "It's decided."

"Bond, you're coming with us," I said. "If you go with them, you and A-Rad will end up killing each other. Either that or Kaley will kill both of you and toss you out of the plane."

They heard about how Kaley tossed one of the brothers out of the plane on the way to Russia. The guys had been impressed.

"If I were going to kill A-Rad," Bond said, "I would've done it by now." He put his arm around him and pulled him close. "We're best mates."

The two were play fighting again.

"It's decided," I said. "Let's get out of here."

A-Rad and Kaley turned to walk to their plane.

"Don't do anything I would do," Bond said to A-Rad, who didn't look back. Only waved.

"I call the pilot's seat," I heard Kaley say, playfully. Clearly this was what she wanted.

"I have seniority," A-Rad said.

"I'll flip you for it."

"Deal."

The whole scene caused me to pause and look back at them. Kaley was giggling. A-Rad had a bounce to his step.

Did I see a spark between them?

We boarded the plane and Alex and I went to our rooms after we were in the air and everyone had settled in. We took turns taking a shower.

When we fell into bed, I said to him, "I think Kaley and A-Rad might like each other."

"I think so too. I saw them in the pool. They were horsing around. Trying to dunk each other. Kind of like we were when we first met on that cruise. Do you remember?"

"How could I forget?"

"I think A-Rad might be smitten. Kaley's a beautiful girl. Inside and out."

"I should've told Kaley to be careful," I said.

Alex laughed. He knew about the whole "Don't be careful" thing between Kaley and me.

"Why?"

My turn to laugh.

"Because not being careful might get you married!"

Not The End

FROM THE AUTHOR

Sorry about the Alex cliff hanger. Not really! Ha, Ha, Ha.

My wife of thirty plus years at the time of this writing is also my editor and beta reader. She reads the manuscript before anyone else. When she came to the part where Brad thinks Alex is dead, she told me, "If Alex dies, we're getting a divorce!"

She was kidding. (I think, anyway)

She also leads a ladies Jamie Austen reading club that meets monthly. She told the ladies about it. They were adamant that Alex can't die. That Jamie has to have a baby. They have to live happily ever after.

That they don't want this series to end.

So we continue on. With more Alex and Jamie adventures. Maybe some Kaley and A-Rad adventures. We'll see.

This book is affectionately dedicated to my wife, Donna, but every book is really dedicated to you, the readers. Without you, these books would not exist either. Thank you for reading them. I love you all, more than you'll ever know.

Terry Toler

Thank you for purchasing this novel from best-selling author, Terry Toler. As an additional thank you, Terry wants to give you a free gift.

Sign up for:
Updates
New Releases
Announcements
At terrytoler.com

We'll send you a copy of *The Book Club*, a Cliff Hangers mystery, free of charge.

READ MORE BOOKS FROM TERRY TOLER

Jamie Austen Thrillers

Read all the Jamie Austen Thrillers. They must be good.
They've been number one on Amazon in ten different countries.
Click on the link below.

THE JAMIE AUSTEN THRILLERS (12 book series)
Kindle Edition (amazon.com)

https://amzn.to/3vmPUy7

Cliff Hangers Mystery Series

Who wants to read a good mystery? We've got you covered! Read the Cliff Hangers where homicide detective, Cliff Ford, solves crimes in Chicago, with help from his wife Julia. These books have everything Terry Toler is known for. Page turning suspense, a hint of romance, and an ending you won't see coming.

The Cliff Hangers Mystery Series (4 book series)
Kindle Edition (amazon.com)

https://amzn.to/36WX3go

About Terry

Terry Toler is an Amazon international # 1 best-selling and award-winning author. He writes clean fiction with a message and life-changing nonfiction. He's a public speaker, entrepreneur, and has authored more than forty books.

Sign up for his newsletter where you'll get free stuff, exclusive content, and news of releases and promotions. He can be followed at terry-toler.com.

If you like his books, please take a few minutes to leave a review on Amazon. We really appreciate it. It helps draw more readers to his books. Thanks!

www.ingramcontent.com/pod-product-compliance
Lightning Source LLC
Chambersburg PA
CBHW020234260626
47156CB00002B/671